"Why are you [...] to my compli[...]

"I can't let you say those things to me," Olivia replied. "I can't, even for a moment, let myself be flattered by your pretty words."

Nick was close enough to her to reach out a hand and lay it on the side of her face. "Why can't you let me tell you how I feel?"

Olivia's disgust at the injustice of the situation rolled forth in a consuming wave. "How could I expect you to understand what I'm saying when no one knows?"

"Knows what?" he asked with a furrowed brow.

"Nothing." She'd already said far more than was safe.

"I thought we were done with the secrets."

"I still have a few more," she said quietly.

"You're going to have to trust someone eventually," he told her as he withdrew his hand. "I was hoping you might let it be me."

She turned to him, with her dashed hopes, fear and sadness in her eyes. "It can't ever be you," she whispered.

MANDY GOFF

began her foray into the literary world when just a young child. Her first masterwork, a vivid portrayal of the life and times of her stuffed animals, was met with great acclaim from her parents…and an uninterested eye roll from her sister. In spite of the mixed reviews, however, Mandy knew she had found her calling.

After graduating cum laude from North Greenville University with a bachelor's degree in English, Mandy surrendered her heart—and her pen—to fulfilling God's call on her life…to write fiction that both entertains and uplifts.

Mandy lives in Greenville, South Carolina, with her husband and three-year-old daughter. And when she is not doing laundry or scouring the house for her daughter's once-again-missing "Pup-pup," she enjoys reading good books, having incredibly long phone conversations and finding creative ways to get out of cooking.

MANDY GOFF

The BLACKMAILED *Bride*

Steeple
Hill®

Published by Steeple Hill Books™

STEEPLE HILL BOOKS

Steeple
Hill®

Recycling programs
for this product may
not exist in your area.

ISBN-13: 978-0-373-82858-6

THE BLACKMAILED BRIDE

www.SteepleHill.com

Printed in U.S.A.

For, lo, the winter is past, the rain is over and gone.
—*The Song of Solomon* 2:11

To Daniel and Brie. I could never eloquently convey how much I love and thank God for you both. I am blessed beyond measure.

Acknowledgments

Thanks to Mom and Dad, for giving me the freedom to dream crazy dreams and for providing me with the support and encouragement to achieve them. To Megan, whom I am prouder than I could say to call both sister and friend and who has believed in me when I didn't believe in myself. To Dennis and Sue, for accepting me into their family long before I married into it. To Elizabeth Mazer, my editor extraordinaire, for being wonderful and long-suffering and for seeing possibilities in the mess. And to Cheryl, who has been my professor, mentor and finally VBFF, and someone I could not thank enough for everything even if I were to say it again…and again…and again.

Chapter One

"You should probably stand up now." Lady Olivia Fairfax looked at the gentleman kneeling by her feet and barely resisted the urge to kick him.

"Not before you consent to be my wife," the Viscount Danfield said.

She suppressed a sigh. "I'm afraid you'll be there for quite some time, then." Rising from her chair, she moved several steps away, ill at ease with the young man so close to her. "I could ask someone to fetch a pillow for your knees, if you wish—I assume the floor will grow uncomfortable eventually."

Viscount Danfield was unfazed. "You jest with me."

"I assure you, I do not," she argued.

He blinked. "Surely you see the wisdom in this arrangement."

"I doubt I, or anyone else, would call a union between us wise." Olivia hated her necessary cruelty but, goodness, this was his third proposal.

"But your brother has consented," he said, grabbing the corner of a table and struggling to his feet.

"Marcus agreed you may *ask*. He never guaranteed my answer."

Judging from Lord Danfield's confused expression, he didn't understand the difference.

At the less-than-discreet sound of a throat being cleared, both Olivia and Danfield turned toward the open door of the morning room.

Gibbons, the family butler, stood in the entryway with a brocade pillow. "I see I have not been quick enough," the elderly man said with a sigh. "Should I leave this here for the next time he proposes, Lady Olivia?"

Olivia smothered a laugh, grateful—for once—for Gibbons' penchant for eavesdropping. "That will be fine."

After depositing the pillow on the nearest chair and turning to leave, Gibbons looked back at Danfield. "Next time, my lord, might I suggest a bit of poetry and perhaps a song or two?"

The obtuse viscount furrowed his brow. "Would it work?"

"No. But I, for one, would find it vastly more entertaining than your usual attempts."

Danfield stared after Gibbons's retreating figure, trying to discern whether he'd been insulted. It took him a surprisingly long time.

In spite of her aggravation, Olivia couldn't help but feel the faintest stirrings of pity for the young man. "I think we would better part as friends," she suggested. Perhaps niceness would make her refusal easier to handle.

Never one to take unnecessary chances, however, Olivia edged her way toward the door, hoping he would follow.

"We *have* always been great friends, haven't we?" he agreed, a little too enthusiastically.

She nodded, wondering how two months in London gave the man leave to claim anything of permanence between them but willing to agree in order to speed his leaving.

"Which is why we should marry," he said with a nod. "It's just as Mother said this morning, 'The best marriages grow on mutual indifference that is rooted in the soil of friendship.'"

"Your mother is…profound…beyond comprehension." Which was the least insulting thing she could think to say about the staid, arrogant matriarch.

A smile lit his face. "I'm glad you agree. And when I tell you Mother has graciously agreed to instruct you on the art of governing the household affairs after our nuptials…well, I can only imagine how delighted that must make you," he said.

"How magnanimous," Olivia muttered through gritted teeth, wondering who he thought had overseen the affairs at Westin Park for the last five years. Whatever inklings of pity she'd felt dissipated.

Danfield missed the warning in her tone. "We—Mother and I—are also concerned over your tendency to bury your nose in a book. That can't be healthy for a woman. You'll go blind. And, really, Lady Danfield suggested you learn to think before you speak. Your frankness is fairly scandalizing."

Olivia rolled her eyes. "Is it, now?"

Danfield stiffened. "Most women would be grateful we are prepared to help."

"Well," Olivia said, brushing her hands together, "you should begin looking for this other paragon. For the last time, Lord Danfield, I will *not* marry you."

The refusal seemed to register. His smile fell, and his shoulders sagged. "Will anything change your mind?"

She shook her head.

After a pause, he said, "I think, perhaps, *this* might."

He strode toward her, smoothly stepping around the furniture obstacles, and Olivia had no recourse but to retreat, until she was flush against the wall. Danfield's hot breath puffed against her face.

He was going to kiss her. And her reaction when she realized this was purely instinctual.

She flailed her arms behind her and grabbed a vase off a side table.

And hit him in the head.

Hard.

The young man fell to the floor with a dull thud, covered in bits of broken pottery.

Wonderful. She'd killed a peer of the realm.

Olivia knelt beside the viscount, wondering if she should loosen his cravat, find some smelling salts or perhaps retrieve a wet cloth for him. Although she doubted any of those considerations would be helpful if he were dead.

Reaching out, Olivia shook his shoulder gently, hoping to elicit a response. A groan? A flinch? An apology perhaps?

Nothing.

If the worst had happened, however, Olivia reasoned that as the sister of an earl she would get special privileges in Newgate Prison. Such as an extra cup of water a day. Or a stick to beat back the rats.

She was so engrossed by her bleak future as a prisoner of the Crown she jumped at the pained moan of the supposedly dead viscount.

"Lord Danfield?" she asked hesitantly. No response. "Are you quite well?" Still nothing.

Olivia stood. If the man weren't dead, he didn't appear to be in a hurry to leave. She hadn't the time to wait on him to do so, either.

There was nothing to be done but tell her brother. If she caught him in a jovial mood, Marcus might find the situation amusing.

Although, she thought, probably not.

Fortunately—or perhaps not—her brother was easy to find.

"Through already?" Marcus, the Earl of Westin, asked, startling her as he approached from behind.

"I suppose you could say that."

He chuckled. "Amazing. I thought we would have to knock him out and drag him away just to get him out of the house."

"I suppose you could say that, too." Olivia wrung her hands together.

Her brother appeared oblivious to her distress. "An old friend of mine will be joining us for luncheon today..." But an anguished groan echoed through the hall, interrupting his thought.

"What was that?" Marcus walked in the groan's direction.

"Let me explain before you—" Olivia tried, hurrying after him.

She winced as Marcus bellowed her name before she could catch up with him.

Marcus fixed her with a hard stare. "What happened in here?"

"There was a bit of an accident." She wouldn't meet his gaze. "At least he's alive," she offered.

Marcus stopped his pacing. "Was that ever in question?"

Olivia thought it best not to comment. But then, she heard the crunch of a shard of vase under Marcus's heel and cringed.

Olivia watched as her brother knelt to pick up a fragment of his artifact. "Please tell me that's not my Ming Dynasty vase in pieces on the floor?"

"All right," she said slowly. "It's not—" only to be silenced by a wave of his hand.

"Never mind that," he huffed. "We have to get him back to his house."

She and Marcus were studying the unmoving viscount when Gibbons reappeared in the doorway. "Lord Westin, Lady Olivia, his lordship, the Marquess of Huntsford is here."

Nick processed the scene before him in less than two minutes. Then, he spent sixty seconds deciding whether he should turn and walk back out the door. His friend Marcus was staring

at his butler, who was stifling a chuckle. What appeared to be the recently deceased Viscount Danfield was lying on the floor with pieces of pottery sprinkled around his head.

After years of acquaintance fostered through attending the same schools and the same endless society functions, Nick could well sympathize with the desire to hit Danfield over the head with whatever came to hand, yet he couldn't help but wonder who was responsible for the attack. Marcus certainly appeared murderously angry, but his eyes glared daggers at the butler, who was showing no signs of sorrow at the loss of Danfield's company in such a permanent manner. And as for the last person in the room…

The lady in the center of the fray made Nick forget everything else he'd seen. She was staring at him, her expression a mixture of surprise and something he couldn't identify, couldn't name—wasn't sure he wanted to.

The butler finally broke the silence. "You requested earlier, my lord, that I show his lordship in immediately upon his arrival."

"Would it not have been prudent to make sure our last guest had departed first?" Marcus asked.

"Perhaps if the two of you would refrain from rendering your guests immobile, such conflicts could be easily avoided," Gibbons sniffed.

Nick's head swiveled back and forth between the two combatants.

Before Marcus could retort, the gentleman on the floor decided to make a last, impressive rally. He struggled onto his elbows and groaned. "Wha-what happened?"

Nick waited to hear the explanation himself, but neither brother nor sister answered.

"You," Danfield said, looking at the Lady Olivia. "You did this." He remained propped on one elbow and used his free hand to massage the back of his head.

Every eye, including Nick's, turned to look at the young woman who appeared to be trying to edge behind her brother. In spite of the seriousness of the moment, Nick felt a chuckle lodge in his throat. The dainty lady hardly looked capable of physical violence. But the evidence was rather irrefutable.

He didn't know whether to applaud her handiness or say a prayer for his own well-being.

"It was a misunderstanding," the young woman defended.

"My…my mother will hear…" The words died as the butler slid his foot out to knock the man's elbow from under him. Without the support, Danfield fell back to the floor, bumping his head again on the way.

The siblings and Nick turned to stare at the butler.

"He was starting to aggravate me," the older man said with a shrug.

Marcus looked around at the occupants in the room. "Has everyone lost hold of their senses?"

"I still have mine, I think," Nick said as he knelt over the viscount and raised the man's eyelids one after another, looking at them intently.

At least he appeared to be still alive. "We should get him home before he wakes up again," Nick suggested.

"I'll have a carriage brought around," the butler intoned, disappearing into the hallway.

After carrying the viscount to his carriage, Nick stood back while Marcus slipped several banknotes into the driver's hands and whispered instructions. Seconds later, the coachman flicked the reins, and the conveyance rumbled down the road.

Nick dutifully followed the pair of siblings into a sitting room, curious to hear whatever explanation the lady had to offer. Not that he minded a bit of excitement, of course, pro-vided *he* wasn't the unconscious body on the floor.

Once in the room, Marcus's sister, the Lady Olivia, curtsied to him again and began edging toward the door. "I'll leave you

two to yourselves. Surely, there is a great deal of catching up to be done." She then practically ran toward the cracked opening and supposed safety.

"I think you should stay awhile." Marcus's voice stopped her hasty retreat.

"Whatever for?" Her tone suggested he would be wiser to simply let her walk away.

"Allow me first to make introductions." Marcus turned toward Nick. "I hope you'll forgive the rather odd circumstances you found upon your arrival and meet the cause of them, my sister, Lady Olivia."

Nick took a few steps forward and bowed over her hand. "A pleasure," he murmured, smiling to himself when she blushed.

Thick lashes framed her dark eyes, which widened as he spoke. She was more beautiful than he'd originally thought. As she stood close to the window, the sun streaming in made her hair seem as though the rich brown was shot through with threads of amber.

He was unaware he was still lightly holding her hand until she hastily withdrew it. The blush on her cheeks deepened, and Marcus's sister glanced with apparent nervousness at him and then her brother.

"And, Olivia, this is Nick, my old friend and the new Marquess of Huntsford."

Nick watched as she dropped a flawless curtsy.

"Well, I suppose I should leave you to your meeting, brother." She briskly turned on her heel and this time made good her escape before her brother could stop her.

Nick was sad to see her go.

He turned back to Marcus, who was looking at the open door with a mix of harried resignation and amusement. Nick was familiar with the look—Marcus often wore it when they were in school together, while reading letters from his sister.

"Your sister is an interesting woman," Nick commented.

Marcus stared at him for a long moment, then grinned.

"*Interesting* is a good word. If she weren't my sister I would maybe say *troublesome*…" Marcus let the sentence trail off.

"Are you implying there's been more than one suitor found unconscious on your floor?"

His friend shook his head, "No, but I've fielded a fair amount of offers for her."

Nick could understand that. Lady Olivia was a beauty. A beauty who probably had an uncommonly large dowry, and came from an old, highly respected family. Those factors combined would be enough to have every young buck and eligible bachelor knocking on the front door.

"I can't see how that would be anything but good. Isn't the point of the Season to marry off all the young, single ladies?" Nick asked.

"If it is the point, someone needs to tell Olivia that. She's determined to spurn the offer of any man who asks. And I nearly have to twist her arm to get her to attend a ball."

The lady grew more puzzling with each revelation. Wasn't it every woman's ambition to marry? To enjoy a glamorous Season in London, filled with balls, dinner parties and elegant luncheons?

And if those weren't her aims, why was Marcus insisting on her attendance?

What reason would any sane man have for enduring—even wanting—to experience the fripperies of the Season?

"Don't tell me you're here looking for a wife," Nick said in mock horror.

Marcus shuddered. "Absolutely not. I've no interest in marriage. At least not right now. I'd like to see Olivia settled with a suitable gentleman before I turn my own ambitions to the marriage mart."

If finding a husband for his sister was his friend's goal,

Nick thought Marcus was going to have his hands full. If this trip to London was solely for his sister's benefit—who showed not even the slightest inkling of interest in marriage—Marcus would likely end up being in London for a long time.

"What about you?" Marcus asked. "What's made you come to town—to England, for that matter—after all those years on the continent?"

Nick hesitated.

"Other than your father's death," Marcus said before Nick could decide exactly what to say. "I heard about that, and I'm sorry."

Marcus knew the relationship, or lack thereof, between Nick and the deceased marquess. It wasn't good. Not by any stretch of the imagination. As soon as Nick had reached the age of majority, he'd also reached the conclusion that he could no longer abide living beneath his father's roof. So he left, with the intention of distancing himself as much as possible from the scandalous reputation his parents had brought to his family name.

"It was time to retire, so to speak," Nick said. He'd returned because as the only heir to the marquessdom, he had responsibilities that couldn't be taken care of unless he came home. To England.

"Are you going to miss it?" Marcus asked.

Nick didn't have to think about his answer at all. "No." His escape to France had been exactly that, a way to get as far from his father as possible. While he might have enjoyed the work at first, the excitement had waned, giving way to an aching hollowness.

But Marcus didn't really know what he was asking. He knew Nick's reasons for leaving, but didn't know exactly what he would be doing while he was away. The Home Office was strict about who was allowed to know about his activities—the espionage he'd performed in the service of his country.

Which was, essentially, no one.

And since it wasn't common knowledge what Nick had been doing for the past six years, there'd been some rather colorful tales circulating about his activities. Nick hadn't been home a week before he'd begun hearing whispers about himself.

Not surprisingly, they weren't whispers about his valor or cunning. The *ton* speculated on the number of women he'd seduced between the docks of London to the ballrooms of Paris.

But Nick didn't want his oldest, and most loyal, friend believing the nonsense.

"I worked for the Home Office," Nick announced suddenly.

Marcus didn't give any visible reaction. Nick could have just as easily said he preferred chicken to pheasant.

"I was a spy," he tried again. Worry settled in the pit of his stomach. Maybe Marcus wouldn't want anything to do with him after this revelation. Nick was as much a God-fearing man as his friend, but that didn't mean that some of the things he'd had to do for Crown and Country didn't look suspect. Maybe Marcus wouldn't want that taint anywhere near him or his sister.

"Were you a good one?" Marcus asked finally.

Nick nodded.

Marcus grinned. "I always knew you were a bit crazy," he said, "but I'm pretty sure this proves it."

Nick chuckled but still waited for the final either endorsement or condemnation of his chosen occupation. "So…"

Marcus's expression sobered. "Nick, I don't care if you were a juggler in Napoleon's court. I'm just glad you're back."

Because of Marcus's ready acceptance, Nick felt the burden of uncertainty roll away. He'd been more concerned than he cared to admit that Marcus would no longer want to be associated with him.

"If you don't mind, I need to finish a few papers before we leave. It shouldn't take long," Marcus said to Nick.

Nick assured him he was fine to wait.

"Feel free to peruse the library," Marcus offered. "Although I must warn you to watch out. Olivia might be in there, and there's no lack of vases in the room."

The earl smirked as he walked out of the door.

Rather than being cautioned by this warning, Nick felt his pulse speed up…no doubt in response to the possibility of talking further with the lady. And he was surprised to find he'd risk bodily injury for the opportunity.

Olivia strained on tiptoes, struggling to grasp a book located on a too-high shelf. She muttered under her breath and let out an uncharacteristic huff.

"Stupid book," she grumbled.

Then she thought better about it; the book could hardly be blamed for where it had been placed. So she amended, "Stupid shelf."

That didn't seem quite fair, either…

Rather suddenly, she felt a presence behind her.

"Allow me," the presence said, and its hand effortlessly plucked the volume from the shelf.

She turned to find herself staring at the Marquess of Huntsford's chest. And as much as Olivia had always prided herself on her self-possession, she couldn't help but blush as she stepped away.

The Marquess of Huntsford was devastatingly handsome.

His dark hair was mussed, as though he'd recently raked a hand through it. His face was perfectly chiseled; Olivia doubted an artist with the skill of Michelangelo could have crafted a sculpture to do the reality justice. And then, his eyes…before, she had thought them blue, or perhaps gray, but now she could

tell, from where she stood, that they were green flecks of crystal that were shrewd, piercing and utterly captivating.

"Thank you," she mumbled.

"My pleasure," he said as he took a small step back.

"I didn't hear you come in," she explained feebly.

"I only entered a moment ago. Marcus wanted to finish some papers before we ventured to Tattersall's to look at a new pair of bays for my stables. I sought to amuse myself here, but I can leave, if you wish to be alone."

"That's not necessary, my lord."

"Perhaps you could call me Nick?" His smile was roguish and made her feel a bit light-headed.

"Gentle ladies shouldn't be so familiar with men," she deferred.

"I was under the impression gentle ladies shouldn't bash others with vases, either." While his face remained impassive, Olivia detected traces of laughter in the lines around his eyes.

She narrowed her eyes at him. "It's not very gentlemanly to bring that up."

He leaned forward menacingly. "Perhaps I'm *not* a gentleman."

Olivia's mouth gaped. She stared at him in shock before he began laughing uproariously.

"I'm sorry," he said in between bouts of guffaws, "but you looked truly horrified just then."

Her blush was fast and made her feel hot to the roots of her hair. "Well…" She tried to defend herself but could think of nothing to say.

"I was simply teasing, Lady Olivia," he clarified.

She stood there for a moment, trying to pretend she wasn't watching him. He *was* handsome enough to be a rogue, she thought.

"Weren't you going to read that book?" he asked with a half

smile. So, he'd noticed her staring at him in spite of her attempts to hide it? "Would you like me to leave?"

"No," she sputtered before she could stop the word. Olivia couldn't understand her own desire to be near him. The men of her acquaintance were generally easy to dismiss. Nothing about any of the gentlemen she'd met in London appealed to her quite the way this one man did. The instantaneous attraction was disconcerting. And inexplicable. And uncomfortable. It seemed dangerous in the worst sort of way. "I mean, you're our guest," she finished lamely.

He didn't say anything but gave her another aggravating half smile.

"I'm going to take this to the garden." She gestured out the window with the volume, resolving herself to do without his company. "So, you enjoy yourself."

"I have been," she thought she heard him say as she left the room.

She refused to admit to herself that this was the first conversation she'd had with a man since this silly Season had begun where *she* had enjoyed herself, too.

Chapter Two

Several days had passed since Lord Danfield had been escorted from her house, and Olivia was just beginning to breathe a bit easier. She stopped expecting Gibbons to open the door to an irate Lady Danfield, and she no longer anticipated the scandal sheets announcing her violent tendencies.

The young man, it would seem, had decided to suffer in silence.

"Lady Olivia, there is a *person* awaiting you in the drawing room," Gibbons announced as he entered her small parlor.

She looked at the butler in expectation. The old fear returned. "It's not Danfield, is it?"

The butler shook his head, but his face offered no other visual assessment on who was calling.

She entered the drawing room to find Lord Finley, their closest neighbor to their estate in Yorkshire and someone she'd known for years. Her smile of greeting was genuine.

"Lord Finley," she said.

"Lady Olivia, you're looking well," he returned with a smile as he took her proffered hand. "Very well indeed."

Olivia was accustomed to Lord Finley's words of flattery; in truth, his compliments were so silly she usually didn't mind

them. "I'm surprised to see you here. I'd not heard you were in town."

Lord Finley was a baron, and his land adjoined the Fairfax holding Westin Park on the north side. When the boys were children, the two were close friends. But that had been a long time ago.

Olivia herself valued her friendship with Lord Finley. After her mother's death, he'd been a constant presence at her home, offering comfort and solace in the dark days that followed.

But she was confused as to why he'd chosen to leave his estate and come to town. Most years, Lord Finley bypassed the amusements of the Season. His complete disregard for the entertainments and activities of town life was another similarity they shared.

"My wish was to come see for myself how you are adjusting to life in London." His gaze was appraising…and appreciative. "You don't look worse for the experience."

"I've not moldered away from lack of the country, yet," Olivia said with a sad smile, thinking perhaps "not moldering" was the best she could say. "But I certainly have not kept my wish to return a secret."

"Then why do you not go home?" Finley asked.

"Care for some tea?" she asked, ignoring his question. And at his nodded assent, Olivia crossed over to the bellpull in order to summon a servant.

Once the request had been dispatched, Olivia faced the baron; his stare was unnerving, and she remembered she'd yet to answer him. "Marcus wishes to remain in town. I certainly wouldn't try to convince him to stay here without me." After the ridiculously grand plans Marcus had devised for her, demanding to return to Westin Park would crush him.

At her brother's name, the baron grimaced. She thought she heard him say, "Ah, yes. Wouldn't want to upset Marcus would

we?" But the statement was muttered, and Olivia couldn't be sure of exactly what he'd said.

"Did Marcus say what inspired his sudden interest in town life?" he asked.

Confessing Marcus wanted her to make friends seemed rather embarrassing, so she shrugged as though to say his reasoning was a complete mystery to her.

"Did he know how vehemently you opposed leaving home?" Finley pressed.

The line of questioning made her uncomfortable. Finley's fascination seemed something more than friendly curiosity.

"He knows my wishes, but he feels an obligation to introduce me to society," she said in Marcus's defense.

Finley stalked around to a side table, picked up a trinket, looked at it and quickly set it down. The movements were jerky, and his breathing was harsh. His back stiffened and his arms angled against his body. Olivia wondered if perhaps he were going to have an attack of some kind.

"Marcus didn't tell you I came to see him before you left for town, then?" The words were clipped.

"No," she answered cautiously.

His brows lowered, making angry, dark slashes, which obscured his eyes. "I thought as much."

"Was there something he should have told me?" she asked. It was unlike Marcus to keep anything from her, and now, she was curious.

"Yes. You should have been consulted before our meeting was over," he answered hotly.

The subject of their meeting and her role in the matter were a mystery. The only thing that could possibly have necessitated her involvement would have been if Finley were propos—

Oh, no, not that.

Finley was a friend, but he would never be more. While she liked him quite well, there was no tension, no attraction…

nothing deeper than admiration and respect. And while admiration and respect were essential in a marriage, Olivia wanted something completely unfashionable in hers—love. And she'd certainly never led the baron to think she harbored any romantic feelings for him.

They'd been familiar, of course, but far from suggestive. The thought made her breathe a bit easier. Finley knew her views on marriage, just as he knew she did not feel that way about him. So something else must have been a subject of interest between the two men.

A maid entered with tea, and Olivia was able to busy herself with the preparation of their cups. She didn't ask for a reminder of how he liked his as this was a scene they had played many times in the past. Although perhaps not with this level of discomfort.

"Would you care to tell me now what it is you were discussing with Marcus?" she asked as the baron took a seat.

Finley paused, as though he were not certain of what should be said. "Yes. You have a right to know," he returned. "I wished to consult with your brother on a matter very dear to my heart—"

What? This was becoming the most peculiar conversation she'd had in some time.

"But your brother wouldn't give me the time to explain my case before denying my request," Finley continued, clearly agitated. "Now, I ask you, what kind of gentleman does not grant a serious proposal his full consideration before offering an answer?"

Olivia didn't have a response.

"After abruptly and unfairly turning me away, Marcus didn't want you to see me and hear what he'd done. That's your reason for leaving the country so quickly." He nodded once, apparently already convinced of the truth of his explanation.

"I still don't understand."

"I petitioned Marcus to let me make you my bride."

Her stomach plummeted. She could think of nothing to say in response.

It would have been much easier if Finley had accepted Marcus's refusal…something she needed to discuss with her brother later. How dare he not tell her about Finley's proposal? Had he done so, at least she would have been prepared.

Because, by all appearances, Finley was unwilling to abide by Marcus's ruling, and it seemed she must be the one to say the words.

"You wished me to be your wife?" she asked unnecessarily.

"I still wish it. Why else would I have followed you here?"

His declaration would have sent most women collapsing into the nearest chair in a flutter. What woman didn't wish to hear such tender words? Finley was titled, wealthy, handsome and charming. His blond hair was always perfectly arranged, his blue eyes were bright and his features were pleasing.

"I am honored by your offer…truly I am…"

Perhaps he sensed her impending refusal because he hastened to add, "I have feelings for you I'd not thought myself capable of. And I think, were you to give this matter your full consideration, you would see we are well suited for one another."

She managed nothing more than an indrawn breath before he continued. "You would be taken care of and would have anything you wanted. I can assure you. You could live wherever you wished. *I* wouldn't presume to tell you what to do with your time."

"I have no doubt you will make a very attentive husband," Olivia rushed on when she saw his self-assured smile. He thought he had swayed her so easily with a few pretty words.

"But I'm afraid I must decline the offer. I am your friend, but I wouldn't make you a good wife."

Finley's mouth was a tight line.

"I really am sorry," she hastened to add.

He cut off any further apologies with a slash of his hand. "You should give yourself time to adjust to the idea. It does you credit that you are not overly eager. I would like for my future wife to weigh her decisions carefully."

Did he have to make this any harder for her? Had she not had enough groveling with the Viscount Danfield? Why were men so determined to believe that when a woman turned down their proposal the no was negotiable?

"I'm certain, in time, you will meet a woman whom embodies all of those qualities," Olivia said.

"You *are* that woman." Finley's voice burned with such intensity she instinctively shied away.

"I count our friendship very dear," her assurances continued.

"And would it not be the natural extension of our friendship to commit our lives to each other?" he asked. "You've told me you are closer to me than anyone else…save your brother," he snarled the last word. "Imagine how comfortable we could be together."

"I could *never* be that comfortable with you." Olivia's voice was shrill, several pitches higher than normal, an indication of her frustration. "I will *not* marry you. A union between us is both unwise and impossible." She had to stop herself before any more words tumbled out.

"I see." Finley's response was toneless, an odd counterpart to the emotion so evident in his voice earlier.

"I don't mean to hurt you, Julian," she said his name quietly. "Especially not after you have done so much for me."

His eyes met hers, and she was surprised by the venom there. "Yes, I've done quite a bit, haven't I? I looked after you when

no one else could be bothered. Your father and mother both gone…your brother busy with something else more than not."

"Marcus had estate matters to attend to," she argued.

He waved away her excuse. "I was there for you whenever you needed after your mother's unfortunate *accident*." He sneered as he said the words.

"I will be forever in your debt for helping me over the years. But you'll have to accept my gratitude because that's all I have to give." She hoped he'd take the proffered olive branch.

His smile was swift but lacked its earlier charm. It was sinister, and Olivia couldn't help but wonder what had happened to her friend. "Why would I settle for gratitude or friendship when I want so much more?" he asked.

"It's all I'm going to offer," she repeated.

"A shame. I'd hoped this wouldn't have to get unpleasant." He shrugged. "I can see I've been too optimistic."

Unpleasant?

"Let me be clear," he continued, "you have something I want, and I think you'll find I have something you want as well. A wedding between the two of us will guarantee our mutual happiness."

"What could you possibly have that I would want now?" Olivia was starting to get angry. This didn't have to destroy their friendship, but Finley seemed unwilling to leave any strand of their former relationship intact. "Why," she continued, "would I consent to being your wife when you have shown such disregard for my wishes today? I don't appreciate being ignored and bullied."

"You will be my wife, and I don't care if you're agreeable. When we come before a minister, you will say your lines and you will not argue. And you will at least *look* happy."

Olivia couldn't help herself. The demand was so ridiculous, she laughed.

Finley's hands clenched.

"I'm sorry," she said between chuckles she couldn't seem to stem. "It's just…you're jesting aren't you…that's not very nice."

Finley sighed. "I'm not jesting. And I have to ask you to stop this foolish display. We have much to discuss before I leave."

The next bubble of laughter died in her throat, choking her. "Lord Finley, I grow weary of having to say it and am running out of ways to do so. I will not marry you. Not now. Not ever."

Finley paid the outburst no mind. "You do not wish to make me unhappy. You won't like what I have to do if you displease me."

Olivia ground her teeth together, "I can't imagine any threat that would make me agreeable to becoming your wife."

"This is becoming tiresome. Unless you wish me to share with the world what I know about your mother, I suggest you silence yourself."

The words *your mother* sent an icy pang of fear straight through her. *He doesn't know, does he? He couldn't possibly.* She wanted to laugh at the ridiculousness of the notion but didn't because she feared ever being able to stop again.

"I see I have your attention now." Finley's smile was smug— and satisfied. "It really would be a shame to have your clever intruder story discredited. I'm sure someone went to a lot of trouble to make that look authentic."

He does know.

"Whatever you are trying to insinuate is ludicrous," she scoffed.

"Is it?" he asked, walking around her in a wide circle. His stride and manner were predatory. Stalking her fluidly, the baron had disposed of the vestige of the debonair gentleman.

"Perhaps you should leave now." Her voice remained firm despite her insides churning with worry and the fear of discovery.

Finley shook his head, the gesture patently sorrowful and clearly mocking. "I'm afraid I'm not going anywhere. You and I need to talk about your little secret. Or should I say—*our* little secret?"

"There's no reason to waste my afternoon discussing your madness."

Finley clapped his hands together, as though she were an actress on the Drury Lane stage. "Brava. Should you turn down my offer, and find your family disgraced and penniless, you could tread the boards for your living. Your acting skills are sublime."

He stopped his applause. "Because I will," he threatened. "Disgrace you, that is, if you continue to refuse me."

What was the point of pretending she didn't understand?

So she said, "You couldn't prove it."

"Couldn't I?" He raised his eyebrows, daring her to contradict him.

Olivia counted to three, hoping to calm herself and the rising hysteria. Then, she supposed it was better to be certain she was composed and counted to ten.

She stopped at twenty. "What supposed proof do you possess?"

"Rather condemning proof. Something our peers would find quite fascinating."

"You don't have anything," she countered. But inside, she was reeling with the implications of what he said—if his words were the truth. Her mother *had* left behind a letter, explaining to whoever had found her that she still loved her family and begged their forgiveness for what she planned to do.

Could that be his proof? It had to be. But how had he gotten his hands on it? The letter had been safely kept at Westin Park.

Three steps brought him right in front of her. His hand reached and caressed her cheek, and she couldn't stop her small tremor of revulsion.

"Don't touch me," she bit out.

He didn't withdraw his hand. If anything, his smile grew wider. "You're not in the position to make demands."

"This is my house."

"That may be, but you're going to be *my* wife."

She felt sick. "I'm not going to marry you," she protested, but the words sounded weak and unconvincing.

"You don't have a choice." His voice was mild, as though they were discussing the pleasant turn of the weather. He had her and knew it. "Unless, of course, you wish for the world to know your mother wasn't murdered by a burglar, but instead committed suicide."

She cringed at the word.

Finley saw the response and correctly interpreted it. "I thought not," he said.

"Don't make me do this." Her voice was pleading. Olivia doubted that beseeching would make any difference, but she had to try. "I'll hate you," she threatened.

"Don't blame me. We could have done this amicably...." He trailed off. Of course, she was the one at fault for making him stoop to blackmail. "And your hatred bothers me not in the least."

"But I don't love you!" She slumped against a table, defeated. She doubted he would be bothered by her lack of devotion, either.

He wasn't. "That's not a requirement. It might have made things easier for you, but I'll get what I want out of this anyway."

What did he want? Money? Finances seemed the most obvious motivation. Her dowry was uncommonly large, something

that couldn't have been a secret among the wagging tongues of the *ton*. Of course, gossip also claimed that he was wealthy on his own merits, but perhaps his fortune was as much a sham as the kind demeanor he'd always shown her up until now.

"I can pay you for the proof," she offered.

"Tempting," he said, "but you wouldn't be able to give me enough. I'm getting more from this than just the money you'd bring me."

The hand that had been lingering on her cheek moved lower to caress her jaw, the side of her neck, settling eventually at the base of her throat. His fingers were smooth—and cold—but there seemed to be steel underneath the skin. He squeezed, the tiniest bit, and without any real pressure. The intended message, however, was clear. She was powerless against him.

"I need time," she stammered.

He looked at her, and his eyes were skeptical.

"To prepare," she rushed on, but a new thought was forming. A small, minuscule seed of hope that was barely visible through the haze of her despair. Perhaps he was bluffing about the letter. He might have seen it but not taken it.

"My brother will not be happy to hear of this," she continued. "I wish for some time to try to change his mind about you. I would rather not have my brother and future husband—" she gulped at the word "—at odds for the rest of their lives."

Finley considered the wisdom of eventually attaining Marcus's blessing and nodded his assent. "Fine. I don't wish to wait forever, though," he warned.

"A few days, that's all I require," she affirmed. Olivia desperately wanted to clutch at this delay. Once she convinced Marcus to take her home, she could see for herself whether the letter was safe. If what she hoped were true, she could return to town and challenge Finley.

If the baron was telling the truth…well, she would think of what to do then.

"I expect to hear from you within a few days," Finley reminded her as he took his leave.

Olivia was proud of herself. She waited until the front door clicked shut before bursting into tears.

Nick and Marcus were preparing to play a game of billiards when Marcus's sister nearly ripped the door from its hinges.

"Marcus," she gasped. Her chest rose and fell heavily, and Nick thought she must have raced her way up the stairs.

Nick snapped to attention when she entered, some instinct driving him to want to protect her from her obvious distress.

Marcus obviously agreed with Nick's silent assessment. "Do you need a physician?" her brother asked.

"I need to go home," she said. Her eyes darted frantically around the room. And when Nick shifted from his place in the shadows, she noticed his presence for the first time. He could tell from the subtle widening of her eyes.

"Please, Marcus." Her voice dropped lower.

"What is wrong with you?" her brother asked, shaking his head.

Before she could answer, Marcus's butler opened the door to the room. The servant's gaze swung around and landed on his mistress. "My lady, Lord Finley left before retrieving his hat and gloves." The butler let the statement dangle in the air. "Would you like me to send them with a messenger?"

"Finley was here?" Marcus growled. Nick understood the anger. He wouldn't let Finley anywhere near his sister, if he had one.

"Briefly," she answered. The look she gave the butler was withering.

"When did Finley arrive in town?" Marcus asked the room in general.

Gibbons shrugged. "I work for you, my lord, not him."

Nick didn't know, and Olivia didn't appear to be open to sharing.

His friend muttered something unintelligible. "Go pack your things," he told her shortly. "I will take you back to Westin Park."

Marcus's sister looked so relieved, Nick thought she might faint, or worse, cry. Before she could turn to leave, however, Marcus grabbed her hand, stopping her flight.

"Did Finley say something to upset you?" he asked.

She shook her head and tugged herself free from his hold.

Nick stared after the beautiful woman as she departed. The gentleman in him knew that the proper thing to do would be to ignore her distress, and let her have the comfort of believing her discomposure had gone unnoted. But he couldn't deny that there was a part of him that wanted to go after her, to hold and comfort her until she was no longer afraid.

What was wrong with him?

Marcus still had his attention focused after his sister. "I'm sorry for that," he said. "She's not usually so…frantic."

Nick brushed aside the apology. "When will you leave?" he asked.

"I guess at first opportunity. Perhaps in the morning. It's several days' journey to Westin Park." Marcus put away his cue. The game of billiards now forgotten in the wake of Olivia's appearance. "Can you spare the time?" Marcus asked.

"I suppose so, why?"

"Come with us. We've known each other for years, yet you've never seen my home."

Nick considered the offer. He had no wish to intrude upon the siblings' time together, but he couldn't deny there was something infinitely alluring about escaping the scrutiny of town for a few days. And while he could have easily visited his country estate, Nick wasn't ready for that yet. Wasn't ready for whatever memories awaited him there.

"I don't guess anyone will miss me." And Nick was surprised to find he was swayed by the thought of having more time to study the fascinating Olivia.

The idea appealed to him more than it should.

Chapter Three

It wasn't there.

The letter she'd believed would be in the rosewood box in the library at Westin Park was missing.

For a moment, Olivia could think of nothing. She stared at the dark velvet lining of the empty container as though the parchment would somehow mysteriously reappear. Olivia watched for several moments, waiting for one of the miracles Marcus so believed in to happen.

It didn't.

The severity of her predicament overwhelmed her.

What was she going to do? Unfortunately, there were few choices…and none of them held much appeal.

Ignoring Lord Finley was definitely what she would prefer to do. Perhaps if she could keep her distance from him, making sure that he never had cause to be alone with her, he would give up his quest to make her his wife. But even as Olivia thought that, she knew the baron wouldn't cave so easily. He would expose them. For herself, Olivia didn't much care. She had no use for society or its good opinion. Marcus, however, would be laughed out of the House of Lords, unable to push through the legislation he'd been working on. And when her brother

decided it was time to marry, no eligible woman would want to link her name with such a damaged and scandalized family.

So pretending she and Finley had never even talked wouldn't work—much as she might have wished otherwise.

That left confessing this to her brother. But what would he say when he realized the secret she'd been harboring for years? Telling him the truth was the only option, wasn't it? With Marcus's help, she could devise a way to nullify Lord Finley's threat and prevent their family disgrace from becoming common knowledge. Perhaps her brother could write him a bank draft. Or maybe they could figure a way to get the letter back, which would make Finley's accusations—should he make any—seem like nothing more than spiteful fabrications.

But what would the revelation do to Marcus? Would he be reduced to the person she'd let herself become? Would the truth strip him of his faith in a God who would allow such things to occur the way it had to her? And what would he think of *her* part in the charade, and the fact that she'd hidden the truth from him for so long?

Marcus would be disappointed. Well, *disappointed* was probably not the right word. But she refused to consider a harsher emotion, one that would forever change the way Marcus looked at her.

She'd become a liar in order to protect him, never anticipating he'd discover the truth…either about her mother or about her.

She wasn't sure which revelation would crush him more.

I could accept Finley's proposal.

The thought repulsed her.

But was it worse than confessing to Marcus?

Could she bear to hurt her brother when she had another option?

No, she couldn't.

Olivia thought she'd cried all the tears she had, but a few

slipped down her cheeks anyway. Consigning herself to a love-less marriage—one built on deception and manipulation—was a heavy decision. But it was one she would make rather than becoming the instrument of disillusionment for her brother.

This was all because of that stupid letter. Had their mother only kept her last words—her selfish confessional—to herself, Olivia wouldn't be in this predicament.

But no sooner had the hateful thought taken root than she chastised herself. She should have burned the letter immediately after reading it all those years ago. As long as those precious, final words remained undestroyed, Olivia had assumed the risk of someone finding it.

It was her fault. She'd been too weak, too overcome with grief and loneliness to destroy the last tangible link to her mother.

And now, it appeared she would pay for her weakness.

"How long have you been in here?" Marcus's voice startled her so much she jerked, and the lid on the box slammed closed.

Turning, Olivia thrust her hands behind her back as though they were holding something worth hiding. How long had her brother been watching?

"Just a few moments," she answered.

"Have you been crying?" Marcus asked in near horror as he came closer to examine her face.

"Perhaps." She couldn't stop the following sniffle.

"Would it be too much to ask why you are weeping in the library?" His voice was mild.

"I've missed my books." It wasn't exactly a lie. She *had* missed her books. She'd miss them even more soon—along with the library itself, and the house and the life she'd be giving up when she married Finley.

"You took most of your books to London with you," Marcus returned.

"Just my favorites," she argued.

"I think we carried at least fifty volumes with us." He was beginning to look less suspicious and more amused.

"I have a lot of favorites."

He shrugged. "I believe Sarah is unpacking your things in your room. Do you wish to lie down for a few minutes?" he asked, eyeing her skeptically. "We're not dining for many hours yet."

"No, I'll find something to amuse myself until then." Or, more likely, she would obsess about what she was going to do, until she realized there *was* nothing to be done.

Then, she would cry some more.

"So you don't have any pressing plans at the moment?" he asked, moving to one of the settees and sitting rather indecorously. He rested his head against the back of the piece of furniture.

She shook her head, wondering if he could see her with his eyes closed like that.

Apparently, he could.

"Excellent," her brother said. "I planned to take Nick around the estate on horseback. Would you care to join us? I know how much you've missed being able to ride."

She could tell Marcus she didn't want to spend any more time with his friend than she had to, but her brother would chastise her for her rudeness. She didn't know what was wrong with her. The marquess was just a man, one she barely knew. But she didn't like the way she felt when he was near. Nervous. Jumpy. Fluttery.

Olivia had counted herself fortunate Marcus and Lord Huntsford had decided to take their horses on the journey to Westin Park. She'd ridden in the carriage alone, which had been preferable to having to share a confined space with the marquess.

But they had still taken a few breaks, allowing Olivia to exit the carriage and stretch her legs. The marquess had the

annoying tendency to seek her out during those moments. Much like when he'd found her in the library back in London, Lord Huntsford was nothing but cordial...so she couldn't explain *why* he made her feel so unlike herself.

But she couldn't avoid the gentleman indefinitely. She wasn't going to stay locked in her room for days, and running into him or having meals together was inevitable.

Besides, London *had* offered limited opportunities to ride. Olivia didn't care much for the sedate, stately stroll through the park. She liked to feel the wind in her hair, whipping it around and into a nest her maid would complain about later. Would she still be able to ride like that as Finley's wife? She shuddered at the thought of the restrictions that he, as her husband, would be able to place on her freedom. But no, she wouldn't let herself think about that today. She wasn't Finley's wife yet—she still had time to enjoy all the things she loved.

So she agreed.

"Excellent." Marcus hopped up from his seat. "Shall we meet in half an hour?"

Olivia nodded. And she looked at her brother, thought about how much she was going to break his heart and couldn't stop the impulse to hug him. Which she did.

Perhaps a touch too tightly.

"Olivia?" he asked.

Marcus was probably wondering if he would need to have a doctor come and examine her.

"I love you," she told him. She might have sniffled, but if so, it was done very, very quietly.

He patted her on the back, used to her spontaneous shows of affection. "I love you as well." He pulled back and looked at her face. "Perhaps the fresh air will make you feel better. You look peaked."

She looked like a wreck. Leave it to Marcus to try and soften the ugly truth. He'd been protecting her all her life.

It was her turn to do so for him.

"You're right. The country air will be refreshing. The carriage ride must have unsettled me." She wondered if he could see signs of her deception in her face, but Marcus looked oblivious.

"See you shortly," he called after her as she left the room.

Fortunately for her, once her back was to him, he couldn't see the fresh tears that had started to fall.

How was she going to tell Marcus?

Not about their mother—no, she'd resolved that Marcus would never learn about that. But to keep the secret meant accepting Finley's proposal, and if the way he'd rushed her out of London was any indication, Marcus would *not* be pleased with the news. What words could she possibly speak that would make him agree to her marrying Finley? How would she handle his disappointment? How would *he* handle his disappointment?

The litany of unanswerable questions kept her mind busy and her stomach churning. She could think of nothing that would make her task easier.

But after her maid Sarah helped her into her riding habit, Olivia had to scold herself. She couldn't spend the rest of her life moping around. For the moment, she was still free and would enjoy herself. And for right now, that meant spending the afternoon with her brother.

"You look lovely," Marcus greeted a short time later as she joined him and Lord Huntsford outside.

After thanking Marcus, Olivia forced herself to give Lord Huntsford a cursory glance. In deference to his presence, she inclined her head and murmured a greeting.

If Marcus noticed her rudeness, he didn't comment on it. Olivia felt a pang of guilt and shame, but her coldness was for her own defense. Something about the marquess was irresistible.

Certainly, he was handsome. But her attraction to him wasn't purely physical. He exuded a strength and mystery that she found alluring. That appeal put her in an unenviable position.

She wasn't free to develop any interest in him.

So she would keep her distance.

"Care for a race?" she asked her brother with a smile after they'd ridden along the length of the west perimeter of the property. The happy expression didn't feel quite right on her face, but neither of the men noticed the subtle difference.

Marcus shuddered dramatically. "I don't think so. I have enough pride to want no one to witness me losing to a woman." Then he grinned at her.

Olivia could almost pretend as though she'd altered time and returned to her life as it was a few days before. She felt carefree and uninhibited.

Which, surely, was the reason she turned to the marquess next.

"What about you, my lord?" she asked.

Lord Huntsford turned the full force of his smile on her, and Olivia had to remind herself to breathe. "Now I feel I must, if only to prove I could do better than Marcus," he said.

"*Anyone* could do better than Marcus, my lord," she exaggerated, simply because Marcus prided himself on his horsemanship—with just cause—and she knew it would aggravate him.

Marcus's friend laughed. "Do you wish a lead? It would only be gentlemanly of me."

Marcus laughed this time.

Olivia smiled and shook her head no. "To the stone wall to the east." She pointed out a straight path with her hand. "Shouldn't be too difficult, my lord. I'll see you when you get there."

Marcus called their start, and Olivia took off. Hooves pounded the ground, sending clumps of earth flying. She laughed and

felt the sound trailing out behind her. It almost seemed as if she were leaving all her troubles behind. For this one, brief moment, she allowed herself to be happy.

Lady Olivia won the race. And if she suspected that Nick might have pulled on his reins just a bit at the end, for the sheer pleasure of seeing her victorious smile, then she had no way to prove it. He was basking in that smile when the lady realized that Marcus had been waylaid along the path, leaving the two of them to return to the house together without his moderating presence.

The realization seemed to make her uncomfortable. The young woman shifted in her sidesaddle several times and fidgeted with the reins.

"You have a beautiful home," Nick commented after a long stretch of silence.

"Thank you. I've always thought it was uncommonly lovely here." Her sigh seemed wistful, and the forlorn noise drew his eye to her.

Mercy. She was uncommonly lovely herself. Their breakneck ride had completely mussed her hair. Tendrils framed her face, both wild and flattering against cheeks slightly pink with exertion.

"Are you staring at me, Lord Huntsford?"

Nick looked quickly away, a reflex more suited to a child who'd been caught peering at presents hidden in a closet than a powerful noble. But her question was quiet, genuinely curious. Flirtation didn't appear to be her aim.

What kind of woman is she?

"I apologize," he said. "I was merely thinking of how different you are."

"That doesn't sound very complimentary."

"It is a compliment of the highest order. The ladies of my acquaintance wouldn't be content to ride through the country

when the amusements of town are within a day's travel distance," he assured her.

Olivia pursed her full lips. "London holds no allure for me."

"We are kindred souls in that regard."

"Then why do you stay in town?" she asked with an arched eyebrow. "You answer to no one. You may come and go as you wish. I should think, were I you, I wouldn't step a toe inside the limits of London."

He smiled at her and wished it were so simple. "Since my father's death, I must take all the responsibilities of the marquessdom—unfortunately, that includes business in town. The mantle is heavy and not one I wear joyfully."

Her expression instantly sobered. "I'm sorry about your father. How long has it been?"

"A year," he answered. "I would have returned to England immediately after his death, but by the time news reached me, I was mired in business I couldn't leave unfinished." Why did he feel compelled to offer an explanation, vague though it might have been?

She didn't ask what kind of business.

He wouldn't have told her if she had.

"I didn't wear mourning for him." The confession was out before he could think of any reason why he would tell her this.

"I'm sure he would have understood your decision," Lady Olivia said.

"I'm sure he wouldn't." Actually, the deceased marquess would have seethed with anger to know his son didn't wear all black for him.

Nick had been so consumed with his own rage toward his father, he couldn't fathom showing him that level of respect. "Our relationship was…strained."

The woman at his side still said nothing.

In the silence, Nick warred with regret at a broken relation-ship with his father. But his father had insisted Nick yield to his wishes. Nick couldn't do that.

So he'd left.

Which had created an even larger gulf, not just physically, between them. The only heir to the marquessdom running away to foreign lands, doing things nobody wanted to imagine… his father had been furious Nick would risk his life, and most important, risk the title leaving the immediate family if some-thing were to happen to Nick.

Nick determined not to look at Lady Olivia, but when he felt a slight pressure on his hand, he looked down to find she was touching him to get his attention.

"I understand." The two words held a wealth of untold sym-pathy. And he felt as though she truly did.

They both turned at the sound of an approaching rider.

"Apologies," Marcus said as he came abreast of the pair. "One of the tenant farmers wanted to ask about repairing his roof. He stopped me before I could catch up with you."

"That's all right," Lady Olivia said. "Now that you can finish giving Lord Huntsford a tour, I should probably return inside."

If Nick thought her manner was abrupt, he had no reasonable explanation for the behavior. Just moments before, she'd been perfectly cordial.

Marcus, however, seemed concerned. "Perhaps you *should* rest before dinner."

She nodded, but Nick noticed she didn't voice an agreement. With a quick turn of the reins, she had her horse pointed back in the direction of the house. She waved a brief farewell then kicked her horse into motion.

Marcus had begun a conversation—something about the crops he was planning for the upcoming season. Nick listened as best he could with his attention diverted. Why was it that

Lady Olivia could alternately be so charming and agreeable, but the next moment seek the quickest way to escape his presence?

Her retreating figure didn't offer any clues, however. And while he hated the fact that he couldn't seem to do otherwise, Nick stared at her even after she could no longer be seen in the distance.

Chapter Four

The next morning, Olivia wandered through the countryside just beyond the gardens at Westin Park. Traipsing feet had left trails through the growth, making it easy for her to simply meander. The day was beautiful. The green hills stretched as far as she could see, and the trees swayed with the gentle, rifling breeze.

She felt herself calming. She'd not cried this morning at all. She could do this. She would agree to Finley's proposal. Olivia had no other choice.

But she wouldn't let it destroy her. Finley was only a person after all.

And hadn't she faced worse?

And done so alone?

"Lady Olivia, is that you?"

Olivia started at the voice, wondering who had intercepted her on the path. She turned toward the sound, finding the parish vicar strolling behind her.

"Reverend Thomas," she greeted. The minister had been in his position since before she was born. He was a grandfatherly man. And while she no longer ascribed to his particular view of God, she was glad to see him.

"It is an unexpected pleasure to see you," he said, coming abreast of her. "Is your brother in residence as well?"

"Yes. We returned this morning."

"Have you given up on London already?" he asked with a conspiratorial wink. He knew how Olivia had fought to stay home after Marcus's decree.

"I'm afraid we'll be returning in a few days."

"Will you be coming to the service tomorrow?" he asked hopefully.

The thought made her uncomfortable. "I am not certain what my brother intends."

"Well, we've certainly missed you here," the minister said.

She smiled at him, hoping it reached all the way to her eyes. "I can't tell you how difficult it's been being in London and knowing I must stay there until the end of the Season."

"Surely it's been enjoyable as well?" he asked her.

"I prefer the assemblies here over the balls there. And nothing compares to an evening staring at the sky and the stars from my bedroom window at Westin Park."

Reverend Thomas smiled knowingly. "Well, I, for one, am surprised some gentleman hasn't swept you off your feet yet."

"Actually, Reverend, I swept one off *his* feet," she said, thinking of the Viscount Danfield. That evoked perhaps the first genuine smile of the day. She wondered if the young man had recovered from his mishap.

But thinking about proposals made her mind naturally wander to Finley's, which erased the smile.

"I'm not surprised to hear that," he answered. But then Reverend Thomas scrutinized her, sensing the change in her mood. Olivia could feel his old, almost rheumy eyes on her. The man was much too perceptive.

"How have you been faring, dear?" The concern in his gaze

was genuine, and, at his caring expression, she felt the tears well and threaten to spill over.

"I'm not entirely sure," she confessed.

He nodded sagely. "Understandable."

"Do you have a cure?" she asked with the glimmer of a smile.

He stopped, and the suddenness had Olivia backtracking to stand beside him. "Would you want the one I have to offer?" he asked.

She didn't have to think about her answer. "No."

It seemed her destiny was to disappoint everyone whose path she crossed today. The vicar looked absolutely crestfallen.

"I wish you would talk to me about it, Lady Olivia. We have known each other many years, have we not?"

She nodded.

"I can bear the weight of whatever pain you carry. Or better, we'll give it to God. He can shoulder it better than both of us." His tone was hopeful, as though she might decide to trust him after five years of faith in nothing.

"Christ had His cross, Reverend," she said, thinking back on the days when the words of the Bible meant something to her. "This one's mine to carry."

"Because you refuse to lay it down," he said quietly. She heard him anyway.

Olivia was comfortable enough with Reverend Thomas to be abrupt and honest with him. "I don't wish to talk about this anymore."

The old man nodded but added, "God loves you." He spoke slowly, as though she were a child.

"Not enough." While anyone else might have needed further explanation, Olivia knew Reverend Thomas didn't. He didn't agree, but he understood.

"Don't blame God for the actions of men, Lady Olivia."

How little did Reverend Thomas know that she blamed God *and* her mother.

"I'll grant you God didn't pull the trigger that ended my mother's life, but did He not hear all my prayers for her before?" Olivia couldn't have foreseen the suicide, but she had feared her mother would drink herself into an early grave. And where had been the deliverance God supposedly granted to those who needed it?

"I can assure you, child, He heard your prayers."

"Oh, did He not care enough to answer them, then? Is that it?" Her frustration, anger and latent grief made the words harsh. "How long can you talk to someone who never answers back?"

"Perhaps He didn't answer," the vicar allowed with a subtle nod. "Or perhaps, for reasons we may never understand, His answer was no."

"It's not fair," she said quietly.

"Nor is it easy," he said in agreement.

"So, I ask you, what can I expect from the hands of such a *loving* God?" she sneered.

"Grace, mercy and forgiveness," he answered without hesitation.

But she doubted the truth of all three.

Nick ambled down the country paths, enjoying for himself the lush beauty of Westin Park. His friend's estate created in him a stab of longing for his own country lodging—the estate he hadn't seen in more than five years.

His country home should have been the first place he went upon returning to England. Instead, he'd opened up the Huntsford mansion in London. And he'd kept promising himself he'd return as soon as his affairs were in order.

But he knew that for the stalling tactic it was.

No longer was he the frightened five-year-old boy, jumping

at shadows and cringing at the jeers and leers from his father's friends. Nor was he the twelve-year-old, convinced he was a man already, who had to confront the truth that his mother's appetites for deviance were no more refined than her husband's. Nick wasn't even the angry twenty-three-year-old who'd stormed from the house in a cloud of disgust and righteous indignation.

So why hadn't he been back?

He wasn't sure.

Perhaps he worried that his parents had desecrated the place of his childhood beyond redemption. Would he be able to walk down the halls and through the rooms without feeling that the lewd images of "parties" and drunken festivities had been imprinted on the very fabric of the house?

Maybe before he went back, he should hire a decorator to strip everything inside and refurnish the house.

And it was in the midst of his internal debate over what to do with his inherited estate that he heard two voices coming from the other side of the trees. The man's voice was unfamiliar, but the woman's voice was immediately recognizable. Lady Olivia.

Perhaps it was badly done of him, but there remained too much of the spy in Nick for him not to still immediately and remain absolutely quiet to hear what was being said.

What struck him, immediately upon overhearing the exchange, was that Lady Olivia's words revealed a young woman who was hurt, angry and no longer trusting of God's goodness. His heart ached for the bitterness and pain laced through each word she spoke. As before, he felt the uncommonly strong urge to reach out and comfort her. But within moments, the opportunity slipped away as the lady began walking back in the direction of the house.

Nick's feet were moving before his mind fully recognized what he planned to do. Crashing through the brush and foliage,

no longer caring to conceal his presence, he went after Lady Olivia. Nick couldn't see her any longer, but he took a few steps on the worn path, figuring she must have been walking back home.

"Hello, there!"

Nick turned around and barely managed to stifle his grimace at being interrupted in his quest. He'd completely forgotten about the vicar once he'd seen Lady Olivia in tears.

"Hello," Nick returned, striding back to where the minister stood in the middle of the path. He introduced himself, waiting impatiently while the Reverend did the same.

"What has brought you to Westin Park?" the older man asked. His eyes were full of genuine curiosity.

"I've come with my friend Marcus. I've only recently returned to England and wanted a bit of time away from London."

The minister smiled. "There seems to be quite a bit of that going around."

Nick wasn't sure what else to say. He never used to have a difficult time making conversation, but with Olivia's flight weighing on his mind, his concern was finding out what was wrong.

He figured he might as well ask.

The worst Reverend Thomas could do would be to not answer his question.

"Was that Lady Olivia I saw leaving?" he asked.

Reverend Thomas smiled, but his eyes still look worried. "Yes."

"Was she unwell?" he asked.

The older man looked as if he wasn't going to answer the question. Nick was quickly losing the tenuous hold he had on his patience. Trying not to think of his friend's little sister crying somewhere in the woods by herself, he waited for the minister's answer.

"Lady Olivia has had a difficult time adjusting to leaving home," he finally said.

Nick already knew that, and he thought he understood part of the reason why. Judging from the snippet of conversation he'd heard, however, Olivia sounded as though she had more to worry about than just being homesick. Marcus's sister genuinely sounded bitter…and upset with God.

But Nick knew the family confidant wouldn't tell him anything further than the surface truth. For all he knew, Nick was a stranger, and had no right to ask anything about Lady Olivia.

And he was suddenly, and surprisingly, disappointed to realize that he had no right at all.

Chapter Five

The next morning, Olivia rolled over in her bed, looked at the open drapes over the window and groaned. The bright sun streamed into the room, and she squinted against the light. All she had to do was roll over again and bury herself beneath the blankets, but sleep seemed far beyond her reach.

"Sarah?" she said to her maid, whom she heard bustling in her wardrobe.

"Yes, my lady?" the young girl asked.

"What time is it?"

"Time for you to get ready for church."

"I'd really rather not," Olivia grumbled, pulling the blanket over her head. It was a futile attempt to stop the inevitable; before long, Marcus would enter and drag her out of bed.

Sarah stopped at the head of the bed, and Olivia didn't have to pull the cover down to see the look of indecision she knew would be on the young girl's face.

"My lady?" Sarah asked.

"Yes?" The covers muffled the word.

"His lordship wanted me to come and help you dress for service."

"I don't feel well," Olivia hedged. In truth, she felt sick to

her stomach, though she knew it was an illness no amount of rest would cure. It had been years since she had been truly at peace with church attendance, but she had always borne through it for Marcus's sake. Yet now, the idea of attending services in the church where Finley would likely expect her to stand as she pledged her life to him…no, she could not bear it. Not yet. Not today.

"Do you wish for me to inform the earl?" Sarah's voice plainly begged her to say no.

"I'll tell him when he comes in." Olivia suppressed a smile at the girl's sigh of relief.

"Thank you, my lady."

Olivia didn't have long to enjoy the sanctuary of her bed before Marcus came striding into the room.

"Wake up," he said unceremoniously.

While Olivia was contemplating feigning sleep, her brother moved closer.

"I see Sarah has failed in her duties," he said from directly above her. "I suppose I shall have to dismiss her."

"You wouldn't dare," Olivia said as she flung back the covers. She looked around, ready to stop her maid from leaving. But Sarah was already gone.

Marcus smiled. "I could, but I won't. I just wanted to prove you were awake."

"Hateful," she muttered.

"So you say." He picked up her cup of chocolate and handed it to her. "You had best hurry or we'll not make the service in time."

"I have a headache," she said, trying to convince him to let her stay home.

"Convenient." He dismissed her imaginary illness without another thought. "Now get out of bed. I shouldn't have to fight with you as though you were still twelve."

Olivia pursed her lips. "Fine, I'll be downstairs shortly."

"Sarah will return to help you dress," Marcus said on his way out of the room.

Two hours later, Olivia sat between Marcus and the Marquess of Huntsford on the church pew. If there were a God, surely He was laughing at her now.

Both men barely noticed her presence once the minister began his sermon, but every other eye in the building was firmly fixed on the back of their heads. The congregants were, of course, used to seeing the earl and his sister, but this new visitor was something altogether different. Olivia didn't have to turn around to know nearly every woman eyed the marquess speculatively. It didn't help that Lord Huntsford walked in the chapel as though it were something he had been doing every Sunday of his life. His self-confidence and total lack of discomfort were aggravating.

Almost as aggravating as his cheery facade first thing in the morning.

"I trust you rested well," he had greeted her with a beaming smile once she descended the stairs.

She had inclined her head, but nothing more.

And now, nearly two hours later, she was irrevocably stuck with him. Lord Huntsford was planted firmly on her right, Marcus on her left. Olivia wished she had sat on the aisle, so she wouldn't feel so confined by the two large men. Not that either of them was aware of her distress.

The congregation stood, singing one last hymn, and Olivia, as usual, only mouthed the words. The marquess's voice, however, sang loud and true—his clear baritone rising high into the chapel. She tried not to listen to him, tried not to think about how inevitably soon her voice would fill this very space as she pledged herself to Baron Finley as his wife.

It had been years since church had symbolized any sort of refuge for her, but now it seemed to represent the trap she'd fallen into that would bind her for the rest of her life. The very idea made her feel truly ill. So instead of dwelling on the horrible future that awaited her, Olivia devoted her attention to the meticulous counting of panes in the glass windows.

By the twelfth pane, she could barely hear the singers through the suddenly shrill ringing in her ears. The noise was so deafening she almost clapped her hands over her ears to stifle it. Olivia stopped herself when she realized that probably wouldn't help at all.

At twenty-eight, her stomach roiled, and she forced herself to resist the urge to sit back on the pew.

At fifty-seven, she swayed, luckily catching herself in time before she pitched forward into the people in front of her.

Something was sitting on her chest, cutting off her air supply. The pressure was a vise. Her heart beat an irregular rhythm, and Olivia tried to ignore the *thump, thump, pound* sensation. Her lips were still moving, still attempting to appear as though she were singing, but Olivia doubted anyone, if he were to look closely, would be fooled.

"Are you feeling unwell?" Lord Huntsford leaned over and whispered in her ear.

She shook her head.

He grunted in disbelief, and while she didn't dare venture a look at his face, she knew he'd look skeptical.

Olivia hardly cared to try and convince him. She was still trying to hold the impending feeling of panic at bay—and was failing miserably.

Lord Huntsford might have still been singing, but Olivia could feel his eyes firmly on her. And when she swayed—just the smallest bit of unnatural movement—his hand reached out to steady her.

"Come with me" was his whispered order. He set down his hymnal and took her by the elbow.

Her protests were irrelevant, and Marcus, so engrossed in his singing, didn't notice the two of them leaving.

Olivia held her head high as they exited toward the rear of the sanctuary. Her eyes were trained ahead, avoiding meeting anyone's gaze. She could hear the whispers as she walked by, but the man at her side didn't seem to mind them, so she supposed she could stand the scrutiny for a few seconds.

Lord Huntsford led her outside, guiding her to a stone bench nestled in the church's garden.

She resisted the urge to take large, gulping breaths once outside in the fresh air. The gasping would only confirm Lord Huntsford's suspicions. She couldn't even thank him for his help without admitting that she'd needed the escape he'd offered.

"Are you unwell?" he asked gently, kneeling beside her.

"I'll be fine," she said, but her voice was breathy.

She sank back farther into the bench. Outside the walls of the church, the ache inside began to abate. And now, inhaling deeply the scent of roses and gardenias, her heart wasn't pounding so fiercely.

"You looked quite ill in there," he persisted. "Are you certain you're feeling better?"

"The closed space made it hard to breathe," she said, hoping he would let the matter rest. Olivia concentrated on the pace of her breathing, trying to steady the gasps so he'd not have any further reason to be suspicious.

"Sometimes I feel that way when I'm hiding, too." His voice was barely a whisper, and he could easily have been speaking solely to himself.

"I've no idea what you're talking about." But she tried to offer a smile in gratitude so the words didn't sound harsh. He was being very conciliatory, after all. And she had the oddest feeling that he *did* understand. That he sympathized with her

struggle and disillusionment. But surely that was just a cruel trick of her imagination, fooling her into believing she wasn't quite so desperately alone. "Feel free to return inside—I just need a moment."

"I'll sit here with you…if you don't mind," he added as an afterthought.

But Lord Huntsford gave her no chance to answer. She stilled as he took up the remaining space on the bench, afraid if she moved the slightest fraction of an inch, she might brush against him.

"I really think some time alone would help me feel better," she ventured. Regaining her composure was impossible with him sitting in such close proximity.

"I have no intention of leaving you out here alone." His crossed arms declared he would brook no argument.

Fine.

She would simply pretend he wasn't there. Something that, in theory, seemed relatively easy. But as he sat beside her, also in silence, Olivia found her eyes involuntarily moving to watch him. Each time, she would wrest her gaze away. Not that it did any good, of course; she was certain the marquess realized each time she did so.

"Did you see the two of them?"

The whispered question floated on the wind to Olivia and Nick, and both immediately straightened.

"How could you not see them? Shameful. And in church, no less."

"Now, Josephine," came a third voice, "they were hardly doing anything shameful. They were sitting in front of God and the whole congregation."

"Well, where are they now?" one of the other women—Olivia assumed it was Josephine—shot back.

Silence followed. Apparently this question stymied the other two ladies.

Olivia started to rise, prepared to step from behind the shelter of the towering rosebushes and into the women's path, but Nick laid a hand on her arm, stilling her. His touch scorched her skin. But she didn't recoil from it.

"Well," the third woman, who Olivia was beginning to think of as her champion, began, "I'm sure they both have a perfectly innocent explanation. Perhaps Lady Olivia had a headache," she offered.

One of the other women made a ribald joke, and Olivia cringed. Humiliation alone was bad enough, but humiliation in front of the marquess was unbearable.

"Well, I'm not surprised," another voice returned. "The marquess has quite a way with women, at least that's what I heard from Eleanor at the dressmaker's."

Their advocate scoffed. "The man was in *church*."

The cynical woman laughed. "Probably looking for an innocent woman to corrupt." She made the statement as calmly as one might if she were suggesting he'd gone to the market to select produce.

Judging from the fact that the voices had stopped wafting to her from different points down the path, Olivia knew the women were standing not too far from where she and Nick were sitting.

"I wouldn't be surprised," one returned. Olivia was beginning to lose track of who was speaking. "Alfred was telling me all sorts of lurid tales of the marquess's exploits in France. Shocking," she added unnecessarily.

"Well, he won't be able to parade about in polite society for long. He's no better than his parents. And his bad blood will out eventually."

Lord Huntsford's grip on her arm tightened, and she looked at him in surprise. His jaw was clenched, and while Olivia didn't know him well enough to be able to decipher his moods with any accuracy, he looked furious.

What would he do? Charge out from behind the bushes and defend her honor? Defend his? But the marquess had been correct in the beginning; it was best they remain undiscovered.

She laid her hand atop his, hoping to both comfort and subdue him. It was the least she could do after he'd set himself up for this sort of slander just by helping her out of doors. Besides, it certainly wouldn't do for the three women to happen upon them. Or for him to step out and confront them.

Once Lord Huntsford felt her touch, he turned to look at her, and his pursed lips and set jaw were the only visible signs he was warring with indecision. Casting another glance to where the women had resumed strolling by, he sighed. As he looked back at her, his face softened. He ventured a tentative smile, and Olivia couldn't help but return it.

She wondered how he had managed to so completely erase the anxiety and panic she'd felt only moments earlier. Yet even with a feeling of peace and contentment stealing over her, a small voice in the back of her mind cautioned against softening toward him and warned that she'd have to double her efforts to stay away from the marquess.

Chapter Six

Later that evening, past the time when everyone should have been abed, Olivia opened the door to the hallway, looked down both sides to make sure neither her brother nor the marquess were loitering about and stepped out. She pulled her wrapper tighter around herself and padded on bare feet down to a scarred wooden door that remained closed at the end of the hall.

Her father's study.

She approached it with a sort of reverence, as though the room she was about to enter was holy in its own right.

With her hands braced on the frame, she leaned her forehead against the cool wood of the door.

Breathe, she instructed herself.

How many years had it been?

Five, already…

And she still felt the fear and uncertainty of the past, while only standing outside.

She pushed the door open and didn't immediately notice there were a few candles burning in the room.

Her mind was too consumed with other images. Brief, fleeting pictures from that night, ones she couldn't banish from her memory—no matter how hard she tried to erase them or dull their influence.

Olivia sank into a chair, one closest to the door. She noticed the faint light in the room now but didn't give much thought to why it was there.

What thoughts had her mother had that evening five years ago? Olivia couldn't begin to imagine.

They'd all been mired in grief. Her father had passed away from a sickness a few months before her mother decided she couldn't live anymore. Her devotion to her husband so complete, she couldn't bear to part with him—even in death.

And Marcus, the earl for three short months, had to assume another role…her guardian.

Most of the room was still cast in shadows, making the memories more eerie than she'd thought they'd be. No one ever asked why she avoided the room. The assumption was that fear kept her away. Of course, to hear everyone talk about it, this was the room the countess was murdered in—by an intruder who had only upended some drawers and strewn around some papers before he left the dead countess sitting at the desk.

Olivia was surprised anyone had believed that.

The story had been as flimsy as a gossamer thread.

But it had held.

And Olivia had to live with not only the lies and deceptions, but also the weight of her mother's crime.

"Oh, Mama," she choked. She put her fist to her mouth, stifling the sound. She wasn't sure if it was a plea or a condemnation…perhaps both.

"Olivia?" a voice echoed from the shadows.

She jumped. Her brother sat forward. He'd obviously been reclining, and neither had noticed the presence of the other.

"What are you doing here?" she asked, hoping her voice didn't sound as shaky as it felt.

"I don't know," Marcus confessed.

She squinted into the darkness at him, rose from her seat

and crossed to sit with him. He obligingly moved his legs off the settee, so she would have room. "I don't know, either."

"It's funny, isn't it?" he asked after a few minutes of silence.

"What is?"

"That the one room that holds such grief for us is the one we can't stay away from." He stared off and around the room, as though looking at something only he could see.

Olivia doubted it was anything like what she could see when she closed her eyes.

Olivia lost track of how long they sat together. Eventually, she rested her head against his shoulder, and he put his arm around her. For a minute, they were not the Earl of Westin and Lady Olivia Fairfax. They were a brother and sister who hurt.

More than either of them knew.

Olivia felt her eyes growing heavy-lidded. She was relaxed with drowsiness and knew she should return to bed. But she wanted to talk to Marcus. Wanted to in some way prepare him for what was going to happen.

She roused herself enough to lift her head and look at her brother. She was surprised to find he didn't look the least bit tired.

"Do you mind if I ask a question?" Olivia began, driven by some courage she didn't realize she had.

In spite of the dim lighting, she could tell his look was wary. "I suppose."

"Why didn't you tell me Finley had approached you to ask for my hand?"

Marcus tensed as an immediate reaction to her words. "Finley told you that?" Although it wasn't asked with a very questioning tone.

She nodded, knowing he could feel the movement against his arm.

"I gave him my answer and I didn't think you needed to be bothered with the matter," he said.

"You've always consulted me in such things. Why didn't you see fit to so much as mention it?" she pressed. Maybe he would tell her something that would allow her to nullify Finley's threat, such as proof that the man was truly a pirate with a bounty on his head. Or a traitor to the Crown.

Either would work for her.

"I didn't see the purpose." He was using a tone she'd only heard a few times. It was the tone that suggested—strongly—she let the conversation drop.

She wasn't going to. "Why do you dislike him so much?"

"I have many reasons" was the curt reply.

His discomfort was no match for her current burst of tenacity. "I would like to spend some time with him. To see if we suit," she said on a gulp.

Had the situation been less serious, she might have laughed aloud at her brother's appalled expression. "Are you jesting?" he managed after several moments of his mouth hanging wide. His voice was strangled, as though invisible hands were wrapped around his neck.

"No."

"I forbid it," he sputtered.

Olivia leapt to her feet, her tiredness seemed a thing of the past. If they were going to quarrel, she'd rather not do it sitting down. He followed to his feet soon after.

"I'm afraid that would make me very unhappy." She strove to keep her voice level.

He was flummoxed. "You've never shown the slightest bit of romantic interest in him. Why now?"

"I've known him for a long time," she began, searching for something complimentary to say that wouldn't make her choke. "He was very, ah, attentive after mother's death." *Too attentive, obviously,* she added to herself.

"Gibbons was attentive as well, do you wish to marry him?" Marcus asked.

"Don't be ridiculous," she snapped.

"I could say the same to you."

She slammed her hand down on a nearby table in frustration. "I'd hoped you would be reasonable about this. I can see my faith in you was misplaced."

She could tell the words stung, but her brother didn't let the hurt dissuade him. "I'm sorry to disappoint you, but I'm not changing my mind about this."

Of course he wouldn't. It would be far too much to hope that this aspect of the deed would be done swiftly and without quarrel. Why did Marcus have to make this more difficult? Was it not enough that what she had to do made her skin crawl? Could she not at least have had no interference from the one person whose good opinion she desired above all others?

"I am an adult," she informed him quietly.

A muscle in his jaw ticked furiously.

"And I'd rather this not become an argument," she continued before Marcus could lose his temper. His clenched hands, narrowed eyes and set jaw were all omens of an impending explosion.

"And I'd rather not issue any ultimatums. So I will simply advise you to stay away from him, or…" He didn't finish the threat. His voice had risen to a near yell.

Hers wasn't very quiet, either. "Or what, Marcus? Will you disown me? Cast me out on the streets to fend for myself?" She knew she should lower her voice, help calm the situation. At this volume, it wouldn't be long before their guest, and probably Gibbons, would be coming in to see what was amiss. But she couldn't bring herself to back down.

Marcus scoffed. "Now who's being ridiculous?"

"Well, you're being obstinate," she snapped.

His answering sigh was heavy and heartfelt. "I've no wish to

fight with you. Do you not trust me enough to at least obey me on this? You know I would only say no if I had a good reason to do so."

Olivia said nothing. She couldn't give him the words he wanted to hear, but she refused to make the moment worse by saying something to needlessly hurt him.

When she didn't answer, Marcus eyed her. "You *will* stay away from him," he said, resolved.

"What if I love him?" she asked in a whisper.

The horror on his face stung. "Do you?"

She vacillated between honesty and the lie that would perhaps, in some small way, make her brother more reasonable.

She opted for honesty. "No, I don't."

His relief was palpable.

"That doesn't change anything, though." As soon as she spoke the words, Marcus's face fell back into its stern mask.

"You know my feelings on the matter," he said, striding to the door of the study. "I trust you'll make the right decision. Good night."

As the door swung shut behind him, she said, "Don't trust me too much," knowing he wouldn't be able to hear her.

"You would be my second if I required it, would you not?" Marcus asked Nick the next morning after Olivia had left the dining room. The trio had plans to return to London later in the day, and while Olivia had been subdued at breakfast, he didn't credit her absence with anything other than a desire to relax before they left.

But his friend's odd question had him wondering.

"Whom are we planning on dueling?" Nick asked.

"Julian Finley. Perhaps you remember him." Marcus raised an eyebrow. He knew well that Nick had not forgotten the rogue.

Nick grumbled in response. "When would you like me to have your pistols ready?" He was only partially joking.

In spite of the obvious stress, Marcus couldn't suppress a grin. "Don't you wish to know why I would challenge him?"

"Since it's Finley, I can only imagine what new dastardly business he is up to. But also, since it's him, I don't have any doubt your claim is valid."

"He wants to marry Olivia," Marcus answered, as though Nick had indeed asked the question.

Nick laughed.

"I'm serious," Marcus said.

Nick had to force himself to stop chuckling. "What did he say when you told him no?"

Marcus shrugged. "What you would expect from him. He ranted and finally stormed out of the house."

"At least Gibbons didn't have to throw him out." Nick allowed himself a moment of silent amusement, envisioning the scene.

Marcus flashed an immediate smile in response, but he quickly sobered.

Why was Marcus so despondent? "You know you made the right decision," Nick assured him. "There'd be no inducement that would convince me to let Finley pay suit to any woman under my protection."

"I know that." Marcus scrubbed his hand over his face.

"What's the problem then?" Nick asked. "Finley has asked, and you have refused. There should be no more to say on the subject."

Marcus laughed, but it held no amusement. "You make the mistake of thinking Finley would abide by my decision. He has not. Instead, he has approached Olivia directly with his suit."

Something seized in Nick's gut. Anger, certainly, was there. Including the ne'er-do-wells he'd met while in France, Nick couldn't think of many in his acquaintance he had a lower

opinion of than Finley. But another emotion tumbled with his rage, fighting for precedence. One that was harder to name. Or perhaps he merely didn't want to identify it.

"Well, has he desisted at *her* refusal?" Nick asked.

Marcus said nothing for several moments. Nick stared at the mantel clock and tried to convince himself he wasn't personally interested in what Olivia had to say. Other than for the sake of his friend, of course.

"She has not refused him," Nick said for Marcus. The nod of acknowledgment from his friend was unnecessary.

It was inconceivable. Nick couldn't reconcile the headstrong, viscount-disabling woman he'd met with someone naive enough to fall for Finley's guiles.

"Did you explain your position on the matter to her?" Nick asked.

Marcus nodded again. "For my life, I can't understand why she won't listen to me. But, as I'm sure you'll agree, I can't allow the two of them to wed. It would be disastrous."

A large understatement.

"He's a snake in the grass," Nick agreed.

And Nick knew both he and Marcus were thinking about an earlier incident involving Finley. When the three of them had been away at school, Finley had seduced a professor's daughter. When everyone discovered she was with child, Finley refused to marry the young woman, even though the protection of his name was the one thing that would save her from public ruin.

Finley's father had been prepared, those years ago, to force his son's hand. Unfortunately for the young girl and her child, the elder baron died in his sleep before he could do so.

An attack of the heart, they said.

And no amount of persuasion from the professor or tearful pleas from his daughter could change Finley's mind. He'd left the woman, alone and ruined, and didn't appear to feel the slightest pang of remorse.

No, Olivia couldn't be allowed to wed someone who would treat a woman so callously, who would most likely not be faithful to his marriage vows, who enjoyed spirits and questionable amusements far too much.

"I attempted to remove her to London after Finley broached the subject of their marrying. I'd hoped the distance would hinder him," Marcus said into the silence.

"But he followed you instead," Nick finished. "That was why you agreed so quickly to leave London when you learned that he had called upon Olivia there."

A curt nod was Marcus's reply.

"Why is he so willing to garner your displeasure? I can't believe he loves her—simply because I don't believe him capable of the emotion."

"I have to agree," Marcus said. "My guess is Olivia's dowry is the reason for the dogged pursuit. My sister has much to recommend her, of course, but I've heard Finley's been liberal with the funds his father left for him."

Money. Of course that would be the baron's motivation. But what about Olivia? What reason would she have to want to marry him?

"What foolishness has possessed her?" Nick ranted aloud. "Why would she want to be married to a wastrel of a man who will eventually break her heart?" Nick knew his fury was out of place. Why should he care if Lady Olivia was determined to ruin the rest of her life? But he did care. More than he was going to admit.

"Olivia and Finley have known each other for years," Marcus explained. "After our mother…" He paused for a moment. "Once mother passed away, Finley was very attentive to her. More so than I was, I'm ashamed to admit."

Nick could sense his friend's guilt. "So she thinks he's a dashing, compassionate gentleman?"

"I don't know what she's thinking."

It was fairly obvious to Nick that she *wasn't* thinking…not at all. But she had to be under the delusion that Finley was something other than a snake. He could almost understand her defying her brother if she thought her suitor was honorable and supportive. Of course Olivia, who was naive in the motivations and thinking of men, would have tender feelings for a man who feigned sympathy in the time of her despair.

But Nick knew the man better. Knew what kind of hidden viper he was.

"What are you going to do?"

Marcus splayed his hands in front of him. "What can I do?"

"Forbid the match." Nick made the statement as though the answer was the most obvious thing in the world.

Marcus almost smiled. Almost. "I know you don't think Finley would care what I decree. And well, you've met my sister."

Nick thought about the feisty young woman who'd intrigued him so effortlessly. And he had to concede that she wouldn't be deterred because her brother said no. The couple could run to Gretna Green at the earliest opportunity, and it would be too late for Marcus to do anything.

"You need to keep her away from him," Nick said, thinking to limit the likelihood of an elopement.

"Do you have any brilliant ideas as to how?" Marcus snapped. But he immediately apologized. "Forgive me, Nick. My anger isn't toward you. I'm only frustrated. There's no place I can take her that he won't try to follow. I thought removing her to London would send a message. But what does he do? Follow us. If we remain at Westin Park, he will trail after us again."

"So what will you do?" Nick asked, unsure of which option he would choose were it his decision to make.

"There is more to do, more to occupy her in London." Marcus

sighed. "Perhaps she will meet with some other gentleman who is more suitable."

Nick found himself bothered by that thought as well. He shook off the errant aggravation.

"Finley will shadow her every move," Nick warned. His time as an agent of the Crown had taught him to think ahead, to anticipate the enemy.

Finley was definitely the enemy.

Marcus leaned back in his seat. "I know I'll have to be glued to her side to be certain Finley doesn't worm his way in."

Nick saw the flaws immediately. "That won't work. You are just one person. You can't be with her at all times. Acquaintances will seek to talk to you, she'll have dance partners…" He let the statement trail off. An idea was forming in his mind. Nick wasn't an impulsive man. He was levelheaded, meticulous and cautious.

But right now, with the anger clawing at him, he was being none of those.

"Let me help," Nick said after a few seconds of thought. "I can be with her when you aren't. Between the two of us, we should intimidate Finley enough that he won't dare approach her."

Marcus pondered the plan. He steepled his fingers and tapped them against his chin. "Don't you think Olivia might be a bit suspicious of that?"

Nick shrugged. "We would attend the same events, and she's my friend's sister. She might believe I'm aiding you in your protectiveness, but if it keeps Finley away…" He shrugged his shoulders again.

"What if she believes you're courting her?"

Nick didn't have a good answer for that. And this was where his rashness might become a problem. He couldn't deny to himself that she appealed to him, but Lady Olivia wasn't the woman for him. From what Marcus had told him, she was in

a delicate spiritual place, and Nick was firm in his belief that Christians should not be linked with nonbelievers.

If things were different…

"Your silence doesn't bode well," Marcus said.

The marquess cleared his throat. "I will be careful to ensure she sees me as a friend—nothing more. Truthfully, this might not be the wisest plan, but it's the only one we have."

Marcus said nothing.

Nick wondered over the source of the silence. "Are you worried my reputation will negatively affect her?" Nick knew the gossips would be vicious.

Marcus seemed surprised, if his expression was a true indication. "That's the last thing I'm worried about. I know what they're saying isn't true. So it doesn't matter to me what sordid tales the gossips have concocted."

Nick nodded in satisfaction. While he tried not to let the ridiculous stories and speculations disturb him, he was gratified to hear his friend believed in him wholly.

"I shudder to think of what Olivia will say if she finds out what we're up to," Marcus said by way of an agreement.

"I guess we'll have to take the chance," Nick said, wondering why he'd assumed the mantle of responsibility so quickly but knowing he was loath to remove it. Something about being involved with the siblings made him feel a little less lonely.

And something about being near Olivia appealed to him immensely.

Chapter Seven

Olivia turned the page of the latest Mrs. Radcliffe novel. And she muttered to herself about Danfield's pronouncement that she read too many books for a lady. Nothing was wrong with seeking innocent entertainment.

But that didn't stop her from shoving the book under a cushion when she heard someone approaching. Really, couldn't she finish a whole chapter without some sort of interruption?

She looked up guiltily, expecting to see her brother, but was startled to find the Marquess of Huntsford before her. She hadn't seen him since they'd returned to London three days earlier.

His presence and her discomfort made her grumpy.

"Hiding something?" he asked with a hint of a smile.

"Of course not," Olivia retorted. But she flashed a quick look at the cushions to make sure she had not left a corner of the book poking out.

"What are you doing here, anyway?" she asked ungraciously, wondering where Gibbons was. Most likely asleep.

"I thought you might enjoy a ride." Lord Huntsford seemed unperturbed by her hostility.

She barely resisted the urge to roll her eyes.

"I've brought you a gift," he continued, pulling a wrapped package from his coat.

Olivia took the present with the reluctant stirrings of curiosity. She was used to men bringing her flowers, but this was something new.

She tore the wrapping off gently, gasping in delight when she saw what lay beneath the paper.

"A copy of *Twelfth Night?*" she asked, trying to keep the excitement from her voice. The play was her favorite of Shakespeare's. She had read her own copy so much it was tattered and falling apart.

He smiled at her. "Do you like it?"

She nodded, not quite trusting herself to say more.

"How did you know?" she asked finally.

"I noticed you had a copy sitting on the table at Westin Park. It looked as though it was in dire need of retirement, so I thought you would appreciate a new edition."

Olivia cradled the volume in her hands, enjoying the feel of the cool leather binding. The thoughtfulness of the gift overwhelmed her.

"Thank you." She forced herself to meet his eyes.

"My pleasure," he replied, and when Lord Huntsford said the words, she believed them.

She wanted to rise from her seat, uncomfortable with him towering over her. His nearness was unsettling. The marquess was too attractive for his own good. And the well-chosen gift also showed him to be perceptive and kind. All of that made for a heady—and dangerous—combination. It would be best for her to keep her distance, in every way. But he was too close for her to stand without brushing against him, so she remained seated.

"Are you sufficiently grateful to accompany me to Hyde Park?" he asked.

It would be best for her to refuse. Reason dictated that nothing good could come from pretending she could be a normal woman and enjoy the company of a charming man.

Her mind clearly didn't care about reason. "Let me fetch my bonnet," she said, ignoring the fact that Nick suddenly looked like he had single-handedly defeated Napoleon at Waterloo.

As she was walking toward the door, Gibbons intercepted her. His eyes were still bleary with sleep. "My lady, the—" he squinted at the card in his hand "—Marquess of Huntsford is here…again, it would seem."

"I noticed," she said, her hand perched on her hip.

"Well, I see there was no need to rouse myself then," he mumbled as he left.

"I'll return in a moment," Olivia said to the marquess, following after the butler, but she was unable to resist stopping at the doorway and giving Lord Huntsford one more smile.

Nick had smiled back, pleased she had, if just for the moment, softened toward him. He'd been nervous in bringing her the book but wanted to give her something. And no, he didn't stop to analyze his motives.

"Sorry for the delay, my lord," Lady Olivia said, standing in the doorway, ready for their outing. He was struck again by how beautiful she looked. The pale pink of her morning gown complemented the creaminess of her complexion, and her dark hair made her eyes have even more of an impact.

"I hope you'll forgive the impropriety if I say you were worth the wait." Nick smiled at her, and he led her out to where his curricle awaited. Several carriages slowed down, and the occupants inside craned their necks to get a glimpse of him and Olivia.

Once she was seated, he moved to climb aboard himself.

Nick didn't notice something else held Olivia's attention until he heard her speak.

"There's Lord Finley," she said, watching as the man strolled down the sidewalk toward her house. The baron caught sight of her, and his mouth formed an O of surprise.

Nick wavered between staying the horses and slapping the reins to leave Finley standing behind, watching them drive off.

He slapped the reins.

"That was badly done of you," she chided as she held fast to her seat.

"What was?"

She gave him a look.

"Oh, *that,*" he said. "I was just ensuring that my plan for a drive with you remained uninterrupted. In my line of work, proper planning means the difference between life and—" Nick stopped himself in mid-sentence, hoping she had not been listening to him. He could have kicked himself for not guarding his tongue.

Luck wasn't with him.

"Your line of work?" she echoed. "I didn't think powerful lords worked."

"We don't," he said somewhat hastily. "I simply meant my responsibilities with the estates and such. Your brother is one of those powerful lords, too." He looked at her out of the corner of his eye to see if she believed him. "Surely you know how much effort he puts into his own lands and the people there."

"Of course I do." But her tone was too light for Nick's comfort. "Forgive me, I simply thought since you had only just returned to England you wouldn't have had time to assume all your responsibilities."

She was clever; he would give her that much. "Yes, well, I was able to learn from my father before I left."

It was the only thing of value the old Marquess of Huntsford had taught him, and the only lesson he'd been willing to learn. The rules of seduction and debauchery, ever his father's favorite pastimes, had fallen on deaf—and disgusted—ears.

"Why did you leave?" Lady Olivia asked then, and Nick

couldn't help but feel he had dodged one bullet only to be struck by another.

"For exploration."

"Exploration of what?"

"The world."

"I should think your father would have had numerous reservations about allowing you to go on such a venture. You were, after all, the sole heir to the marquessdom," she said.

While he admired her tenacity, he could not claim he was comfortable with the direction their conversation had taken. There were things—particularly things in his past—he would rather not discuss with her. She should never be touched with anything so sordid as his memories of his father.

"I can't say he was happy to see me go."

An understatement.

Nick still carried the small, upraised scar on his forearm where his father had attacked him with a knife after his pronouncement. The old man had stood between Nick and the door, waving his weapon erratically and threatening to kill him. But Nick had been faster and not muddled by liquor. He'd managed to disarm his father with only the minor injury. The scar reminded him of the depths to which the old marquess had fallen.

And his own determination to escape.

"I believe my brother was also upset by your abrupt departure," she confessed, and Nick felt the guilt piling on him again. Had he been a decent friend, he would have stayed to help Marcus deal with the loss of his own father and mother.

The elder marquess's lunacy had grown so pronounced, however, that Nick had feared being murdered in his bed if he had stayed. His father had dismissed the entire staff, hiring new servants who felt no loyalty to his son. He had tried to isolate Nick from all of his friends. Marcus had been the only one to stick beside him.

"I hoped your brother would understand," he said finally. Marcus knew, like few others had, of his father's depravity. And while Nick left without bidding anyone farewell, he'd prayed that he would be forgiven by his friend when he returned.

"He did." Olivia rushed to reassure him, making him wonder how much information she had been privy to. "But it was still a difficult time for him."

"Was it not for you?"

She squared her shoulders and clenched her jaw, as though she could hold at bay the bad memories. "I am not my brother."

Her comment confused him. "I certainly wasn't trying to make that insinuation."

"What I mean is," she said on an exhale, "it didn't shatter me, because I'm not so foolish as to believe life is perfect."

"And you think Marcus does?"

She twisted her reticule between her hands. "I think he allows his misplaced belief in his *God*—" she said the word with a sigh "—to convince him that all things work for the good."

"You disagree?"

"I'm sure it is nice to believe that."

He wasn't certain what to say but felt as though he should say something. Should argue with her and try to convince her that faith made one strong—not weak. But he doubted, after hearing her conversation with Reverend Thomas, she would listen. And the last thing he wanted was to sound pious and cause her to retreat into her shell.

Help me find a way to reach her, Lord, Nick prayed. *For Your sake, and for hers.*

"I do have a question," Olivia said after a long silence between the two of them.

"Yes?"

"It's about what the ladies at the church were talking about."

He merely nodded.

Olivia sighed. He obviously wasn't going to make this any easier for her. "Was any of what they were saying true?" She knew how offensive she was being just by asking the question, so she rushed on. "I normally would never bring up such a matter, but I've been wondering…" She trailed off. She was making a muck of it.

"What do you think about the things people are saying?" But the statement wasn't a challenge, a gauntlet thrown at her feet. He seemed genuinely curious.

"I think they're lies," she said after a thoughtful pause.

He rewarded her confidence in him with a dazzling smile.

"And I think you are uncannily astute," Lord Huntsford returned.

"But why would people be saying those kinds of things anyway?" Olivia knew that some of the *ton* lived for scandals… some even manufactured them for entertainment. But was there any particular reason the marquess had been singled out? Any suspicious evidence? Or was it simply the unfounded ramblings of people with too much time and too little scruples?

Lord Huntsford pulled his curricle to a stop and turned to look fully at her. "Sometimes, Lady Olivia, things aren't what they seem. Sometimes, they aren't even close."

The answer mystified her. "Then why don't you put a stop to the rumors? I wouldn't be surprised if the lies have spread through half of London."

"It's not worth the waste of time it would take to discredit. I know the kind of person I am. God knows even better. That's good enough for me."

God again, she thought with a small measure of disgust. "Aren't you worried someone will actually believe the drivel?"

"I can't stop the ladies at church—or anyone else—from believing it. So why should I bother?"

Olivia's frustration rose with his very nonchalant remark. "Don't you understand? You could be ostracized if those rumors became common knowledge?" This was the very dilemma she faced with the *ton* knowing about her mother. The very reason she'd gone to such lengths to protect Marcus. His title would be worthless if he didn't command the public's respect. Lord Huntsford's would be as well.

"I'm not overly worried about that. Truth be told, I don't much enjoy balls and parties."

"But you're in the House of Lords now. There are your peers to consider."

"I don't understand why you are so upset about this," he said. "The rumors, while completely unfounded, would hurt only me."

"I'm upset because it's just not fair," she cried. "You shouldn't have to be punished for something you didn't do!"

His face softened. "I have faith eventually my character will speak for itself."

She digested his words. What kind of person thought so little of the opinions of others? He seemed to believe God would reward his silence by revealing the truth eventually.

And maybe, she mused, *God would.*

She wished she could test the theory for herself.

Chapter Eight

Several days later, Nick waited for the butler to open the door and grant him admittance to the stylish Mayfair House. And he tried to quiet the unease he felt standing outside. Five years had passed since he'd been here.

Who knew what reception he'd receive?

A staid-looking butler opened the door, and a slight lift of the eyebrows was the only indication the servant was surprised.

"Smithson," Nick greeted with a smile.

"My lord." The butler inclined his head and motioned for Nick to come in the house.

"If you'll wait just a moment, my lord," Smithson said. Turning to grab the attention of a hovering footman, the butler dispatched the other servant.

Nick was then ushered into a decidedly feminine drawing room. He smiled at the frills and profusion of lace covering nearly every available surface.

"Nicholas!" a woman cried as she walked into the room.

He turned at the voice. "Aunt Henrietta," he greeted.

The older woman embraced him in a swirl of perfume. Nick wrapped his arms around her and squeezed. And the memories he'd feared would assault him upon seeing her stayed

on the periphery, enough out of sight that he wasn't bothered by them.

"Your uncle will be sorry he missed you," Nick's aunt said as she took a seat and motioned for him to do the same. "But he had a meeting with his solicitors this morning."

Nick nodded in understanding.

Then he stared at his aunt. The last five years had been kind to her, but then again she'd been the beauty of the family from the beginning. A fact that had always needled his mother. Oh, there was some resemblance between his deceased mother and his aunt—they were sisters, after all. But anyone who had seen the two while both were living would have to concede his aunt had inherited the loveliness of the Holbrook family.

While her face still retained much of its youth, however, her wardrobe left a great deal to be desired. Her morning gown was a garish orange, which was accompanied by a bright purple feather bobbing from an otherwise fashionable green turban.

It was an ensemble to make a man's eyes bleed. But it was quintessentially Henrietta. Her love for bright colors in shocking combinations was her one departure from the good sense and good taste she showed in every other respect.

"I would ask how long you've been in town," his aunt said as she dispatched a footman for a tea service, "but I already know."

Nick smiled. "I'd be surprised if you didn't."

"I have my spies all over London."

Nick stiffened at the innocent remark. His aunt and uncle knew about his wartime excursions, but the issue of his occupation had never been openly discussed. Was this his aunt's not-so-subtle way to steer the conversation? It took only a moment to realize he was being edgy and foolish.

"I'm sorry I didn't come by to visit sooner, Aunt," Nick said. "I've had quite a lot to occupy me."

Her smile turned speculative. "I've heard things about that as well."

The tea service arrived then, sparing Nick from having to comment right away. Aunt Henri didn't ask for a reminder of how he took his tea. She dropped two sugars in the cup and handed it to him.

"I've missed you, Aunt Henri," Nick admitted.

Her face softened. The eyes lost their teasing glint and instead shimmered with unshed tears. "I wrote you many letters while you were gone. But I never knew if you got them." Her face was hopeful.

He hadn't gotten them. Never had been in one place long enough to receive any correspondence. Even if his missions and contacts didn't have him constantly on the run, his cover wouldn't have withstood a barrage of missives from his family. Pretending to be a defected Englishman was difficult enough without explaining constant letters from family he supposedly no longer had contact with.

"I was busy while I was gone," he hedged.

Silence stretched between them. He could tell, by reading his aunt's face, there was something she wanted to say to him.

"Go ahead," he prompted with a smile.

She didn't bother to ask what he was talking about. "Your uncle and I saw your father before he died."

Nick clenched his hands. Some pithy remark waited on the tip of his tongue, but he bit it back. Was he supposed to ask, hopefully, if his father had experienced a deathbed conversion? Or to see if his son's name had been on his lips before he passed? He didn't know what kind of reaction Aunt Henri wanted—if she wanted any—from him, so he said nothing.

"He wasn't much changed when we last parted ways," she said delicately.

Nick let out a breath he didn't realize he'd been holding. And the hope he didn't want to have, died. "I'm not surprised."

"You've grown into a fine young man," his aunt said after a few moments of contemplative silence. Obviously, she'd decided they weren't going to be discussing the past and its shadows this afternoon.

"Thank you, Aunt Henri."

Her eyes crinkled at the corners as she smiled. "So, you were busy then, and you've been busy now. But I have a feeling now has less to do with business and more with pleasure."

Sitting his teacup and saucer on the polished mahogany table, Nick forced his gaze to remain steady. Of course his aunt was prying, that was how the lady occupied much of her time—keeping a watch on everyone else.

"I guess you've been busy, too." He smiled.

Aunt Henri covered her smirk with a well-timed sip of tea. "You won't be able to distract me, so you might as well talk."

"You remember Marcus Fairfax, don't you?"

"I remember hearing about him. His father passed away years back, then his mother was murdered. A shame," she said.

"Well, he's in London as well. I've been spending a great deal of time with him."

She didn't bother trying to hide her smile this time. "And his sister," she said.

The statement wasn't a question.

Nick nodded. "Yes, and his sister."

His aunt was silent, no doubt waiting for him to expound on his unusual attachment to the young lady.

Nick said nothing.

"And?" she prompted.

Stifling a chuckle, Nick knew his aunt's agitation was only going to grow with his continued silence. "And what?"

She set her cup on the saucer with a jarring clatter. "Don't play games with me Nicholas Robert Stuart."

Nick strove for an innocent expression, but he could tell from Henri's face it wasn't working.

"Tell me about this Olivia girl," his aunt demanded.

"I would have thought you'd know everything there was to know by now," he returned.

She wasn't amused by his witty banter. "I'd like to hear it from you."

Nick threw his hands in the air. How did he explain Olivia or how he felt about his role in her life? "I don't know, Aunt Henri."

"Well, *I've* heard the young lady's rather arrogant. Snobby, I believe, is what they call her." His aunt regarded him with cool, impassive eyes.

Blood thundered in his ears. His fists clenched, almost of their own volition. "Who's saying that?" he asked, but didn't give her a chance to answer. "Lady Olivia is a caring, lovely young woman."

No one knew Olivia. So how dare they judge her and deem her aloof?

"Are you okay, Nicholas, dear?" Aunt Henri asked.

"It's just ludicrous. Whoever's saying that obviously doesn't know her and doesn't deserve to."

"Well spoken, my dear." Henri clapped her hands together.

And Nick recognized—too late—the trap for what it was and acknowledged his fall into it was inevitable.

"Don't get any ideas, Aunt Henri," he warned.

She feigned innocence—poorly. "I have no idea what you're referring to, Nicholas."

"I'm serious about this," he insisted.

She held out her hands, a show that she had nothing to hide. "I'm merely commending you for your speedy defense of the young lady. It's very honorable of you." She paused and raised a finely arched eyebrow. "And considerate."

"Don't try to read anything into it, Aunt Henri."

She made another "I would never" gesture.

He was unconvinced. "Besides, Lady Olivia is fascinated with Julian Finley."

"Bah," his aunt said.

If only it were so easy to dismiss Olivia's unusual attraction to the rake. "I'm not sure what she sees in him," Nick confided. Perhaps he should have felt awkward discussing the situation with his aunt, but the marquess had always found her wisdom and insight to be invaluable.

"Finley's about as slimy as a serpent," his aunt said.

Nick couldn't have agreed more and said as much.

Henri wasn't through, however. Something sparked in her eyes, and her expression grew less disgusted by their topic and more speculative at the turn the conversation had taken.

"Personality and morals aside, however, I suppose he's attractive enough…if one enjoys a blond Adonis-like, incredibly good-looking man."

"You're really not helping right now, Aunt Henri." Couldn't they go back to talking about how repulsive Finley was as a person?

Henri patted his hand. "I wouldn't worry about it, dear. You're handsome and titled, as well."

Nick opened his mouth to retort, to inform his aunt he had no wish to ever be compared to Finley. His aunt didn't give him the opportunity.

"No, if you *were* interested in this Lady Olivia—despite her unfortunate attraction to Baron Finley—"

"I never said she was attracted," Nick felt compelled to interject. "I said fascinated."

"Whichever. If you were interested in Lady Olivia, I would advise you to make an attempt to win her affections." She raised a brow. "Unless you believe Finley—despite his snakelike qualities—is more adept in the art of romance than you."

Nick refused to fall into another of Aunt Henri's traps. "She's only a friend," he said, trying to sound decisive.

His aunt smiled. "Whatever you say."

The sky foretold the impending rain.

Olivia ducked into the milliner's shop, in need of a new bonnet and eager to finish her Bond Street expedition.

"Good morning, Lady Olivia," the shop owner greeted her warmly.

"It's nearly afternoon, I'm afraid," Olivia returned with a smile as she took off her gloves.

"True enough, my lady. Now, what might you be interested in seeing today?"

Mrs. Dunwittle was the owner of the milliner's shop and was patronized by many of the women of the *ton*. Not only was her manner pleasant and inviting, but her hats were the height of fashion. Olivia enjoyed slipping into the shop and buying herself a new present whenever she felt low.

And the reality of her impending marriage to Lord Finley made her feel incredibly low.

The owner left her largely to her own devices, having dealt with the young lady often enough since her coming to town to know she would browse and ask questions if needed. Olivia fingered a bonnet, admiring the pretty shade of blue. She was in the process of deciding what walking dress she had that would match, when she felt someone approach her from behind.

Before she could turn around, the newcomer said, "Perhaps I should accompany my cousin on her errands more often." Lord Finley.

"Lord Finley, this is quite an unusual place to meet you." Was he following her? She was acutely aware of the fact she'd yet to give him an answer to his "proposal."

The baron gestured at a young girl, a child really, certainly no more than sixteen years old, who was talking quietly with

one of Mrs. Dunwittle's assistants. "My cousin, Anna. My aunt imposed upon me to take the girl to Bond Street." He glared at the back of the girl's head.

"I didn't know your cousin was in town as well. Might I have an introduction?"

He glanced between the two females. "While I'm certain Anna would be flattered by your request, I assure you, you would be disappointed."

Olivia was too shocked by his hatefulness to respond.

But her silence made Finley reconsider. "If you must," he said on a sigh, grabbing her elbow and propelling her forward.

Olivia wondered if he knew how tightly he was gripping her. She tried not to wince as he maneuvered them past displays and toward the young girl.

"Anna," he barked.

As the girl spun around, Olivia was struck by the fear in her gaze.

"Have I done something wrong?" Anna asked worriedly.

"Not yet." There was no smile to belie his words. "Lady Olivia would like to meet you."

Anna's eyes widened, perfect, dark circles in her pale face. "I'm honored," she stammered.

Finley flicked a dismissive glance over his relative. "Lady Olivia, this is my cousin, Miss Anna Finley." He sighed. "Anna, Lady Olivia Fairfax."

The young girl curtsied, and as she did, Olivia noticed her shoes were worn.

"It is very nice to meet you, Miss Finley."

The young girl cast a tentative look at her cousin but he was distracted by something outside the window, so she offered a small smile.

"I pray you will excuse me for a moment, Lady Olivia," Finley said, with his attention still focused outside. "I see an acquaintance I must speak to."

Olivia watched Anna as Finley walked toward the door of the shop. With each step the baron took, the girl relaxed her rigid stance.

The two ladies stood together uncertainly, and Olivia finally took the younger girl's hand, leading her to a display of straw bonnets.

Anna visibly suppressed an "ah" of delight at one of Mrs. Dunwittle's creations. "It's beautiful," she breathed, rubbing the ribbon between two fingers.

"It would look lovely with your complexion," Olivia agreed.

"Julian did say I could purchase a new bonnet," Anna looked at her cousin's friend apologetically. "I'm afraid most of my clothes were too countrified, as he said."

Olivia didn't know what to say.

"I didn't wish to come to London in the first place," Anna said in frustration. "But I had to come after the trouble at home—" It seemed as though she were going to say more, but she promptly snapped her lips shut.

"Well," Olivia said briskly, taking Anna by the arm, "I think you are going to enjoy your time here immensely." Just because Olivia wasn't having a splendid Season herself didn't mean young Anna was doomed, as well.

Anna, still fascinated with the bonnet, called out to one of the shop assistants, inquiring about the price.

"Ten shillings, miss."

Anna blanched. "That's far too much," she whispered to herself.

Olivia took the bonnet in her hands and practically drug Anna to the front of the store.

"Mrs. Dunwittle," she called.

"Yes, my lady?" the woman asked, bustling to the front.

"We'll be taking this. You can put it on my account," Olivia said, raising her voice to drown out Anna's protests.

"Very good, my lady."

Olivia handed the bonnet to an embarrassed Anna. "You really shouldn't have, my lady," she protested.

"Nonsense. Consider it my welcome gift to you. And, please, call me Olivia."

Anna flushed, and Olivia hoped it was with pleasure and not mortification.

"You are a very nice lady," Anna said quietly.

Olivia smiled in response.

"I had thought you would be like my cousin," the girl continued.

A chill skittered along Olivia's spine. "Why would you say that?"

Anna looked at the ground, studiously avoiding Olivia's eyes. "I shouldn't have said anything. It would be best if we forgot I mentioned this."

"If you say so," Olivia said slowly.

Anna waited a few moments, visibly struggling with whether she should continue. "My cousin's not very nice," she began, but stopped abruptly.

Olivia didn't have to look up to know Finley had reentered.

"I hope you have not been making a nuisance of yourself, Anna," he said as he rejoined them.

"Of course she hasn't," Olivia said with a smile she wasn't certain she felt. Anna's sparing words were still bothering her.

"I see I shall have to add patience to your list of virtues," he said.

Anna looked hurt by the words. And Olivia's fist coiled automatically at her side. "I think I must be going now," she said tersely.

Anna thanked her again and bid her a good day, but Finley insisted on seeing her out of the shop. "Don't fret," he told her,

once the door was closed behind them and the two were standing under an awning. "I will be sending her back along with my aunt next week. I've had about all of the silly chit and her mother that I'm willing to take."

"I rather enjoyed meeting her." Olivia gave him a disparaging glance. "I find her company much preferable to other's in her family."

Finley's lips pursed and turned white. "You'll hold your tongue, you impudent…" He paused and took several deep breaths. When he continued, his voice was subdued but still possessed the edge of his anger. "Have you forgotten what I can do to you?"

"You'll have a difficult time convincing me to marry you then," she said. Olivia had been avoiding this conversation, dreading it actually. But it was inevitable.

"I will do no convincing. I've laid my offer on the table. It is your turn to decide what you are willing to sacrifice to keep your little secrets and lies."

She couldn't look at him as she said the words, so she stared at the hanging sign of a shop in the distance. He was right. She had no choice. Marcus would be angry, may even refuse to speak to her once he found out, but her family's reputation wouldn't suffer. Marcus's career wouldn't suffer—nor his faith.

"I will do it," she said.

"Smart," he said.

"But I have a few conditions of my own."

He raised his brows in question.

"You will wait to make any announcements of our betrothal," she said.

"Why would I do that?"

Olivia thought about knocking him on the head with her reticule but figured that might cause talk were anyone to see.

"Because Marcus will not be happy. He needs time to adjust to the idea." Like *that* would ever happen.

"Marcus's happiness is of no concern to me."

"You are a fool, then. My brother is a powerful man."

Finley seemed to consider this. "I won't wait long," he acceded.

"Just a few weeks," she assured him.

"You'll stay away from the Marquess of Huntsford," Finley said before she could walk away.

His command stopped her. "How do you expect me to accomplish that? He's Marcus's friend," she said, her back still to the baron.

"I will not be made to look like a fool," he warned. "So you will not parade about with that man like a common strum—"

Olivia spun around and interrupted him before he could finish. "You need me, Lord Finley. I suggest you don't forget that. And I also suggest you not cause a scene. That would ruin my reputation just as effectively as sharing the family secrets. And then, I'd have no need to bow to your blackmail." And not because it mattered to her, but because she was unwilling to surrender everything, she said, "I will not sever ties with anyone. You may have my hand in marriage, but you won't have my life."

"Make a fool of me, or yourself, and I will ruin you," he threatened.

He stepped away from her and, without a word of goodbye, walked back into the shop.

Chapter Nine

"Do you feel more like a member of the peerage now?" Marcus asked with a grin once he and Nick took their seats at a table by the window. They were sitting in White's, the gentleman's club that was always littered with male members of the *ton*.

"Yes. You know, I've been asking myself why this didn't feel *right* yet. Now I can see it's because I've not been to White's in order to waste time and money. A true rite of passage."

Marcus chuckled. "It's a necessary evil, my friend. Like it or not, this is the place to be seen and talk with influential people."

"You do realize *we're* the influential people, don't you?" Nick asked. The statement was without conceit and was actually rather surprising to Nick himself. Because the truth was, though Marcus had been a recluse and had not traveled far from his country estate for years, and Nick was a rumored debaucher and despoiler of innocents, the two of them held a pair of the oldest and most distinguished titles in England.

Yes, before much longer, they would be inundated with requests for introductions. It was only a matter of time, and an issue of who was able to work up the courage to approach them first. Nick knew he looked rather intimidating—such

was his intent. He had few friends in London, and Marcus was the only one currently in the room. He saw no need to make himself approachable to men who wished to make use of him for his wealth, his position or—even worse—the notoriety of his name.

A young man who looked better suited to a schoolroom than a club approached Nick and Marcus then. "Huntsford, I thought that was you over here."

For his life, Nick couldn't remember the boy's name. Marcus was no help—he didn't seem to know him at all.

"How have you been—" Nick fumbled for his name, tried out *George* in his mind, and thought that fit "—George?"

George—Nick thought the last name might be Chase—looked pleased. If Nick remembered correctly, the man was the fifth or sixth son—something unfortunate like that—of an earl with an estate close to Nick's home. He didn't appear to be in the army or a member of the clergy, popular choices for lesser sons, and Nick wondered what he did for his living.

"It has been a long time," George replied. "It's good to see you back in England."

Nick thanked him, wondering what George wanted. He wanted George to leave so he and Marcus could continue their discussion. But from the way George had helped himself to a chair, that didn't seem likely.

"Sorry about your old man," the newcomer said. "Went to one of his parties a couple of months before he passed away. Had a great time, but then I'm sure you can imagine."

Nick could, although he wished it were otherwise. The infamous parties had been his father's favorite form of amusement. And as with anything relating to his sire, no one with an ounce of decency or a shred of morality would have wanted to be within a stone's throw of the festivities.

"Was there something in particular you wanted, George?" Nick asked.

The unwelcome acquaintance from his past looked mildly offended, but the flicker of emotion passed quickly. "Just wanted to see how you were getting along," he defended.

"Well enough." If the man were waiting for Nick to open a dialogue, George was certain to be disappointed.

"But undoubtedly," George tried again, "you haven't had the time to enjoy being home. Tons of invitations, I'm sure."

Nick didn't comment.

George turned his attention to Marcus, obviously assuming his inane commentary would be more welcome on that side of the table. Nick knew he should probably introduce the two men, but he didn't. Doing so would only give George an additional reason to linger.

"Huntsford, here, has been pretty busy since he returned to town," George told Marcus.

"Has he?" Marcus asked, his voice bland.

"Yeah, but that's no surprise. Like father, like son, eh?"

Nick sighed. How long would he be compared to the dead marquess?

George, wisely enough, didn't give Nick an opportunity to answer to the insult. "Hey, Huntsford, a couple of the guys and I were…talking, and I was wondering if you'd help me out."

Nick raised an eyebrow. "How would I do that?" *And why,* he thought to himself.

"Some are saying you've already got your eye on some chit. I'm wondering how confident you're feeling about your ability to woo her."

Nick stiffened, and he saw, from the corner of his vision, Marcus narrow his eyes. "I don't know who would be saying anything like that."

George started, but then, thinking he understood Nick's game, laughed. "I get it. Don't want to tip your hand. Smart move." The man leaned back in his chair, balancing his considerable girth on just two legs.

Nick thought about kicking the seat out from under him.

"But you can trust me. I'm just wondering because some say this Westin girl is a harsh one." George grinned, waiting on Nick to give him an answer.

"That's my sister," Marcus said. His voice had a hard edge to it.

George didn't miss it. "Oh, I—uh—I'm sorry." The man cast a frantic look to a group on the other side of the room. "I better go. Just—uh—forget about the other." And he was gone before either Marcus or Nick could say another word to him.

Not that Nick particularly cared.

"It's happening already, I suppose. The gossip." Marcus sighed.

Nick managed a shrug. "We knew it would. Just a bit sooner than I thought."

"You don't know how grateful I am for your assistance," Marcus said. "You're a good friend to help me this way."

Nick felt somewhat uncomfortable. Of course, he was doing this to help his friend…but he didn't like to think of the time he spent with Olivia as being part of a job, or a duty.

Because he liked her.

Quite liked her, as a person. He found Olivia fascinating, and beautiful, and witty, and charming.…

She was unlike most women he knew. While many of the ladies of his recent acquaintance didn't know the real him and were after what they thought he had to offer them, Olivia seemed to appreciate him for the person he was—not the one he was purported to be.

Nick didn't realize Marcus had been studying him during his long moment of silence until he looked up and his friend looked away guiltily.

"I don't want you to feel you have to do this." Marcus's voice had dropped.

The significance of the situation, and the importance of his

answer, wasn't lost on Nick. He knew that the words out of his mouth next would dictate a rather large step.

"Olivia's my responsibility, and I can keep her safe." Marcus pushed onward.

And before Nick knew exactly what he was doing, he tumbled headlong into a future with Olivia's continued presence. "The two of you would kill each other before it was over, if I didn't help."

"Perhaps," Marcus allowed. He sat back, relaxing into his seat. And Nick hadn't realized until then how much Marcus was dreading hearing his answer.

A waiter arrived with their food, and after depositing the china plates on the table, he faded away.

"I will say, though, that I hope your assistance in this matter is not going to cause problems for you on the marriage mart," Marcus commented.

"What are you talking about?"

Marcus shrugged. "I didn't know if you came to London because you were ready to settle down and find a wife. Are you looking? For a wife, that is."

Nick didn't know if he liked Marcus's overly unconcerned manner. The nonchalance made him feel as if there were several layers to the question he couldn't understand.

"No. Not right away. Eventually, of course," Nick knew he was rambling but didn't stop. "I'm happy to help as long as it's needed."

Marcus's speculative look wasn't making Nick feel any more at ease.

"What about you?" Nick asked, hoping to deflect some of the attention, and heat.

"What about me?" Marcus asked, returning to the plate of food in front of him before changing the subject.

Nick didn't have time to answer before Marcus was speaking again. "Well, again, I appreciate your help with Olivia, but you

can consider yourself on vacation this evening. I'm escorting Olivia to the theater, and I doubt Finley will show for that. I don't think he could afford the box."

"He might be with friends." Nick didn't know why he was trying to talk himself into an invitation.

Marcus shrugged off the concern. "Eh, I don't really see Finley as a fan of Shakespeare. I certainly wouldn't go if I didn't have to. Olivia will be safe enough. I didn't mean for this venture to take up all your time."

Nick wanted to argue...insist he should come. He knew Marcus was trying to give him a break, but Nick *wanted* to see Lady Olivia, to experience her reaction to watching the work of her favorite playwright brought to life on the famous Drury Lane stage.

But he said nothing.

What was wrong with him?

Nick studied his plate in order to hide his tumult of thoughts. Perhaps he was getting sick. That would explain the pang in his chest at the thought of missing an evening spent with Olivia.

Perhaps he was simply losing his mind.

Chapter Ten

"Are you almost ready?" Marcus called from outside Olivia's bedroom door.

"Nearly," she returned. She scrutinized the dress, deciding she rather liked the deep blue with the ivory gloves. And Sarah had spent what seemed like hours pulling and tugging her hair into place.

She should feel silly for caring about how she looked. Finley wouldn't be at the theater—not that she would dress to impress him anyway—and attracting the attention of other men would get her in trouble.

Although, she thought—as a certain marquess came to mind—if things were different, she might not object...

She cast one last look in the mirror before leaving her chambers and descending the steps.

"You look wonderful," Marcus said as she joined him.

"I must say, you don't look too poorly yourself." Olivia took his arm, allowing him to lead her outside to their carriage.

"I hope we can have a pleasant evening," he said, no doubt frustrated that the past several days—since their disagreement and return to London—had been spent in a kind of tenuous but still strained peace.

"I don't see why we can't." In truth, she was in a rather good

mood. Although, she wasn't quite sure what contributed to her sudden change in disposition.

"Marvelous."

As they arrived outside the Drury Lane theatre, Olivia's enthusiasm rose higher. She always loved the theater but had yet to attend one of the *ton*'s fashionable stage productions this Season.

In spite of the people trying to angle her brother into conversation, they made fairly unhindered progress to their box. Olivia took her seat, leaned over the railing and peered at the swarming crowds below. How much longer until the curtain rose? Her excitement mounted with each passing moment.

"Nick, I didn't think you'd be joining us tonight," Marcus suddenly said.

Olivia whipped her head so quickly to look behind her, she felt a stabbing pain in her neck.

The Marquess of Huntsford entered their box. "I hope you'll forgive the intrusion, but it was rather dull sitting alone in my box. I thought I might join the two of you."

Olivia looked back from the marquess to her brother and tried to decipher the small grin on her brother's face.

"Of course," Marcus replied. He swept his hand out at the few empty seats around them. "We have plenty of room here. And company," he added slyly.

Lord Huntsford opened his mouth to respond, but he stopped at the sight of her. Olivia forced herself to remain still under his scrutinizing gaze. It wasn't offensive, merely appraising.

He spared Marcus a distracted thank-you and moved to take the seat behind her. Olivia fought a blush as he approached, remembering her thoughts from earlier, when she'd wondered what it would be like if she were free to win the admiration of this man—this handsome, charming man who shared her interest in Shakespeare…and who hadn't taken his eyes off of her since entering the box.

But I'm not free, she reminded herself, and looked away.

The marquess leaned forward to whisper in her ear. "You look beautiful," he said.

She turned to him, searching his face for any signs of sarcasm. He looked sincere, at least. "Thank you," she mumbled. She diverted her attention again to the floor below, hoping to hide the embarrassing blush.

Marcus cleared his throat. Olivia swung around to look at him, but he didn't appear to be studying them too closely.

Lord Huntsford was acting as though they were alone in the box—and in the theater. He leaned forward, not so far to be sitting in her lap, but far enough to make her uncomfortable. "You're the most beautiful woman here." But his voice wasn't pitched low enough. Marcus raised his eyebrows, obviously having heard the exchange.

"I suppose I see someone in the hallway I should talk to," her brother announced, rising from his seat abruptly. Olivia thought he muttered under his breath as he passed by them and flung open the door to the box. She couldn't make out the specific words and wasn't sure she wanted to.

"Lord Huntsford," she said primly, "I wasn't aware you were a fan of the theater." She strove to ignore his close, close proximity.

He sat back—just a little. "I'm an admirer of many things."

"I hear Kean is sublime," she pressed on.

"As are you," he returned.

She looked at his face, took in his startled expression, and surmised that he'd not intended to voice the compliment. She blushed and ducked her head so he couldn't see the signs of her embarrassment.

"Behave," she warned, hoping to lighten the sudden seriousness of the mood. She should put some distance between them. But Olivia's traitorous body refused to move as little as an inch away.

"It turns out I *didn't* see someone in the hall who required my attention," Marcus announced as he reentered the box and looked at both of them.

"Am I interrupting something?" her brother asked after a long, awkward moment.

Olivia jumped guiltily. "Of course not."

"Hmm," came from Lord Huntsford, who seemed back to his normal, charming self.

"I feel like an extra player on this stage," Marcus continued good-naturedly when the marquess didn't sit back in his chair.

"I don't suppose you could be a character with no lines?" Huntsford asked.

Marcus smiled.

"Would both of you be silent, please? The curtain is about to rise." Olivia moved forward in her seat, peering through her opera glasses.

The actors took the stage, captivating with their flawless performance. From the moment the players began speaking their lines, she was engrossed in the drama unfolding beneath her. She didn't hear her brother and the marquess whispering through most of the play, nor did she notice the curious stares from others around them.

Olivia didn't sit back until the curtain fell for intermission. Then, she rose from her seat and joined the throngs of people littering the hall. Marcus and Lord Huntsford were still speaking with each other when Olivia took her brief leave, claiming a need of fresh air.

But fresh air was the rarest commodity in the crowded hallways. The paths were littered with people. Matrons meandered through the crowds, peering imperiously down their noses at people whose dress they considered gauche or whose manner they found offensive. Young men prowled the halls in pursuit of various game. Some were after heiresses to refill or supplement

the family coffers. Others had a more licentious end in mind for their prey. And the young women, most ushered by their eager mothers, were in the market themselves, searching for the often-elusive perfect husband—wealthy, titled, handsome and chivalrous.

Olivia didn't belong to any of those groups, and for the most part, the other occupants kept their distance. She was, therefore, able to navigate through the crush with the deftness of a weathered captain charting through choppy seas. Not having to sidestep any of the young men who usually came to speak to her was refreshing as she had no desire to converse, but it was also unusual.

"You can stop trying to walk so fast," Lord Huntsford said from somewhere behind her. "I'm accompanying you."

The man was relentless…and probably the reason for the lack of other men in her vicinity. She noticed him scowling at a gentleman who looked ready to walk toward them.

Seeing a column ahead that would afford them some privacy, Olivia maneuvered the two of them through the people and on to the other side of the impromptu hideout.

"I know I shouldn't bother, but I really have to ask why you are chasing after me," she said on a sigh.

"Can it not be as simple as my desiring the pleasure of your company?" he asked instead of answering her.

She laughed at his pitiful expression.

An elderly couple passed by then, with both heads turning to look in direction of the laughter.

Lord Huntsford seemed not to care what anyone—including her—thought. He was content to stand there, one hand on the column above her head. She shook herself; she couldn't be charmed by him without disastrous results.

"This really must stop," she insisted.

"Why?" The gleam in his eye unnerved her.

"It's unseemly." Not to mention should Finley become any

more suspicious there would be more consequences than she wanted to contemplate.

He chuckled, a low, warm sound that made her stomach do an odd turn.

"I'm serious," she persisted.

He cupped his hand to her face, an action that seemed to surprise even him. Olivia forced herself to resist the urge to turn into his touch or cover his hand with her own.

"You should stop," she whispered, knowing her voice lacked heat and resolve.

But he didn't remove his hand.

"Why don't you want to be around me?" While the words were said lightly, there was vulnerability in his eyes.

He was giving her the opportunity to hurt him.

And, though the thought nearly brought her to tears, she was going to have to take it.

Otherwise, he might not leave her in peace.

And she was in enough turmoil without his constant, disarming presence.

"While I find your company not…unpleasant, I think, considering your background, it would be best if we weren't seen so often in each other's company."

She regretted her necessary cruelty the moment the words were spoken.

"My background?" he echoed.

"Well…that is to say…I…" she stammered.

"Explain yourself." He leaned forward menacingly, and Olivia had the absurd fear he would strike her—not that she wouldn't deserve it. But she had to make sure he would cease whatever plans he had for the two of them. Even friendship would be too risky. Finley didn't want her with anyone who could be perceived as a threat. And as she'd been reminded over and over again, she was in no position to bargain with him.

There was nothing for her to do but brazen it out. "I just

mean, with all the women in France, and your father…" She knew those few words would cut deep.

He stepped away, hurt momentarily visible on his face before his expression locked down into blankness.

"If you believe that, you know nothing about me," he said quietly.

Regret overwhelmed her. What had she done?

"I'm…" she began, unsure what words she was going to speak but halfway thinking they were going to be an apology.

She never got a chance to hear for herself what she was planning to say because he speared her with a glare and stalked away.

He stormed through the crowd, the masses seeming to part to allow him easy passage. And he didn't spare her a backward glance. She ignored the burning sensation behind her eyes. She wouldn't cry. This was the way things should be. It was better for everyone if he ended his odd fascination with her anyway.

"Lady Olivia?" A young girl approached her out of the milling, but thinning, crowd.

After a few moments, Olivia recognized the girl as Finley's cousin, Anna.

"Are you all right?" Anna asked, coming closer and peering at Olivia with so much concern, Olivia felt like crying all the more.

"I'm fine," she answered automatically. "How are you?" This was followed with a brief flare of worry. *Is Finley with her? Has he witnessed anything between myself and Nick?*

Anna still looked skeptical about Olivia's well-being, but she answered, "I'm well. My mother was invited to the play by some old friends, and she let me accompany her."

Olivia sagged with relief when she realized Finley was probably not in attendance then.

"Are you enjoying the show?" Olivia asked, wondering why she couldn't seem to form anything more significant to ask.

"Yes." The word had the slow pace of question. "I'm not trying to be a bother, but are you certain you are feeling well?"

"I'm certain."

Anna chewed on her bottom lip. "I saw that man storming away. Had he said something to upset you?"

Quite the opposite. "Oh, no. He simply had somewhere to be." Somewhere far, far away from her, she figured.

"Oh. Well, that's all right then," Anna said.

Olivia wondered what Anna planned on doing if Olivia had insisted Lord Huntsford was the cause of her troubles. Hunt him down? Give him a shy, but stern, lecture?

Olivia was obviously not thinking soundly.

She cleared her throat and looked at Anna, who was still peering at her curiously. "You won't mention what you saw, will you? To your cousin…" She hated to ask, but if Finley caught word…well, that didn't bear considering.

"I don't talk to Julian unless I must," Anna confided.

"I appreciate your silence." Olivia reached out and gripped her hand in gratitude.

Anna smiled, and Olivia thought how pretty the girl looked when she was happy. "I must return to Mama, before she comes looking for me," she said with a hint of an apology in her words. "But I hope to see you again soon."

Olivia bid her goodbye. And on legs that were still shaky from her confrontation with Lord Huntsford, Olivia returned to the box. Marcus noticed his friend's absence and looked at her with raised brows.

She shrugged as though to say his disappearance was a mystery to her as well. It was easier. She didn't want to lie to her brother, so it was best not to speak at all.

Chapter Eleven

Olivia couldn't remember a time when she'd felt worse about the way she'd treated someone.

She knew, as soon the words had come tumbling forth, that what she said was going to hurt the marquess. She knew the implied accusation was untrue. Neither of the two had prevented her from saying it.

But she had to do something to keep him away, she reasoned. Lord Huntsford seemed determined to integrate himself into her life. And while she didn't necessarily understand his motivation, she was all too aware of what would happen if Lord Finley grew any more suspicious.

She wouldn't put it past the baron to take out a front page announcement in the *Times* with a printing of her mother's letter in order to publicly disgrace her family.

She watched in the mirror as Sarah fastened the set of sapphires around her neck. The matching earbobs were next.

"You look lovely, my lady," Sarah said.

"Thank you," Olivia said, but she knew she sounded distracted. Too much seemed to hang in the balance, and one gentle sway could bring everything crashing around her.

She would do anything to prevent the secret from being

revealed. But she still knew she had to make amends. Her nagging conscience would accept nothing less.

Marcus had informed her that he was hosting a dinner party, a rather uncharacteristic move, with several influential members of Parliament and their wives. Her brother was petitioning for reforms for those forced to slave away in workhouses, and he needed every available vote to help the reforms pass.

Olivia's duty was to be charming and sociable. The mission didn't seem overwhelming until she walked into the parlor and noticed the marquess standing with some men, talking.

She hesitated inside the door. Lord Huntsford looked directly at her, but she was unable to read his expression. At least he didn't give her the cut directly—turning his back and refusing to acknowledge her attendance.

Perhaps he'd like to. Maybe Marcus's presence was the only thing preventing him from doing exactly that.

She couldn't approach him, not that she was considering being so bold, because an elderly woman with elegantly coiffed, silver hair and dazzling jewels atop a blindingly bright yellow evening dress approached her first.

"Lady Olivia?" the woman whose dress was an insult to subdued society queried as she came within hearing distance.

Olivia nodded, worrying over whether she was supposed to know who the impressive figure before her was.

Marcus appeared at her elbow then, and Olivia could have breathed a sigh of relief.

"Olivia, allow me to introduce you to Her Grace, the Duchess of Leith. Her husband is one of our greatest supporters."

The duchess rapped Marcus on the knuckles with her fan. "As am I, dear boy," she chided.

Marcus bowed his head. "Of course, your grace, my apologies. Please permit me to present my sister, Lady Olivia."

Olivia curtsied deeply, already admiring the woman and her

husband for backing the controversial reforms her brother was proposing. "It's a pleasure to meet you, your grace."

The duchess's smile was sincere and put Olivia instantly at ease. "As it is to meet you, Lady Olivia. I've heard much about you."

Olivia gave Marcus a questioning look.

He seemed as flummoxed as she, but someone called to him from across the room. With a bow and a plea for the duchess's pardon, Marcus went to attend to his guest.

The Duchess of Leith quickly returned to their previous conversation. "My nephew speaks highly of you," she clarified. "Of both you and your brother."

Olivia couldn't have been more lost in the conversation than if the woman were speaking Portuguese.

"Your nephew?" she questioned.

"Nicholas." The duchess pointed into the crowd of people conversing on the other side of the room. "The Marquess of Huntsford." Her tone became increasingly unsure. "The handsome one in the corner…"

Olivia was speechless.

The duchess furrowed her brow. "Forgive me, but I was under the impression he is a friend of the family."

Olivia recovered neatly. "Of course, forgive me. I wasn't aware Lord Huntsford was a relation."

Huntsford's aunt took Olivia's hand in her own. "Don't worry over that dear. Nick can be very secretive. It's that trait that makes him good at what he does."

What he does?

Olivia and the duchess were taking a turn around the room, walking slowly by the other handful of couples who were passing the time until dinner with conversation. Olivia had to force herself not to continue looking in the marquess's direction.

Olivia wanted to ask the obviously open duchess more about Lord Huntsford's mysterious line of work, but knew she

shouldn't express interest in the man. Fortunately, the duchess had already moved on to another topic. "My nephew told me you have spent most of your years in the country."

"Yes, your grace."

"Please don't 'your grace' me. I'd be honored if you'd call me Henrietta."

Olivia assured her she would love nothing more than for the duchess to address her informally as well.

"So how are you finding your time here?" Henrietta asked, returning to the earlier vein of conversation.

"It's been enlightening," Olivia hedged. The last thing she wanted to do was offend her new acquaintance by insulting England's capital city.

"That sounds like a polite way of saying you're miserable."

Olivia laughed. "You are very perceptive."

"I'm old," Henrietta countered. "When you get to be my age, dear, you're lucky to have something to show for the years other than wrinkles and gray hair. I have been duly cursed with both, but I do have a bit of wisdom to show for them as well."

"You are an inspiration," Olivia said with another chuckle and smile.

"Perhaps you can tell Nicholas that. He needs to hear how valuable I am every once in a while."

Olivia caught herself before she fell into the trap of discussing the marquess. "I know your support of my brother means a lot to Marcus."

The duchess looked at her, clearly aware of the desperate change of subject. For whatever reason, Henrietta decided not to pursue the matter. "My husband and I are always stirring up some kind of trouble for the 'radical'—as they're called—rights we want to help the working classes achieve. But for all their grumbling, people still try to garner our favor." She shook her head. "It really can be most tiring."

"I know Marcus keeps his head buried in his work. I've not seen much of him in the past several weeks. I think what all of you are doing is commendable." *And purposeful,* she added silently. Perhaps after her marriage to Finley, she'd be able to take on some charitable pursuits. It would keep her out of her husband's company.

The two conversed a few more minutes before the service for dinner was announced.

As soon as she entered the dining room, Olivia knew that her brother had tampered with the seating arrangements. She'd taken pains to ensconce herself with several elderly guests. And she'd placed the marquess as far from herself as possible.

Beside her brother…at the other end of the table.

Unfortunately, due to the *new* seating arrangements, Olivia was inconveniently situated across from Lord Huntsford.

Olivia glared down the table at Marcus, when what she wanted to do was fling a spoonful of food at his head. Her brother was too entrenched in his conversation with Henri and a gentleman she supposed to be the duke to even notice.

Lord Huntsford didn't show any surprise or disdain at the adjusted seating. He didn't display any kind of emotion at all. He had apparently resolved to ignore her. Something he did with remarkable dedication. Olivia decided not to push him.

She occupied herself by conversing with the man and woman on either side of her. And if her eyes shifted occasionally to the brooding man across from her, she couldn't be held responsible for that.

By the time the dessert course made its way to the guests, she was nearly ready to throw herself across the table and ask for his forgiveness. She resolved to meet with him once everyone had disbanded.

There were a few things she needed to say to him, but asking him to accompany her out of the dining room—while

not entirely scandalous—would certainly set Marcus's friends to talking.

The deed of getting Lord Huntsford's attention must be discreet. Which meant Gibbons couldn't be involved. So she stopped a footman in the hall, asking him sweetly if he would deliver a message to the Marquess of Huntsford. The servant, a relatively new addition to the household staff, seemed eager to please his mistress.

"Try not to let the women hear you," she cautioned.

The footman looked ready to salute her, and she had to smile at his eagerness. But she was overcome with a case of nerves. She wondered what Nick would have to say to her. He would still be angry, perhaps, but she needed to make amends. While she would never be able to be more than his friend—if she even had that luxury—his good opinion of her mattered. For some reason, losing it was more than she was able to bear… she wished she realized that before insulting him.

Olivia waited in the library, pacing across the floor, something she must have learned from Marcus over the years, and wondering what was taking the man so long.

What if Lord Huntsford had decided not to come at all?

Could he be so angry with her he wouldn't give her a chance to explain?

"You summoned?" Nick asked shortly, striding into the library.

Olivia set down her copy of *Twelfth Night,* the one he had given her, he noticed. "Yes, I did."

Nick seated himself in the chair farthest from her. "I'm surprised you'd want to meet with me alone…considering my background, that is."

She winced. "I deserve that, of course." She folded her hands in her lap. Nick assumed it was to hide the fact they were shaking.

He noticed anyway.

She worried her bottom lip between her teeth. And while his anger was due to her callous comment, he couldn't help but pity her awkwardness. He wanted, immediately, to cross the floor between them and take her in his arms.

He resisted the impulse.

"So why am I here?" he asked, more kindly when it seemed as though she was going to say nothing more.

"So that I might apologize." She heaved a sigh, and her shoulders rose and fell with the breath. "I truly am sorry. What I said at the theater—" she stopped, struggling.

He took a breath, ready to end this torture for her. He didn't need to hear the words; the remorse was evident on her face.

"—was uncalled for," she finished.

He smiled, ready to absolve her of her guilt, but she wouldn't let him.

"I hope you know I don't think that," she continued quickly. Her sorrowful eyes stared at him, and he couldn't help but imagine they were beseeching him—for what, he wasn't sure. "No one who has spent any time with you could delude himself into believing anything negative about you." A long, shaky breath. "I was trying to hurt you," she confessed.

This new information puzzled him. "Why?"

As she shook her head slowly, ruefully, some of the hair carefully piled into the top knot slipped free and caressed the sides of her face. "I can't tell you."

"You can tell me anything." Maybe she would tell him why one moment she seemed amenable to his attention, and the next she'd coldly rebuff him.

"We can't be friends," she said earnestly.

Was she worried Marcus would find something amiss about them spending time together? In truth, he wasn't sure how her brother would handle knowing Nick was developing feelings

for the enigma in front of him. But he highly doubted Marcus would have a problem if they were friendly with one another.

"We can't be seen together much more than we already have." Her voice was plaintive and seemed to catch with unshed tears.

Soon, the two of them needed to have a serious talk. She was hiding something from him—maybe from everyone—and he wanted to relieve the burden it had caused. But he could hear speculation from the other room about their whereabouts, so he was going to have to leave her momentarily.

She seemed to sense that as well. "I truly am sorry."

"I forgive you."

Olivia was stunned. "Just like that?"

He nodded. "Just like that. Does that surprise you? Surely you expected forgiveness when you called me here."

"Well, I—ah—didn't expect it so quickly."

It was Nick's turn to look confused. "Why should I make both of us suffer by drawing it out?"

She seemed to think hard about the question. "Is this one of your Bible lessons?" But the usual disdain in her voice when speaking of spiritual matters was gone.

"It's one of many."

She pondered that for a moment. "I don't understand."

He knew they were no longer talking about just forgiveness. "What would you like explained?" he asked slowly, afraid if he said the wrong thing she would close up again.

She turned her head to peer out the window, and he suddenly wished that he could erase the faraway, pained look in her eyes. "It doesn't really matter. I couldn't ever believe in that again anyway. I've…I've seen things…" she trailed off.

"What things?"

She turned to face him then, and her eyes were suspiciously moist. "Awful things," she whispered.

Nick couldn't take his eyes off of her expression—the

shadows and fear visible in her countenance. His heart hammered in his chest; he was afraid of what she would tell him—afraid that he wouldn't know how to comfort her.

But mostly, he feared that Olivia would decide she didn't trust him enough to tell him anything at all.

She wished she could call the words back once they had been spoken, but they hovered in the room of their own accord. Lord Huntsford studied her face as though it were a map that held the key to a valuable treasure.

Infinite minutes passed, and he said nothing. Olivia wanted to squirm under his scrutiny but forced herself to stay still. His gaze revealed nothing of what he was thinking. The weight was pressing on her again; she wanted him to laugh at her…call her a fool…insist that a sheltered miss couldn't possibly have seen anything so awful as she claimed.

Then she could pretend he was right.

She could push aside the resurfaced memories of her mother—lying in a pool of her own blood. The pistol still dangling precariously in her lifeless grip. She could forget, at least for a while, the rising bubble of hysteria she felt upon stumbling on the scene. The insane urge to scream and scream and scream until her voice broke and nothing else came out.

She could act as if she'd never broken the glass window and disposed of the gun. If she could convince herself she'd not lied and kept secrets, perhaps she could understand and attain this thing that her brother and Nick seemed to have.

They were different from her. And for possibly the first time, she wished she could be someone else. That she could be as deluded as they.

When Olivia had abandoned hope of Lord Huntsford saying anything at all, he surprised her with his own confessional. "I've seen things, too."

"What things?" she echoed his earlier question.

He stood up, moving into a seat closer to her. "Things that made me question how I could ever believe in justice and goodness again."

She leaned forward, hoping he'd continue. How had he overcome his own dark shadows and moved into the light? Could she do the same?

"But I had to come to the place," he continued, "where I realized life wasn't always going to be the way that I wanted it to be, and I wasn't always going to be privy to only the best the world has to offer." He shrugged. "God promised me an abundant life. I could doubt it, or I could accept His word as truth. I'm not a theologian, and I had to decide for myself what kind of person I was going to be. My faith was ultimately greater than my doubt."

She was going to say something but stopped when he held up his hands, splaying them open in the air as though trying to show her he had nothing to hide.

"My anger eventually faded. And here I am—as I am."

He was still watching her, perhaps expecting some kind of immediate metamorphosis. She certainly didn't have anything in that vein to offer. She desperately wanted to change the subject, uncomfortable with the truth of his words, but she couldn't think of anything appropriate.

A thought occurred to her. "What do you have planned for tomorrow evening?" she asked before she could stop herself.

He quirked an eyebrow. "Nothing, although I'm afraid to ask why."

Well, she had come this far, there really was no turning back. Besides, what could it hurt? She could pretend one more evening that she was allowed to have someone like him in her life. Maybe she even deserved it.

"The Sutton musicale is tomorrow. Marcus isn't planning on attending, and I thought maybe you, and your aunt Henrietta, might like to go."

He smiled with what appeared to be genuine pleasure. "I can't make any promises for my aunt, but I'd be delighted."

While her body relaxed slightly with relief, she cautioned him. "I'd advise you not to read anything into this more than what I've asked. I'd enjoy spending more time with your aunt, and, well, I just wanted to show you I truly was sorry."

"If you think agreeing to be seen with me in public will ease your own guilt, I'm even happier to do it."

A general din rose from the direction of the hallway.

"I suppose that is my cue to leave, before everyone descends." He rose from his chair.

She rose, too, ready to accompany him to the door. "I would like to thank you again for accepting my apology."

He nodded. "Think nothing of it." But he turned back to face her, his features set in an inscrutable mask. "And if you'd ever like to talk about the other issue again, I'd be more than happy to."

She nodded. What good would it do to tell him she didn't have any intentions of bringing up the matter again? It would be best for her not to pine for things out of her reach.

Chapter Twelve

Why had she asked Nick to accompany her to the musicale? Olivia thought she must be the most foolish woman alive, or the bravest. Something told her it wasn't the latter.

Worry gripped her that this lapse in judgment would end badly for her.

But all she could do now was either rescind the offer or brazen it out.

For most of the night, she warred between the two choices. Tossing and turning in her bed, she agonized over what could happen as a result of her impetuous invitation.

Finley could decide she was in direct violation of his orders, which she was, and declare their agreement void. He could tell the whole world the truth about her mother, and she and Marcus would be shunned.

Having a family tainted by suicide would ruin everything for Marcus…his reforms and political ambitions.

But would Finley really use the one piece of leverage he had on her over her friendship with Nick? She knew her money was the greatest draw for him. If he were to expose her now, he'd not see a farthing of her dowry.

So why shouldn't she allow herself to enjoy one evening with a man who had become her friend?

Olivia wasn't foolish enough to believe it would ever be more than friendship between them. But since she was going to be tying herself to someone she loathed for the rest of her life, she thought she deserved one evening of happiness, one to hold on to and treasure.

Lord Huntsford seemed the perfect person to create such a memory with.

While she'd never know what could have happened between them had it not been for Finley's interference, Olivia liked to imagine she would have eventually married someone like Nick. Someone her brother found suitable, someone who didn't flatter her with empty words. Someone who didn't think because she read she must be trying to incite a feminine rebellion.

And certainly, she wouldn't have minded tying herself forever to a man who was so handsome he made her feel lightheaded if she looked at him for too long.

"Lady Olivia," Gibbons said, approaching her while she was stealing a snack from the kitchens.

Olivia quickly swallowed the biscuit. "Yes?"

"You have a caller."

Who was it? She wasn't expecting anyone. Dread filled her as she thought perhaps Finley had decided to come and pay a visit. "Is it a man?" she asked nervously.

"I believe it's a peacock, my lady."

A peacock?

Gibbons left the room before he could shed any more light on who—or what—was in the other room. At least she felt relatively assured it wasn't her future husband. Gibbons probably would have had something much more scathing to call him.

The Duchess of Leith was waiting for her in the blue salon.

And she most certainly did look like a peacock. Or perhaps some exotic bird from the east, ones she'd seen paintings of. The lady was robed in a bright-teal morning dress, with several

blue plumes sticking out from her head. This was topped with a fuchsia spencer.

It was, though Olivia had not thought such a thing possible, more garish than the gown from the evening before. She had to avert her eyes, afraid of going blind from staring at the brilliant colors for too long.

"Your grace," Olivia said with a curtsy. "It's a pleasure to see you again." *To see your face, at least.*

"How many times must I tell you to call me Henrietta, or Henri if you prefer?"

"Apologies," Olivia said with a smile. She wanted to chuckle as well. After closer inspection, Olivia decided if there were a color of the rainbow the duchess wasn't wearing, she was hard pressed to name it.

Olivia indicated a chair, and the duchess sat and adjusted her voluminous skirts. When one was a duchess, there was probably little she could wear and be criticized.

"Would you care for some tea?" Olivia asked, ready to call for a service.

"Oh, no, dear, I just came for a little chat."

Olivia smiled but felt apprehensive as well. What could the duchess want to talk about?

"I'm sure you miss home," Henri began, "but I'm selfishly glad you came to spend time in London. After hearing Nicholas speak of you, I knew I had to become better acquainted with you myself."

The gleam in Henri's eyes was speculative, and Olivia knew she was right to be worried. She'd heard tales of the viciousness and ruthless tactics of matchmaking mamas. She didn't suppose matchmaking aunts would be any better.

"I'm very glad you did. I have found my time here in London to be without much female companionship," Olivia returned.

The duchess nodded. "I wouldn't let that worry you. Unfortunately, many of the young ladies here are going to be intimidated

by your beauty, and envious of your wealth and position. It doesn't make the best breeding ground for friendships."

"It seems you and your nephew are rather close," Olivia commented, trying to change the conversation but realizing too late she'd maneuvered it back to the marquess.

"Yes, we are. He often came to visit me when his parents were…otherwise occupied," Henrietta hedged.

Olivia thought that was a delicate way to put it.

From what she'd been able to wheedle out of Marcus, apparently, the late marquess and marchioness were somewhat free with their affections…and not only with each other.

"He must have been relieved to have somewhere to go whenever the situations at home were unpleasant," Olivia said.

The duchess bobbed her head, making the vivid plumes dance with the motion. "Oh, yes. I always wished I could have kept him with us. Henry loves Nick as his own son."

"Henry?" she asked.

"My husband," the duchess clarified with a smile.

Henry and Henrietta. It really seemed too funny and unfair to be true.

"We weren't able to have children, you see." Henrietta's eyes took on a faraway look, and Olivia thought tears were close to the surface. "That was the best gift I could have given my husband, but I was unable to. He loves me still, of course, and always said God sent Nick to us on purpose."

Olivia was mystified by the way Henrietta spoke about God sending Nick to them. That seemed a little out of God's character as well. If He didn't care about her mother drinking herself into a stupor because she was so heartbroken over losing her husband, it seemed odd He would care at all about one couple needing a child to love in their life.

"So I suppose we can credit the marquess's character as the work of you and your husband?" Olivia asked with a smile, more to keep the conversation going than anything else.

"Oh, no," she protested. "Nick was a strong, good boy from the moment he first showed up on our doorstep. He'd already made up his mind he was going to be different than his parents. It's why he risked his life...oh, dear," she finished. Henri looked quite put out with herself.

The curiosity was too much for Olivia to leave alone. "Risked his life? Doing what?"

"You don't kn—" Then the duchess caught herself. She shook her head and the plumes did another exotic, almost hypnotizing dance. "Forget I mentioned anything."

Olivia bit her lip to keep herself from asking any more questions.

"Nicholas told me of your invitation," the duchess said, effectively changing the subject as she gathered her things to leave. "I am thrilled to accompany both of you. The carriage will be round at seven to pick you up."

Olivia nodded, deciding she was too much of a lady to press the issue of Lord Huntsford endangering his life. She wasn't, however, too much of a lady to mention it to the marquess. Perhaps he would tell her what his aunt wouldn't.

Olivia watched Nick from across the carriage as they drove to the musicale, wondering exactly how to bring up what Henri had let slip earlier. She darted a glance at the duchess, but she seemed soundly asleep in the corner. It might have been pretense, an opportunity for the young couple to think they had privacy, but the occasional snore from Henri seemed too real. Olivia decided she would risk a whispered conversation.

"You never did tell me what kept you in France for so long," she began.

Was it her imagination, or did he sit a bit straighter? "I don't recall you ever asking." He darted his own look at Henri.

"Odd, but I would think it would have come up in the conversation at least once."

"No, I don't think it ever did," he argued.

Olivia smiled at his evasiveness. "Would you care to tell me now?"

"What do you want to know?"

Where to begin, she thought. She could come right out and ask him what work he had been doing during the war. She could ask how exactly he'd risked his life, and why it was so important for him to distinguish himself from his parents. She could ask what finally made him leave.

Instead, she asked, "Do you miss it?"

He seemed to think about the question, waiting several moments before answering. Olivia counted how many times the carriage swayed or hit a rut in the road before he answered.

Seven.

"That's a hard question," he said finally. "I enjoyed what I did. To a point. It helped to know my work was keeping people here in England safe."

Her respect for him rose.

"But it was a hard job. I had to go places I would have otherwise never gone, had to see things I think I could have lived the rest of my life without. And I had to do things…well, things I wish I could take back."

What kind of things had been so awful he would regret them still?

He must have seen her questioning look because he clarified. "I tried to make sure not to do anything that would compromise my faith. I didn't have much of a testimony while I was there, I'm afraid. But I had morals, and I was determined to hold on to some semblance of the person I was, even if I were playing a part the whole time."

"Would you do it again?"

He smiled. "You still don't know what it was I did," he reminded her.

"I think I have a fairly good idea."

"Really." He raised an eyebrow and cast his own look at the sleeping duchess. "Care to share your thoughts with me?"

Well, now she'd feel ridiculous if she said what she was thinking and it was wrong, but then she'd feel like a coward if she backed away from his challenge. Which was worse?

Being a coward, definitely.

"I think you were a spy."

Her answer gave him pause. "Is that what someone's been saying?" he asked.

"No, just my own theory. I could be wrong," she hurried to add. "Perhaps it wasn't quite so glamorous as that."

"Being an agent isn't glamorous," he snapped.

She blinked in shock. "No, of course not."

Nick shook his head, as though clearing away the fog. "I'm sorry, I shouldn't have barked at you. But I've seen many die because they wanted to be heroes. Or because they thought the work was much more glamorous than it really was."

Well, he'd answered her question. "I think you're very brave," she told him.

"I'm not brave."

"Yes, you are," she argued.

"I was running away. That's cowardice."

"There were other places to run to," she said quietly.

"They weren't far enough away."

She wanted him to tell her what exactly his parents had done that had made fleeing England seem like the best option. Especially when Nick had an aunt and uncle who loved him like their own son. But because she so zealously guarded her own past and would never push him to dredge up his, the question would never pass her lips.

Chapter Thirteen

"I see why you asked me to come with you," Lord Huntsford said not more than an hour later. "You're trying to kill me."

Olivia didn't look at the marquess, who had been quietly moaning since the first note was struck at the Sutton musicale. "Don't you think you're being a little dramatic?"

The look in his eyes suggested she had lost her mind. "Are you listening to this mockery of Mozart?"

"It's Beethoven."

"You'd never be able to tell. Should I assume Marcus was conveniently otherwise occupied for this very reason?"

Olivia smiled. "Marcus firmly believes the only thing more heinous than being stuck in conversation with one of the Sutton daughters is listening to them play."

"I must say that I agree."

"You didn't have to come," she said with a smile. "You could have refused the invitation."

"And turn down the opportunity to spend an evening at your side? Never."

"Should I suppose you'll hate me by the end of the evening for bringing you?" Her smile was full and wide. She was surprised by how much she enjoyed teasing him.

He leaned over, so close his lips almost touched her ear. "I could never hate you."

Olivia hid her smile and turned back to the girls playing. She didn't grimace as one of the Sutton girls dropped her violin— although she was fairly certain the marquess did. Unfortunately for everyone, the instrument didn't break. The poor girl snapped it back off the floor and continued her frantic sawing with the bow.

"You must owe them some grave debt to listen to this without complaint," he joked, and then flinched at a particularly shrill flute note.

"I do. They are kind girls. And I've found kindness to be a rather extraordinary quality here in London."

The marquess had nothing to say. No witty rejoinder. Which was a first.

He was uncharacteristically quiet afterward. No complaints. No requests for a quick and merciful death. Olivia was proud of his restraint and touched at his reaction to her admiration of the Sutton daughters.

Blessedly, there had been no sign of Lord Finley at the Sutton soiree. That wasn't terribly surprising; Olivia had a hard time envisioning him at something so tame and ear piercing.

It was for the best. Not only was she spared another jealous rage from the baron, but also there was no telling how the marquess would have reacted had Finley shown up. He seemed to be as protective as her brother.

She looked around to find Henrietta, which wasn't a difficult feat. Henri was the only woman in the room with a vividly pink ostrich feather bobbing from her head every time she moved.

The duchess was cloistered with several older women. They tittered behind their fans and pointed out different people.

Olivia suppressed a groan. They were matchmaking. And it wouldn't be long until their searching gazes landed on her and Nick.

Olivia excused herself from Lord Huntsford, claiming a need to take a brief respite in the retiring room. Moving out into the hallway, Olivia enjoyed the feeling of not having so many eyes on her.

She sat on a beautifully upholstered red-and-gold settee that had been relocated to the expansive hall. Olivia watched idly while a few ladies and gentleman milled about. She was hidden behind a monstrously large potted plant and, being such, was concealed from two gentlemen having a discussion a few feet away.

"Did you see who Huntsford had clinging on his arm this evening?" one asked the other.

"Lady Ice?" the second snickered.

"Didn't seem quite so frosty this evening. I'm thinking the old chap might be able to do it after all."

Do what? Olivia wondered.

"It'll be a miracle, George. She's spurned the offers of every man who's been brave enough to ask. Don't know what makes her think her blood's any better than the rest of ours," the second one said.

"I, for one, will be glad to see the marquess take her down a peg or two. It's nothing more than she deserves," George said.

Humiliation washed over Olivia in a consuming wave. Her cheeks reddened, and tears gathered in her eyes. She was grateful they couldn't see her.

"Well, I'm against Huntsford," the second said, and Olivia craned her head toward them, hoping to hear why. "It weren't wise to go against him at White's. But can't change the books now, and I'd hate to lose the quid."

Were they *betting* on her? White's was notorious for its gambling book, used to record all manner of ridiculous wagers. Whether a man would win a horse race. Whether a lady would

disgrace herself in front of her peers by doing or saying something uncouth.

And apparently whether the Marquess of Huntsford would melt Ice Queen Olivia.

The man named George laughed at the foolishness of the second man. "It *was* stupid to bet against Huntsford. He seemed rather sure of himself when we talked at White's."

"Well, I'm not bidding my blunt goodbye yet. He's got to prove she's fallen for him. And I haven't seen evidence of that."

"Oh, you will," George gloated. "A gambling man knows not to bet against the marquess where the ladies are concerned."

Olivia stopped listening. She made the conscious decision to direct her attention and ears everywhere but at the two men on the other side of the plant. Her pride wouldn't withstand much more of their commentary.

She was a fool to allow herself to think Nick was her friend.

If he were, he certainly wouldn't have proposed a wager against her ability to resist him. Oh, she knew men made such petty foolish bets as a way to pass the time, but in her eyes, that didn't excuse the crime or mitigate it.

And she supposed it was no wonder he'd been following her about London, always whispering compliments and making her light-headed with his nearness.

Beneath the anger was hurt as well. Nick was supposed to be her friend, but…it appeared he'd been doing nothing but playing games with her. Not that she thought she'd ever have anything with Nick—Finley had won her through dishonorable means, but she *was* still committed to be his wife—but she'd trusted the marquess.

And he'd been using her.

Well, unnamed gentleman number two was about to get lucky.

Olivia decided there was no way Nick would get through the frosty barrier she was going to erect.

He'd most likely freeze to death first.

Olivia discarded her plans to go back and join Lord Huntsford inside. She had a servant send a message to him, explaining she was no longer in need of his escort. Then, she paid a footman to hail a hack for her. A hired carriage was certainly not the fashionable way to slink home, but it was better than commandeering the duchess's conveyance. She just hoped the vehicle would arrive before Lord Huntsford discovered what she'd done.

She tapped her foot impatiently and wished she had told the footman to wait several moments before delivering the message. With her unenviable luck, the marquess would find her on her way out of the house and demand an explanation.

Her audible sigh of relief once she saw the hack rumble in front of the door could probably have been heard back to where the musicale goers were. Olivia didn't waste any time descending the stairs, hoping to jump in the carriage and take off. Quickly, hardly breaking stride as she did so, Olivia passed a banknote up to the driver's hand.

"Please hurry," she begged.

"Lady Olivia!" Lord Huntsford called as she was preparing to close the door.

She could tell the coachman was hesitating, uncertain whether to leave or wait for the strange man running full charge at them.

She leaned up and rapped on the ceiling of the conveyance. "Go on!" she shouted.

Still another moment of indecision, and Lord Huntsford was almost close enough to reach the door.

She banged—in a very unladylike manner—on the roof, and finally, the coachman flicked the reins. They swayed and rumbled down the cobblestone drive, and Olivia told herself

not to look back at the marquess. She didn't want to know if he was standing there, watching them drive away. She was better off without that image in her mind. She didn't want to think he was watching for her, waiting until nothing could be seen of the carriage against the darkness of the night.

But her resolve lasted mere seconds. She pulled back the small curtain in front of the window and peered around to where they'd just been.

Lord Huntsford stood, his arms crossed over his chest. She didn't need to see his expression to know it ranged somewhere between confusion and anger.

Warring with the two emotions herself, Olivia let the curtain fall. And even though he could no longer see her, she turned her back to him.

The ride was quiet and too long. She didn't want to be left alone with her thoughts for longer than necessary. She needed something to occupy her mind from thinking about her hurt. Finally, her home came into view, and she could have collapsed with relief, knowing she'd be safely inside and among myriad distractions.

But as angry as she was with the marquess, Olivia couldn't stop thinking about his expression as she drove away.

Well, my sin against him wasn't near as grave as his against me.

Funny, but that didn't make her feel much better.

She was dismounting from the carriage when a figure shrouded in shadows stepped forward. The illumination from the oil lamps on the streets fell on Baron Finley's face, making his expression starker.

"Where have you been?" he asked.

Not now. Was she not dealing with enough already?

"The Sutton musicale," she answered, "although I wasn't aware I needed to have you approve my schedule of outings."

He ignored the last part. "Who were you with?"

"The Duchess of Leith," she hedged.

Finley wasn't fooled. "Who else?"

Obviously he already knew, or else he wouldn't be pressing her. "Lord Huntsford."

Olivia watched as Finley clenched and unclenched his jaw. "I believe we have already had a conversation about how I feel about you being in his company."

"And I believe I told you his company was unavoidable. As Marcus's friend, he has become an integral part of my life since his return." She moved another couple of steps closer to the front stairs. Soon Gibbons would hear the noise—if he were still awake—and open the door for her. Then she could sprint inside and leave all memories of the furious marquess and the angry baron on the steps.

In three strides, Finley was beside her, gripping her arm painfully. "My coach is down the road. Come."

"Are you daft? My brother will be expecting me home." And if Marcus noticed anything was amiss when she returned, he might very well schedule an early morning meeting with Finley.

"If you had not left the musicale early, you wouldn't be home for many hours yet," Finley returned, using his bruising hold to steer her down the street.

Olivia looked back to the coachman for help, but he must have missed the shadowy figure approaching and driven off.

Sometimes, she had the worst luck.

"I'll be ruined if someone sees the two of us together," she tried. "You'd not like your future wife to be the subject of vicious gossip, would you?"

"You'll be safe enough where we're going." His confidence was highly aggravating.

He shoved her into his coach and barely gave her enough time to fix her skirts before he climbed in after her. As though

at some unspoken command, the driver flicked his lines, and the carriage rocked into motion.

"Where are we going?" she asked.

"Why, to see the fireworks." He spoke as though they had longstanding plans to do so and she'd simply forgotten.

"The fireworks at Vauxhall?" Olivia knew her face showed her surprise. She also knew that appearing at the gardens of Vauxhall—a place the demimonde adored—alone, with Finley would certainly culminate in her ruination if it were discovered. She glanced out the carriage window before pulling the curtain closed. She'd soon be in enough trouble without being seen beforehand.

Finley turned his face away from her, and for the second time that evening, Olivia felt her temper flaring to unmanageable heights. He meant for her to walk alongside married men and their mistresses, with actresses and their latest admirers. Surely some there would recognize her. He meant to punish her for going out with Huntsford by making her the subject of speculation and rumor.

And, of course, it didn't matter to him. He didn't want her reputation truly ruined—if it was, she'd have no reason left to give in to his blackmail. But it seemed unlikely that he'd mind if she was the target of whispers and speculation from those who might catch a glimpse of her in such a scandalous location.

Finley escorted her from the carriage after a tense and silent ride, and Olivia kept her face down. She stared at the ground in the hopes no one would be able to get a clear look at her face.

"This way, dear." Finley took her hand, intertwining his fingers with hers.

Olivia fought the immediate urge to pull away. The most important thing she could do was avoid a scene—of any size—in order to protect her anonymity.

"I'm afraid we will have to meander along with the common

crowds," he told her with an apologetic shrug. "I've loaned my box here out to some friends."

Olivia recognized the statement for the lie it was. She'd eat her gloves if he could afford a box here.

"Would you care for some refreshment?" he asked her.

"Don't bother playing the dashing gentleman with me. We both know what you are. There's no need to pretend otherwise." She kept her voice low, but she knew he heard every word because he stiffened at her side.

"As you wish." He dropped her hand and swept a ridiculous little bow.

"Stop," she said, taking his hand and pulling him upright. Avoiding attention would be impossible if he kept this up.

They stood there, with couples and people flowing around them on all sides. He eyed her speculatively, knowing precisely what she wished to avoid. "Perhaps we should introduce ourselves around?" he asked.

"No," she whispered. With a frantic jerk of the head, she looked around to make certain there was no one nearby who might recognize them.

He laughed. "Calm yourself. Desperation isn't a look you wear well."

Olivia could have slapped him…*wanted* to slap him and take her chances with whatever the consequences would be.

"Why are we here?" she asked again, allowing him to lead her to a nearby bench.

"To allow me to spend time in your company, of course."

"Surely you don't think I believe that," she retorted. "You couldn't care less about my company. My money, perhaps…"

"You have a point," he said with a shrug. "And speaking of business arrangements, have you spoken to your brother yet? I am a patient man, but you are trying my limits."

Olivia thought it interesting he could threaten in such a mild

voice. "He isn't well disposed to you." *For good reason.* "So it's been rather sensitive bringing up the subject."

Finley leered at a passing woman, whose dress was showing entirely too much, and Olivia was grateful his attention was momentarily turned.

It didn't last, however.

"I don't care what your brother thinks," he said as he returned his attention to her. "I am not allowing you time to change his mind. You asked for time so that our union wouldn't seem rushed and your brother wouldn't be suspicious."

"My brother isn't someone you would wish to make an enemy of," she said, pitching her voice low to match his.

With a beaming smile, he patted her hand and said through gritted teeth, "I'm the one he does not want for an enemy. Always remember that, dear."

Chapter Fourteen

Nick thought if his driver didn't speed the pace, he was going to jump from the carriage and make the trek to Olivia's house on foot.

Once there, he planned on barreling past Gibbons, storming up to Olivia's chamber and demanding to know what her problem was. He'd left his aunt at the musicale, assuming she would be happy to chat with her friends while he came on his reconnaissance mission.

He watched from the window of his carriage as another vehicle went in the opposite direction. Nick happened to notice a pale, worried face looking out of the window as the two conveyances passed each other.

Olivia.

Olivia?

What is the foolish girl doing?

He recognized the crest on the other coach after a moment's reflection—Finley's.

He banged on the roof of his coach and bellowed a command to the driver to follow the other carriage. But it took longer to turn around than he liked.

Had Olivia planned this? Had she spent the evening with him while planning to sneak off to Lord Finley?

What was it about the scoundrel that was so irresistible for her? Why would she choose Finley's company over his own?

He stopped the thought.

This wasn't a competition.

It was a job…nothing more.

He was *not* competing with Finley to win Olivia. Oh, sure, she was exceedingly lovely, and bright, and witty, and…

And, well, she was in need of a good lecture. What could she have been thinking? If she were seen by some members of the peerage—alone with a man late in the evening without a proper escort—her name would be splashed all over the gossip rags in the morning.

The entrance to Vauxhall Gardens eventually came into view. Finley's carriage was there. Nick hopped from the still-moving coach, looking around to try and catch a glimpse of Olivia.

Lord, let me find her, he prayed. *Quickly,* he added in case that part wasn't clear.

He made his way through the crush of people. Men walked and whispered playfully into the ears of women who were not their wives. Some gentlemen, probably on holiday from their schooling, weaved through the crowds, calling at attractive women. They were obviously drunk.

And somewhere in the midst of the melee was Olivia. Would Finley have her secreted into a secluded nook? Was she okay? What means of persuasion had Finley used to trick her into coming here? Was she happy with the baron?

The last question gnawed at his insides.

"Hey, love," a woman cooed from beside him.

Nick turned and acknowledged the woman with the barest nod.

"What's a handsome man like you doing alone?" she persisted, nearly running to keep pace with his long stride.

"Looking for someone." He scanned the crowds.

"I'm looking for someone, too," the woman murmured, taking her ungloved hand and running it along his shoulder.

"Best of luck to you, then." He picked her hand off his coat, freeing himself from her touch.

The woman hmphed.

Nick turned around, seized by a crazy thought. "Maybe you *can* help me," he said.

She smiled, the seductive intent marred by her missing teeth. "That's what I'm trying to do."

He ignored her comment. "I'm looking for a friend of mine. She's young, brown hair…well, it's brown with amber threaded through it…her face…she's beautiful. Amazingly so." Nick could think of no other way to describe Olivia.

"She might be with a gentleman," Nick continued. "Blond. Some would probably call him handsome." The last part was said very reluctantly.

The woman was looking off behind Nick's shoulder. "You mean like that pair?" she asked, pointing out a man walking with a lady who was most definitely Olivia.

He could have kissed the woman.

"Thank you!" he called as he turned and ran toward the pair.

"Olivia," he barked as he came to stand before her.

"Nick?" she gasped.

He wondered if she realized it was the first time she'd used his given name. And he wondered why that was his first thought.

Finley had also turned at the intrusion. But rather than looking angry, Finley merely looked annoyed. "Why must you show up everywhere?" he asked Nick.

Nick ignored the baron. "What were you thinking?" he asked Olivia. "Do you not know the damage your reputation could sustain coming out here with—" he gave Finley a pointed look "—*him?*"

Nick couldn't decipher the look on her face. Was it relief? Annoyance?

"We were just about to leave, were we not, Lord Finley?" she asked her accomplice.

Finley's brows lowered, but he nodded. "Of course, sweetling. Shall we go to the carriage, and I will see you home?"

There was no way Nick was going to let the two of them get in a carriage alone together. "Olivia, you will come with me," he said, and laid his hand atop her own.

She drew back as though burned by his touch. "No. I will not. Lord Finley will see me safely home."

Why was she so angry with him? What had he done?

Other than ruin her planned night out with Finley.

"Finley?" Nick said, addressing the baron for the first time in the conversation.

"What?" the other man barked.

"Can I assume the ride to the Gardens was comfortable?"

If Finley sensed a trap, he was powerless to avoid it. "Yes."

"Excellent, there should be room for one more then." Nick stopped a passing worker and paid him a quid to tell his coachman to await him at the Fairfax home.

Finley looked ready to argue, and Olivia had her back to him. Well, he'd have no allies here. But he wasn't going to let Finley spend any more time alone with Olivia. Not when he was anywhere nearby.

A bright, loud burst of fireworks exploded overhead. The shimmering shoots of lights bathed everyone in a multicolored glow. And while he knew he was supposed to be upset with Olivia because of the danger she'd put herself in, he found much contentment in watching her awe and surprise at the show.

"Lead on to the carriage, Finley," Nick said imperiously after the lights had fizzled in the night sky. He reached to take Olivia's arm, and to his surprise, she didn't fight him.

Finley's eyes narrowed, and Nick could tell he was trying to think of a way to disinvite him.

Obviously, he could think of no good excuse.

"This way." The baron stomped ahead through the crowd to lead them back to the entrance of Vauxhall.

Nick didn't relinquish his hold on Olivia, nor did he allow her to come too close to Finley.

"What are you doing here?" she whispered.

Nick had his own share of anger at Olivia, which bubbled so close to the surface, he had to force himself not to yell at her. "I'm keeping you out of trouble, you little fool," he hissed.

The set of her mouth was mutinous. "I'm in no trouble here. I'm surrounded by people."

Nick stopped, and his hold on Olivia's arm forced her to pull short as well. "Look around you, Lady Olivia. Do you think any of these people would give a farthing if you were in trouble?"

She didn't look around, nor did she meet his gaze.

Nick began walking again before Finley turned and noticed they were no longer behind him. "Why did you leave me?" he asked her quietly.

"I'm not speaking to you," she informed him rather than answering his question.

He snorted at her childishness. "Fine."

They'd made it to Finley's coach, and the baron had already seated himself inside. Nick handed Olivia in, and she took the seat opposite Finley. Nick didn't hesitate a moment before sitting beside her.

"I trust you had a good time?" Finley asked Olivia, clearly intending to ignore Nick for the duration of the ride.

"I did, thank you," Nick answered.

Both Finley and Olivia looked at him. Finley in annoyance, and Olivia—well, who ever knew what a woman was thinking?

"Although I do wish you had chosen a warmer evening for the outing," Nick continued. "It's a bit chilly."

Finley looked at Olivia, seizing an opportunity to be gallant. "Would you care for my coat?" he asked her.

"No, I have my own," Nick said.

"He wasn't speaking to you," Olivia snapped.

Nick arched an eyebrow. "If I remember correctly, you aren't supposed to be, either."

The pretty brunette beside him crossed her arms over her chest.

Nick knew he'd have to repent later, but he found too much enjoyment in agitating the baron to stop. "I daresay the next time we go out, we should try the ices at Gunter's. I've not had an opportunity to stop there yet."

"*We* will not be going anywhere else in the future," Finley said between gritted teeth.

Nick, hoping he wasn't overdramatizing his hand, reached over to put his arm around Olivia. "I'm sorry, darling," he said to her in soothing tones. "Perhaps Marcus will go with us instead."

Olivia, apparently, had had enough. She threw her arms in the air, nearly knocking Nick in the nose with the back of her hand. "What are you doing?" she yelled.

Nick was saved from having to answer when the coach pulled to a stop in front of Olivia's home. Nick, who was quicker than Finley, disembarked and handed her down from the conveyance. She didn't bid either of the gentlemen good-night before she marched up the stairs and inside her house. Nick looked around and found his own coachman waiting for him across the street.

Nick stepped back into Finley's carriage before the baron could signal his driver to go on.

"What are you doing back?" Finley asked. The hostility that was barely masked earlier was now evident…and ugly.

"Explaining something to you." Nick didn't speak loudly. He didn't have to. The menace in his voice was clear.

"Which would be what?" Finley's own voice wavered. Just the slightest—almost unnoticeable—bit.

"I know what your game is. You will never have Olivia."

Finley laughed. "That's not your decision. Or choice."

Nick leaned forward. "Know this. I'm smarter than you. You try and take her, I'll follow you to the depths of Cheapside to get her back. If you think Olivia will come to you without anyone putting up a fight, you're wrong."

"I'm not afraid of you," Finley said. His voice shook, however, revealing the lie.

"Then you're a bigger fool than I thought," Nick said as he left the carriage.

Chapter Fifteen

Olivia had forgotten Henrietta's invitation to her monthly literary evening until the morning of. The very last thing she wished to do was put herself anywhere near where the marquess might be. But when she gave serious consideration to canceling her plans, she decided it wasn't fair to punish her new friend simply because Lord Huntsford was a cad. Besides, it had been two days since she'd discovered his duplicity.

She was past it.

Hmph.

She dressed with particular care. Although she'd never admit it to anyone, least of all herself, she wanted to make sure she looked stunning. In case the marquess was there.

Not that she was trying to impress him, of course.

She had a fiancé, after all.

But Olivia didn't want Lord Huntsford to think she'd spent her time weeping into her soup because she'd discovered his deceit. No, she was going to be stunning and never let on she'd drenched her pillow the past two nights before she finally fell asleep.

He didn't have to know how much it wounded her to discover his friendship was not genuine, was only a means to more money for him, and bragging rights to bolster his pride.

Olivia was going to make sure he lost the bet…and some of that pride.

Her dress was a soft blue, so pale that in the right light it might have looked silver or white. The gown was simple, with no adornments at all, but Olivia brought out the family sapphires to wear with it. Nothing like a bit of jewelry to arm oneself.

The right set of jewels could be as effective as chain mail.

Olivia went alone.

Marcus had isolated himself in his study, preparing his arguments for the reform bills. The moment she walked in the door of the townhome across Mayfair, the duchess abandoned her companions and embraced Olivia warmly.

"You manage to look lovelier each time I see you," the woman said with a motherly smile. "I like to think if I'd had a daughter, she would have been just as beautiful as you."

Olivia thanked her, grateful for the kind words.

"I believe I have a nephew in attendance who would agree with my assessment," Henri said with a sly smile.

Olivia's mouth went dry, and she scanned the room.

Of course.

Lord Huntsford was there. He was leaning against the wall by the fireplace, watching her intently. Had he been waiting for her?

"Shall I introduce you around, dear?" Henrietta asked, taking Olivia's arm and leading her to the first couple without giving her the time to agree or protest. The woman could be an unstoppable force of nature, and Olivia was swept away in the tide.

Olivia smiled and chatted, answering the endless barrage of questions the guests had for her.

Many of the elderly ladies seemed to be unspoken members in a secret club. They whispered and chatted behind their fans, and when they thought Olivia was too far away to hear, they

began to run down a list of eligible suitors they might throw at her feet.

Olivia found herself alone, laughing at the not-so-subtle glances and furiously whispered plans taking place all around her. She saw Lord Huntsford approaching and tried to look anywhere but at him.

"Why are you laughing?" Nick asked, standing right in front of her.

"It's nothing, really." She smiled—the expression patently false—to let him know she wasn't hurt by his ungentlemanly behavior. Not in the least.

"I like it when you laugh," he said, and then grimaced. "But not when you smile like that."

"That's not a very nice thing to say," she chided him as her frown settled fully into place.

"You looked like you were in pain."

"Who's to say I'm not?"

Lord Huntsford appeared to consider whether he'd been insulted and seemed to settle on the obvious truth that he had. "So you're speaking to me now?"

"Only out of necessity. I've no wish to upset your aunt," she told him.

"What have I done to anger you?" he asked.

She still didn't answer him.

"Please tell me," he said, bending down and whispering the words in her ear.

A servant appeared announcing a light dinner was to be served before she could say anything.

Nick offered her his arm, and Olivia wrapped her hand around it before remembering she was mad at him.

He didn't release her until he guided her to her place at the table. Considering Henri's machinations, Olivia wasn't surprised that she was positioned beside the marquess.

What she had not counted on—but was an unexpected

pleasure nonetheless—was that the gentleman on Lord Hunts-ford's other side had some investment matters he wished to discuss with the marquess. Each time Lord Huntsford turned to her, his other table partner launched into a litany on the benefits of American cotton or Indian silk. Olivia enjoyed his frustration more than she would have ever admitted.

But under the table, where no one could see, Lord Huntsford slipped his hand down to hers and gave it a gentle squeeze. She didn't know if he meant to maintain the contact and would probably never know because she snatched her hand away and settled it firmly into her lap.

After dinner, the gentlemen and ladies separated for a few moments before the planned gathering in the large salon. Olivia thought they were going to be reading one of Shakespeare's plays. One of the Henrys…or maybe Richard. Perhaps, if she were lucky, they'd read one of the ancient tragedies where everyone ended up in a bloody heap, or cooked into soup.

It would suit her mood.

The men went into the duke's library to discuss all manner of interesting masculine pursuits: horses, property, saddles for the horses and improvements to their properties.

The ladies didn't fare much better. Olivia noticed with a bit of dismay she was the youngest, and probably the only single lady in attendance. She avoided the other women in an attempt to spare herself a lecture on why she needed to marry. And quickly. Waiting until all of Henri's guests were immersed in their conversations, she snuck out of the room.

Once in the hallway, she sagged against the wall in relief.

"Aren't you worried the guests will wonder where you are?" Nick's low voice, husky with the effort to keep it quiet, made her heart beat just the tiniest bit faster. Or perhaps that was from the shock of his sudden appearance. "Why did you leave?" he continued.

"I needed a moment."

"Is something the matter?" he asked.

"Of course not." She smiled and knew it looked false, but he didn't seem to notice.

"Good." He was still staring at her.

"Is something wrong with *you?*" Before her lips finished forming the words, Olivia wished she'd not asked. Why should she care?

"Me?" he asked distractedly. He ran his hand through his hair, disheveling it. "Lady Olivia," he began but stopped immediately. His unspoken words hung in the air, making her wonder what he could possibly have to say.

"Yes?" she prompted.

"I have to tell you…something has been vexing me…"

He paced the length of the room, seeming to war with himself over how to break the news to her. He stopped abruptly, turning to look at her. His eyes were bleak.

"You have been hurt enough," he began again. "And it was never my intention to add to your pain." Another pause.

She couldn't bear to see him this way. Lord Huntsford was supposed to be charming and affable—not anguished and at a loss for words.

"Please stop," she said, halting his forward steps immediately. "I already know."

"What? You do?"

She nodded. And fought the clawing she felt in her throat and the tears threatening to spring to her eyes.

"How?"

"I heard…"

"You…" he trailed off, moving quickly to stand in front of her. "You should have heard it from me. I doubt it would have hurt less, but it was my responsibility."

"It's all right." She wouldn't let him know how much her heart was breaking. And she tried to remind herself that he

had done the decent thing by approaching her to tell her the truth.

"Please forgive me," he whispered.

"I already have."

"Just like that?" he asked, with the ghost of a smile, echoing her earlier words.

"Just like that," she affirmed but couldn't bring herself to return his smile. He'd easily see the pain in the expression.

"You are a remarkable woman, Lady Olivia Fairfax."

Not remarkable enough, apparently. If he truly thought so, his interest in her would have been more serious than winning a silly wager. But she banished the thought before it could take hold. She didn't want Lord Huntsford anyway. He wasn't right for her. Marriage to someone he loved was his fate.

It wasn't hers.

"I would like to ask a question, though," she said into the ensuing silence.

"Ask me anything."

"What made you decide to tell me?" She held her breath, unsure of exactly what she wanted him to say.

"I couldn't pretend anymore."

Couldn't pretend anymore? Was the charade of being interested in her too much to handle? The feel of a lone tear slipping down her cheek was the first realization she was actually crying. She turned her head, hoping to hide the fact. She couldn't very well pretend she was fine if she were weeping.

Lord Huntsford had already noticed her distress, however.

"Come here." The words were commanding, but his gentle tone was more a coax than a demand.

Her feet obeyed before she could refuse.

"I *have* hurt you," he insisted.

She shook her head.

He wrapped her in his arms, ignoring her denials. Ignoring the fact they were in a hallway someone might enter at any

moment. As he pulled her into a tight embrace, he rested his cheek on the top of her head.

"Please don't cry," he said into her hair.

The minutes crept by, and Olivia, in spite of her efforts, couldn't stem the flow of her tears. His waistcoat would be drenched with her sorrow. How funny, she thought, that she should be so worried over his attire. She might ruin his wardrobe, but he had broken her heart.

Not that she loved him, of course.

Or even liked him more than was proper.

But she had trusted him.

Trusted that, while he had been a spy, he wouldn't be the kind of person to cloak his actions in secrecy...not where his friends were concerned. And while she had never encouraged his attentions, he had certainly paid them. And all the while, he had been counting on her naivete and his powers of persuasion.

She may have forgiven him. But it still hurt.

"Olivia?" Nick queried after what seemed an eternity.

She nodded, wiping more tears on him.

Gripping her shoulders, he pushed her away, and Olivia had to bite back her protest.

"I truly am sorry. The last thing I would ever want to do is hurt you." He stared at her. Shame and remorse were evident in the lines on his face. It seemed he had anguished over this as much as she had.

She tried for a smile. It was wobbly, but it made him offer his own tentative grin.

"I care about you," he said into the silence.

And while the look she gave him wasn't necessarily one of utter disbelief, it was clearly skeptical.

"I *do*," he insisted.

She stared at him, finding herself wishing yet again they

were two different people, or perhaps the same people in very different situations.

She was too close to him. The nearness seemed to cloud her judgment and perception because clearly he couldn't be doing what she thought he was. Her mind was playing some rather funny tricks on her.

For instance, Nick appeared to be shifting nearer. She blinked several times, thinking if she did so his face wouldn't appear to be so close to hers.

Olivia was wrong. Before she had time to protest, or to think about whether she *wanted* to protest, his lips were on hers. She sighed a bit, melting into his embrace.

His arms around her tightened, and she leaned farther into him. She was so lost in the moment that forming a comprehensible thought was impossible. This was everything she'd imagined a kiss would be—what she'd hoped to find with someone eventually.

What she'd never have with Finley.

She wondered if Nick felt as lost in the moment as she....

Olivia stiffened.

Of course he didn't.

This had been Nick's plan all along. He wanted to prove, to himself and everyone else, she could be swayed by his attractions and pretty words. And she'd been more than willing to help him win his wager.

"What's wrong?" he asked as he pulled away, fear coloring his voice.

"Get out," she said quietly. She didn't know with whom she was most upset, herself or him.

"What?" His tone reflected his confusion.

"I said, 'get out!'" she repeated with more force and volume.

"This is my aunt's home," he reminded her, still looking bewildered.

"Shall we ask her if you should stay or go?" She was shaking with anger.

Lord Huntsford stepped back from her but moved no farther. Truly, was her embarrassment not enough? Now he was humiliating her by acting as though she were being irrational.

"If you don't go, I shall…I shall…hit you." She grabbed the closest thing off a nearby table. "With this," she said holding up her makeshift weapon.

"A volume of poetry?" he asked incredulously.

"It's Lord Byron," she defended, looking at the spine. But really, who kept a collection of Bryon's poetry in the hall? A candelabra would have been much more intimidating.

"Is this a joke?"

She knew her expression clearly said it wasn't.

"Well, I believe I shall take my leave then," he said tightly. And before she could call him back—not that she wanted to—he had vanished.

Chapter Sixteen

Nick rode hard through the outer reaches of Hyde Park. He was blissfully alone and had passed no one since leaving his aunt's home.

What had he done?

Well, he knew what he'd done—the better question was why had he done it?

Why had he thought he could get away with just an innocent, comforting kiss?

He should have known the moment he took her in his arms, he was tempting himself needlessly. That he'd stoke a fire that could have consumed them both.

How could he ever ask for her forgiveness? He'd overstepped himself. But seeing her, looking so incredibly sad, he'd wanted to show her she wasn't alone. That he cared about her. Cared about her probably more than he should. And for a moment, it had seemed to Nick that she shared his care, concern—whatever emotion it was. Things had changed quickly for her, however.

She'd been right to push him away.

His better intentions seemed to leave him the moment their lips met.

He had been nearly ready to confess feelings he wasn't sure of…and shouldn't have been feeling regardless.

When he approached the small lake, he slowed his pace. Reining his horse to a halt, he dismounted, leaving his steed to graze nearby. Unmindful of the damage to his breeches, Nick sat beside the lake, throwing nearby pebbles into the water. The stones broke the surface with a single *plunk,* and while the waters rippled, eventually they calmed.

His life had been so orderly before he'd met Olivia. He'd known exactly what he wanted. He wanted to be through with the Home Office, having discharged his duty to Crown and Country. After, he planned to turn his attentions to his estates, bettering life for his tenants. And eventually, he would marry... perhaps not someone with whom he was in love, but someone with whom he shared an easy affection. Someone who would be a good wife and mother to their children, and would help him restore respectability to a name that had been tarnished for too long. Someone who would share his code of decency and morality and—most important—faith.

That person wasn't Olivia. At least not now.

He had no doubt a life shared with her would have been based on affection and admiration. And she certainly would make an excellent mother. Beneath her wounded exterior, she was caring and considerate.

But she had been so hurt, so disillusioned, often he felt he was wasting his time by trying to reason with her. She was so certain she didn't need God in her life any kind of open conversation was impossible. He was in a dangerous position. He had an opportunity to help a young woman regain her faith, and he wasn't setting the example he needed to.

Nick wondered if she would tell her brother about their kiss. Marcus trusted him to protect Olivia, to treat her like his own sister, and he'd taken grave advantage.

Well, he reasoned, if Olivia did say something, perhaps it would be the opportunity he needed to tell Marcus he wasn't sure he was the one best suited for this particular task. Could

he admit he had burgeoning feelings for her without angering his friend?

He wanted to be honest, and he also wanted to safeguard Olivia's reputation.

A serious relationship with her wasn't a possibility right now. He couldn't, and most certainly shouldn't, offer her anything other than friendship.

So there was nothing left for him to do but apologize to her... again.

Olivia sat on a low stone bench, glad the morning sun had burned the dew away and left everything dry. She inhaled deeply, reveling in the smell of the roses directly behind her.

"Good day, Olivia."

Olivia snapped out of her reverie in a trice and found, to her utter dismay, Nick standing at the entrance to the garden. "Go away," she said without hesitation.

"That's not very nice." He smiled tentatively, as though afraid she would throw something at him.

"How unfortunate for you." She turned around, determined to ignore him.

"I've come to apologize for what happened last night." He walked toward her with a smile and hands held open in a gesture of peace.

"Really? Whatever for?"

"Don't pretend you don't remember," he snapped.

"Not a great tone for an apology," she fired back.

He looked at her for a moment before shaking his head. "You drive me mad."

"Well, that's flattering."

Nick stared at her. "Okay, let me start over. I am sorry I kissed you." His voice dropped to a whisper, and Olivia noticed he was edging closer and closer to her.

"Why?" *Confess that the kiss was meant to win the wager,* she mentally begged, hoping he would redeem himself.

He said nothing.

And he *wasn't* going to say anything, she thought with disgust. For several moments, she warred with what to do. Should she remain silent and simply let him walk away?

Maybe she should remind him that she knew. She'd stopped his apology the night before, telling him that she was already aware of the circumstances, but perhaps he didn't realize that she knew the extent of it—that it was not simply the time he spent with her that would win him the bet, but the success of his seduction. If he knew she was wise to his motivations for getting close to her, perhaps he would give up his mission.

"I heard an interesting conversation about you the other day."

Nick quirked an eyebrow. "If you found it interesting, I'm intrigued."

Olivia debated how best to continue.

"I understand you're a gambling man."

His eyebrows rose and pulled together.

She plunged ahead, "I also understand you were fairly confident in your, um, ability, to charm me."

"Olivia, what are you talking about?"

His feigned confusion raised her ire. "You put a bet on the books at White's that you'd be able to make me fall in love with you." She speared him with a haughty glare. "Not that you've been successful, of course."

"*I* put a bet on the books at White's that…what?"

Her face flushed. Apparently he wouldn't simply admit the truth to end her embarrassment. Her humiliation was to be thorough and complete. "That you would make me love you."

"Who did you hear this from?"

"Two men at the musicale."

"Did you happen to get their names?"

"George something, and the other…well, I don't know." she said.

"These men told you I was paying you attention for money?"

"Well, they didn't tell *me* exactly."

He stared at her, his gaze hard.

"So you gleaned, from a conversation you overheard pieces of between a George something and a gentleman you don't know, that I'd set up some kind of wager on whether I'd be able to seduce you?" The hurt in his voice was unmistakable.

Olivia pondered. Put that way, it did sound rather ridiculous.

"I don't need to gamble over a lady's affections to get money," he continued.

When she said nothing, he studied her. "Do you really think I would kiss you for any reason other than I wanted to?"

No, she thought immediately. Huntsford didn't seem the kind to do anything other than because he wished it.

But what about his plea for forgiveness the night he…well, kissed her?

"What about your apology?" she countered.

"My apo—" Nick's mouth dropped open. "You thought I was apologizing for wagering about you?"

"Weren't you?"

"No!" he yelled.

"Well, then what was it?"

This made him hesitate. "I came to apologize for something entirely different."

"Which was?"

"Well, it certainly wasn't for being crass enough to try and make you fall in love with me, or whatever drivel it is you're accusing me of."

She crossed her arms over her chest. "Then?"

He said nothing for a long moment. "I was apologizing

for the false pretenses surrounding my constant presence by your side."

"Exactly," she said as she waved a hand in the air.

Nick looked as though he wanted to hurl something at the stone wall behind her. "Would you listen to me? It's true I've not been completely honest with you, but I'm not the rake you've painted me to be."

Olivia waited.

"I'm helping keep an eye on you." The confession was subdued, and Olivia had to think carefully about what he'd said.

And once she did, her dissipated anger returned in full force. "What?"

"Marcus was afraid you were getting too close to…well, someone, and he needed help making sure you were protected." The marquess looked like a boy being scolded for taking too many biscuits from the kitchen.

She didn't know whom to be angrier with. Marcus, for trying to meddle in her life. Or Huntsford, for being his henchman.

"So you've been a spy for my brother?" She laughed mirthlessly at her choice of words…of course he had. A person couldn't change who they were.

Lord Huntsford, for the first time during their conversation, looked embarrassed. "I don't think spying would be how I would classify it."

"What *would* you call it, then?"

"I prefer to think of my role as more of a protector."

Olivia scoffed. "I don't need your protection. Or Marcus's. What I need is for the two of you to quit meddling in my life."

"We wouldn't have to you if you'd simply listen to reason."

She didn't like his tone. Or the way he was looking at her. Like he wanted to throttle her.

"Was the kiss part of the plan?" she asked quietly, to disarm him and halt the potential throttling.

Her plan worked. He seemed to lose the thread of the former conversation.

"That kiss was me and me alone," Nick said.

The marquess knelt on the ground by her feet. He took her hand in his own larger one. She wanted to tell him to stand up, but he spoke first. "I was wrong to kiss you. I assure you I won't let it happen again."

Olivia was surprised at the sharp pang of disappointment she felt.

Perhaps she was bound for Bedlam after all.

"So are we friends again?" he asked her with a ghost of a smile.

And really, when he looked at her like that, she couldn't help but return his grin. "No more spying or thinking you know better than I do," she warned.

He nodded, a sharp bob of his head. "No more believing the worst of me?"

She mimicked his nod.

He'd still not risen, and his thumb stroked a pattern on the back of her hand. To anyone passing by the garden, they would look like a pair about to be betrothed.

Why did she suddenly wish that were the case?

"Lord Huntsford," she began. The tentative words catching in her throat.

"Yes?" He raised his head to look at her. Was she imagining the tenderness in his gaze? Surely she must be.

"I wish—"

"What?" he asked.

His hand never moved from hers, nor did he make an attempt to sit beside her on the bench. They remained frozen, ready subjects for a passing painter.

She didn't know what words she was about to speak. Olivia

had the suspicion she'd been about to confide in the marquess more than she should. He might be her friend. And she might get away with having a friendship with him. But he couldn't be her confidant or advisor. She doubted she would like the advice and guidance he'd give her.

"What, Olivia?" he asked, more urgently this time.

She didn't correct his use of her name. Fumbling for something to say, she spoke the first words that came to mind. "I wish you would tell me more about yourself."

Although the words were not her intended ones, Olivia was surprised at her curiosity over his response. She knew little of him, other than what Marcus had let slip.

The marquess furrowed his brow. But after a deep breath, he launched into a story filled with abusive, immoral parents and redemptive, saving grace.

Olivia greedily absorbed his words.

And felt a vise around her chest ease.

Chapter Seventeen

"Thank you for agreeing to see me," Olivia told Reverend
Thomas as she joined him in the small garden beside his home.
His housekeeper had directed her outside when she'd knocked
on the elderly man's door. Marcus had been scheduled to make
another trip to Westin Park, something he seemed to be doing
with increasing frequency, and had allowed her to come with
him.

After her conversation with Nick in the garden, and some
thinking, she'd felt the nearly overwhelming urge to speak to
Reverend Thomas. Olivia hoped he'd be able to shed some light
on the shadows plaguing her.

The vicar was kneeling, pulling at the weeds that had found
their way into the otherwise perfect bed of flowers.

"You know you are welcome here anytime." He wiped his
forehead with the back of his gloved hand.

"Need some help?" she asked, kneeling beside him in the
grass.

"Oh, no," he said. "You'll ruin your dress."

She ignored his protests and began to grab weeds. After she
gave a good yank, they ripped free from the soil, and with a
flick of the wrist, she flung them into the growing pile. "I don't
care about the dress, and I'm happy to help."

They worked side by side in silence. Reverend Thomas hummed an old hymn to himself.

He didn't inquire as to why she'd come, which surprised her. How long he would go without asking?

"I can remember you spending hours out here when I was little," she said once the pile beside her had grown exponentially.

"I like working with my hands, and I like tending God's creation. It's satisfying." He wiped more sweat off his face. "Even when it's sweltering."

Olivia didn't feel the heat of the day and paid no mind to the fact that her hair, and most likely her dress, were sure to be wilting. Her mind was occupied with other thoughts. With questions to which she could no longer go without answers.

But she didn't know how to initiate the conversation.

"Something on your mind?" Reverend Thomas asked finally, and Olivia exhaled with relief.

"I've been thinking quite a bit lately."

"That's a good thing."

Olivia chuckled. "You would think so."

Reverend Thomas never once stopped in his mission of ridding the garden of invaders, but Olivia knew he was paying her his full attention. "Want to share any of your thoughts with an old man?"

"Well, they're questions mostly."

"Old men know a lot of answers," he said with a smile.

She sat back on her heels. "I'm counting on it. I came all the way from London to see you, hoping you'd be able to help me."

"Would you like to move inside where we can discuss things?"

Olivia didn't want to; she was enjoying having something to do with her hands. She thought it wouldn't be as awkward if they didn't have to stare at one another across the table.

"Or we can finish tidying up the garden while we talk," Reverend Thomas suggested at her hesitation.

"I think I'd enjoy that."

The minister smiled knowingly.

"I don't quite know where to start," she began.

"Maybe you should tell me what exactly has brought you here."

"It's a man I know."

"Hmm." His voice was rife with speculation.

Olivia blushed. "It's not anything like what you're thinking. He's a friend."

Reverend Thomas nodded, but Olivia thought he still looked skeptical. "Well, what about this friend has you wondering?"

"I want what he has."

"And what do you think that is?"

She couldn't exactly describe what it was about Lord Huntsford she wanted for her own life. And she felt bad insinuating she wanted his brand of peace. Marcus had tried, ever since their mother's death, to bring her back into the fold. He cared for her soul, and she knew he prayed for her daily, prayed she would find her way back.

But she'd always felt if Marcus had known the things she did, he would feel just as lost. He'd wonder where God had been hiding and why He'd chosen to remain silent those five years ago.

But Nick seemed to her a man who had seen worse than she could even fathom. He was ridiculed, the subject of unfair speculation and the son of known wastrels. And she didn't want to imagine the things he'd experienced while on the continent. Yet somehow, he'd managed to keep his faith alive.

Olivia forgot Reverend Thomas was still waiting on her until he discreetly cleared his throat.

"Sorry, Reverend, I was trying to find the words to answer your question." She struggled but decided to plow ahead any-

way and do the best she could. "I've always thought, because of what I've seen, there was no way I'd ever be able to be as close to God as I used to be."

But that wasn't entirely accurate, so she amended, "Actually, I wasn't *afraid* I wouldn't be close to God—I didn't want to be."

Reverend Thomas nodded in what was either encouragement or understanding. Maybe both.

"I figured any God who would leave me without both a mother and father wasn't the kind of deity I wanted to serve." Olivia chewed on her bottom lip. "It sounds rather selfish, now that I say it aloud."

"Your emotions are understandable. I know how badly upset you were."

"I was angry. So incredibly furious with everyone. With my mother, with myself and especially with God."

She inhaled quickly once she realized she'd said she was angry at her mother. Olivia hoped Reverend Thomas missed the unintentional slip.

"Anger is a natural emotion," he said in a comforting tone.

"I have to let go of the fury. I can't explain it, but I can't move on, can't be the kind of person I need to be until I let this go."

Reverend Thomas stopped his methodical tending and looked at her.

"I don't know how to," she finished.

"You have to forgive." Reverend Thomas then chuckled. "Forgive me, I'm laughing at myself. Of course, forgiving isn't an easy thing to do."

"What works for you?" she asked curiously.

"I turn it over to God. And don't misunderstand, there are times when I'm angry at the Almighty Himself."

This unexpected confession captured her attention. "When?"

"When I officiate at the funeral of a baby or child. When I watch a husband abandon his wife and children, leaving them to the mercy of relatives or the community, or perhaps leaving them to starve." He looked at her meaningfully. "When I see a son and daughter lose two parents in a matter of months, I wonder why God would let that happen. And yes, it makes me angry."

She was touched.

Reverend Thomas continued, "In your case, especially, it was difficult. I'd known your parents for years, and having to bury both of them was hard for me. But that was nothing compared to having to watch your brother assume so much responsibility at such a young age. And you…I knew the moment I saw you at your mother's funeral what it had done to you."

"I tried. I really did." She wanted to assure him she had not abandoned her faith immediately.

He nodded in understanding.

"I want it back," she said finally.

Olivia was tired of thinking the worst of life. Her disillusionment and anger had leeched enough happiness from her.

"God wants you back as well." Reverend Thomas seemed to be trembling, with what, she wasn't certain.

"Are you feeling unwell, Reverend Thomas?"

He laughed, a hearty, booming sound. "I'm wonderful, dear. I've been waiting years to hear you say those words."

"Can you help me?"

"I'd love nothing more."

Several hours later, Olivia knew peace once again. She'd talked to God for the first time in years. Talked to Him without yelling or accusing. Reverend Thomas sniffled and wiped away tears the entire time.

"I have to tell someone," she told him once they'd finished eating dinner. "Marcus will be thrilled." She smiled as she

thought about how much joy the announcement would afford her brother.

"I suspect your *friend* will be happy as well," Reverend Thomas said blandly.

The minister was right. Lord Huntsford would most likely be as enthusiastic as her brother. But she felt shy about telling him. For reasons she couldn't figure out, she wanted to wait to share with the marquess…probably because she felt she owed him a grave debt.

Olivia's enthusiasm caused her to do something she hardly ever did, forget her manners.

"I have to leave now, Reverend," she said without pre-amble.

He laughed, not bothered in the least by her haste. "Yes, I suspect Marcus will be wondering what has taken you so long."

She smiled at him. "In more ways than one."

Upon returning home, Olivia found Marcus in his study. And once she laid eyes on him, she hesitated. The excitement and newfound joy she'd felt when returning home was still there, still bubbling under the surface.

But this was the biggest news she'd ever had to share with him. Her brother would be thrilled, regardless of how she told him. But Olivia wanted the delivery to be perfect.

"I'm home," she said as she walked into his dark paneled study.

"You were gone quite a while," he said without looking up from his papers.

"Estate business?" she asked without acknowledging his remark.

He sighed and ran a hand through his hair. "No, just a few bills and such." He brushed them into a drawer quickly.

Odd.

"Did you have a good visit with Reverend Thomas?" he asked, shutting the drawer.

"I did indeed."

He waited for her to say something else, but she pressed her lips together, hoping to stop the beaming smile from breaking through just yet.

"And?" he asked. Marcus rarely enjoyed these kind of games. He never wanted to guess what she was thinking, or take a stab at what wonderful thing had happened on the way home.

"I was reintroduced to someone while I was there."

This piqued his interest. "Who?"

"God."

Marcus, bless him, had to think this through for several moments before grasping the significance of what she'd said. But when he did, he let out a whoop, jumped from his desk and grabbed her in a hug. His strong arms lifted her feet off the ground.

He hugged her until she thought she might faint from lack of air.

Her brother set her down finally, and Olivia had to struggle to keep her balance.

"This isn't some kind of joke, is it?" Marcus asked, looking at her sternly.

She shook her head. "No. I'm sorry I've made you worry. And thank you for not giving up on me."

"I would never," he whispered, pulling her again into another embrace. This one wasn't quite as energetic as the last, but comforting all the same.

Olivia wished her parents could be here for this moment, to see their son and daughter doing so well. She wanted to cry at the thought, but the joy in her heart wouldn't let the tears form.

Marcus gave a little squeeze. "Welcome home, Olivia. You've been away far too long."

Chapter Eighteen

Two days later, Olivia and Marcus were back in London. Nick was at the house, playing billiards with Marcus. Olivia had no desire to intrude on their gentlemen time, so she took Reverend Thomas's lead, went out into the garden and began trimming the roses. She'd been there for what felt like hours when the marquess came out.

"I'm surprised your brother doesn't employ a gardener for that."

Lord Huntsford joined her beside the bushes and delicately held a bloom in his hand.

"Marcus does, I was only looking for something to keep me occupied," she confessed, attacking a dead growth with a satisfying snip.

"Why don't you go riding with me?" he asked. "If you're bored, it's probably more exciting than mauling innocent plants."

The unexpected invitation made her pause. "Riding where?"

He smiled. "I'd prefer the country, but I'm willing to settle for Hyde Park."

"I'll have a groom saddle the horses while I change." She gifted him with her most dazzling smile. Walking into the

house, she admitted to herself that agreeing was probably not the wisest thing she might have done. Finley was an ever-looming threat, of course, but she didn't want to deprive herself of what promised to be an enjoyable afternoon.

No more than twenty minutes later, Olivia was in her dark-blue riding habit, mounting her horse in front of the house. Marcus had barely looked up from his papers when she bade him goodbye. Fleetingly, she wondered what "business" had occupied so much of his time and energies traveling back and forth from London to Westin Park over the last two weeks.

The marquess and Olivia rode through the streets to the park.

"I understand congratulations are in order," Lord Huntsford said with a smile once they had passed the general traffic leading to the park.

"Thank you, they are." She was glad Marcus had taken the announcement out of her hands.

"How do you feel?" he asked her.

"Better." And were it not for Finley looming somewhere on the near horizon, she'd feel perfect. "I have much to thank you for."

"How so?"

"Were it not for you, I don't think I would have gone looking for answers."

Olivia, had she not been looking directly at him, would have thought the blush was merely a trick of the sunlight. "You give me too much credit," he said. "I'm convinced you would have found your way eventually. But I'm happy to be a part of your journey."

Olivia turned to look at him. He was gazing intently at her.

"Why are you staring at me?" she asked, embarrassed.

"I can't seem not to," he confessed. "You are quite a woman, Lady Olivia Fairfax."

She laughed, hoping to dispel some of the awkwardness. "I suppose that could be taken many different ways," she joked.

"I mean it in the best sense possible. Surely you know I admire you greatly."

Olivia lowered her head. Looking into his eyes wasn't the best way to resist the pull he seemed to have over her.

"Care to walk for a moment?" he asked.

She could think of no good reason to refuse. He was off his steed first and came to stand beside her. His hands reached up, gripped her waist and lifted her effortlessly off the saddle. As he lowered her to the ground, she thought she was doing a fairly poor job of keeping a distance…of any kind. He stood a breath away from her.

When she braved an upward glance, the storm in his eyes transfixed her. Olivia regretted the lapse in self-control immediately.

"I thought you wished to walk," she said, hating the way her words sounded a touch disappointed.

He smiled. The man saw too much for either of their good. He took her hand and for a moment did nothing with it…in fact, he held it in his own for so long the warmth of his hand seeped through her glove, and chills traveled up her arm. Finally, he wrapped their arms together.

"Will your horse follow us?" he asked.

Olivia couldn't find the voice to answer the simple question, so she nodded.

They walked near the banks of the Serpentine, the small lake in Hyde Park. She was tempted to search for a stone to skip across the water—a talent she'd mastered during childhood.

"Do I want to know what you're thinking?" Nick asked. A

small smile played at the corners of his lips, and Olivia suppressed the memory of when he'd pressed those lips against hers.

What is happening to me? She'd given her life back to God and yet was battling with improper thoughts of the most dangerous sort.

Her smile was apologetic. "I'm afraid I'm not having any revelations. I was only thinking about childhood pastimes."

Lord Huntsford's face became a blank mask at the mention of anyone's youth.

"It's really quite beautiful out here," she said to change the subject.

"Very beautiful." His eyes didn't leave her face.

She flushed a deep crimson. The sudden burst of heat to her cheeks made her want to bury her head into his chest to hide the embarrassing evidence.

"May I ask you a question?" his voice rumbled.

"I suppose," she said warily. She'd already made up her mind she was going to attempt to be completely honest with the marquess. Insomuch as she was able without compromising her own precarious situation.

"Do you enjoy spending time with me?" Nick's expression was vulnerable.

"Yes."

He smiled at her again, but this time it was...victorious. "Do you like me?"

From any other man, the question would have made her laugh. But the marquess's face was so serious, so open, the moment wasn't funny in the least. "You said you were only going to ask one question," she reminded him in lieu of an answer.

"I was hoping you'd be generous."

She debated.

"I would think the first would answer the second." She

worked to slide her arm out from his, thinking she would only truly be comfortable when she wasn't pressed so tightly against him.

She was sure he'd noticed the way she'd refused to give him the words he wanted to hear. And he only let her slide out her arm a little. He flipped his palm over so he was holding her hand. His fingers twined with hers, and her small hand fit perfectly in his larger one.

She wasn't going to think about that.

"We should probably return home," she said after several moments. Olivia had not removed her hand. Partly because she couldn't think of a way to do so without being awkward. Partly because she liked the feel of it as much as he seemed to.

"Do you think Marcus will be afraid I've kidnapped you?"

"It's just getting late."

The sun was still high in the sky, and Olivia wished she were either more observant or better at making excuses.

He pulled on her hand and used his free hand to tilt her chin until she could look nowhere but at his face. Olivia recognized the look in his eyes. He was going to try to kiss her. She should stop him. Say no. Run as far away as she could manage before his lips descended on hers.

But her heart wanted something entirely different.

She nodded her acceptance.

Nick needed no other encouragement. He dropped her hand and framed her face with both of his. He had no gloves on, and Olivia was aware of the almost rough texture of his skin.

She didn't think as he kissed her. Thinking would force her to halt this temporary madness. Her arms snaked around his shoulders as she leaned into him. Olivia lost all connection with her surroundings; they could have been standing in the middle of a crowded ballroom, for all the discretion she had.

Nick was the one to pull away from her, and instantly, her arms felt bereft.

"We really should be going," she insisted to cover her awkwardness.

With his hands still on her face, he used his thumb and brushed it across her lips. "You know I care about you, don't you?" he asked.

Olivia panicked. Was he preparing to make some sort of declaration? She couldn't allow him to. "I think you are a very worthy individual yourself. And I like your aunt prodigiously well."

Nick smiled as though he knew exactly what she was trying to do. He removed his hands, but Olivia felt as though they were still there, clasping her face.

"Aunt Henri has taken quite a liking to you. It seems to be a family trait," Nick finally spoke, and she heard the laughter in his voice.

Enough.

She could only ever dream about what would have happened if Nick had shown interest in her, but now, hearing him say words that sounded close to a declaration made her realize the unfairness of it all. She should not have one life dangled in front of her when she was being forced to accept another.

"I don't think we should talk about this anymore," she said firmly.

"Why are you so adverse to my compliments?" he asked her.

"There is no benefit to them."

This statement puzzled Nick. "Do you not want me to be honest with you?"

The anguish in her heart grew.

"I don't wish to fight with you," she told him, or maybe—more precisely—*yelled* at him.

"I wasn't aware we were arguing."

"I can't let you say those things to me. I can't, even for a moment, let myself be flattered by your pretty words," Olivia said.

They were still walking their horses down the path, but Nick was close enough to her to reach out a hand and lay it on the side of her face. "Look at me."

She did so. Grudgingly.

"Why can't you let me tell you how I feel? Does it bother you?"

"Yes. I mean, no. I mean, I can't let you say those things."

"You're not making sense right now," he told her.

Olivia's temper, her anger and disgust with the injustice of the situation rolled forth in a large, consuming wave. "Don't you think I know?" she nearly yelled. "How could I expect you to understand what I'm saying when no one knows?"

"Knows what?" he asked with a furrowed brow.

"Nothing." She'd said far more than what was safe already, and she'd not let him get another word out of her.

"I thought we were done with the secrets." The look he gave her was more hurtful than any of his compliments could have been.

"I still have a few more," she whispered. She looked away, down the path at the beautiful trees and flowers ahead. She pretended to study them to hide the fact that she didn't want to look at his face, didn't want to see the disappointment certain to be there.

"You can trust me." The hand on her face moved to tilt her chin so she faced him again. "You have to believe me. I want to help you."

"No one can help me with this." The old Olivia was speaking again, and she hated she couldn't reach out to Nick and let him assist her with the burden. But she'd have to trust God would see her through it. It may be her cross to bear in life, but she would never invite anyone into her misery.

"You're going to have to trust someone eventually," he told her as he withdrew his hand. "I was hoping you might let it be me."

She turned to him, with her dashed hopes, fear and sadness in her eyes. "It can't ever be you," she whispered.

It can't ever be you.

Fine, Nick huffed silently, as he stabbed his dinner with his fork.

Just. Fine.

He'd thought things had changed with her. Thought he would be welcome in his attentions.

Well, things *had* changed for her, but apparently not where he was concerned.

Now he knew why he'd remained single all these years. Who could ever figure women out anyway? They had to be the most confounding, most agitating creatures in existence.

When Marcus had told him the wonderful news during their game of billiards, which Nick had won soundly, Nick felt as though it were a sign from God.

Olivia had been continuously in his thoughts, invading his dreams, with memories of her popping up at the most unexpected times. The hindrance, he'd felt, had been her lack of a relationship with God.

But then…*then,* he was given the news that her faith was no longer an obstacle. No longer would his desire to have her in his life be something outside the will of God. No sooner had the words left Marcus's mouth than Nick was trying to find a way to extricate himself from the game. He wanted to find her. To hug her. To kiss her. He could have slid down the staircase banister in his haste to get to her.

And then she'd agreed to accompany him on a ride. Something probably of small significance to anyone outside the situ-

ation, but after all their ups and downs, Nick felt as though it was the last sign he'd needed.

But Olivia had made it clear she wanted nothing to do with him.

Nick had promptly returned Olivia to her house and left to nurse his wounds at home. There would be other godly women to consider as a bride in the future.

So what if Olivia was perfect for him? If he liked her better than any woman he'd ever met? If life as her husband would never have been dull?

He'd find another. If he decided that's what he wanted.

But who else did Olivia have in mind? Nick wasn't foolish enough to believe she'd never marry. Marcus would want his sister to find someone who made her happy and to start a family of her own. Wouldn't Olivia want that as well?

So if she didn't marry him…not that he was proposing or anything of the sort, of course…then who?

Finley.

Nick should march over to the man's house and demand Finley drop the charade with Olivia. Finley had already stripped a poor young woman of her future, and a child of his father, without the smallest tinge of remorse.

And *this* was the man Olivia had been paying an inordinate amount of attention to? Nick couldn't conceive it. While Olivia couldn't know the details of what had transpired at Oxford, Marcus should have been able to convince her Finley was the last man she wanted to hang her hopes and dreams on.

Olivia, it would seem, was either more stubborn or foolish than anyone had realized.

Fine. He fumed. He'd not waste his time panting after her like some lovesick pup. He'd not be the next unconscious body lifted from the floor of Marcus's home. She could be his friend, and he'd not allow himself to consider anything more.

It is a good thing I didn't have my heart set on her, he

thought to himself. And obviously, he must have misunderstood what he thought were signs from God telling him they were supposed to be together.

No, he decided as he pushed his plate away, he didn't need Lady Olivia in his life. Sure, she might have made it more interesting, might have given him something to laugh about every day—she was an amazing wit, after all—but he'd done without that for years. And he could continue to do so.

He wasn't hurt by this latest, blatant refusal to a question he'd not had the time to ask. He was fine.

As he slammed his chair back up to the table, he wondered who'd believe that story.

He certainly didn't.

Chapter Nineteen

"**I**'d like you to meet a few of my friends before you run along and find some nice young fellow to dance with." Henri, somewhat less than resplendent in a chartreuse gown, motioned for Olivia to follow her after they had been announced at Lord and Lady Ashburn's. The duchess had brought her carriage and accompanied Olivia to the ball since Marcus was away, yet again.

They walked toward the matrons' lair—the corner of the ballroom where the dowagers sat and nitpicked over every minuscule thing about everyone. They had no bias on whom to torment, and Olivia doubted she would be spared their commentary.

"Speaking of young, unmarried, especially handsome gentlemen—have you seen Nicholas yet?" the duchess asked as they walked. Olivia wasn't sure they were necessarily discussing that topic, but she didn't argue.

Olivia could see the group of dour-faced women looming ever closer. "He has more important things to attend to, I'm sure."

"Bah" was the elegant retort.

Henri sighed as she sank down into one of the chairs along the wall. She was then greeted effusively by her friends.

This naturally was followed by greetings from all five of the ladies to Olivia, with each one firing off a rapid succession of questions.

"I hear you and Huntsford are having the banns read this week," from one.

"Have you decided to forsake men and remain unwed?" This, asked a little too eagerly, from a staunchly proud spinster. Olivia wanted to roll her eyes—she was only twenty.

"You should meet my grandson. He's probably about your age," another said.

"I don't know what all this other nonsense is. I heard you were engaged to Viscount Danfield," from the last.

Olivia gave up. She looked at her friend with all the pleading she could muster into one single, heartfelt gaze. After a small show of pretense, Henri released her.

"I know it's wrong to poke fun, but you're too amusing when you're flustered for me to resist." Henri gave her a quick, impulsive hug, and Olivia bid farewell to the matrons and left to find some peace in the ballroom.

The room was decorated in shades of blue and gold, and the candlelight reflected off the gleaming crystal and glass candelabras, casting the room in a romantic glow. Olivia sighed wistfully, wishing she were like some of the other young women in attendance who could feel nothing but pleasure at the prospect of a ball. She looked around enviously.

Olivia might have escaped the dowagers but didn't have time to celebrate her victory, or fully enjoy her surroundings, before the Marquess of Huntsford grabbed her hand as she walked past him.

"Lady Olivia," he said as she stopped.

"Yes?" She tried to extricate her fingers from his grasp, but he wouldn't let her go.

"Dance with me." His voice was husky and sent a chill skittering down her spine.

"It wouldn't be wise." She didn't think she needed to explain why.

He didn't release her. "Just one dance."

"Why?" *Why must he press the issue? Couldn't he simply let me walk away?*

Apparently not.

"Because you look especially beautiful tonight, and because I wish it," he whispered.

She should reprimand him and walk away—quickly. Instead, she merely said, "You shouldn't say those things to me." But the statement was whispered as well and lacked conviction.

"It's only a dance, Olivia."

"You shouldn't call me that, either."

"One dance," he repeated, ignoring her.

She acquiesced.

Still holding her hand, Lord Huntsford led her to the floor with the other couples. The dancers lined up at the beginning strains of a quadrille.

The marquess bowed to her, and Olivia curtsied in return. Then, letting her body take over, she began moving along with the other women, circling and turning with Nick.

"Would you like to talk about the weather?" he asked with a smile when they came close together.

She looked at him as though he were a lunatic.

"We've seen a full three days without rain. I've yet to check any scholarly writings, but I believe the event would classify as a phenomenon," he said.

Olivia didn't have anything to say but was saved when the steps of the dance took her far enough away she couldn't hear him.

"I do fear, however, if the tide of weather fortune does not turn, the beauty of the park will soon wither and die," he continued when she neared again.

"Did you really ask me to dance with the intent of speaking about a drought?" she asked.

Lord Huntsford pondered the statement. "I don't believe I would classify a three-day lack of rain as a drought."

Olivia sighed in a large rush of air. "Lord Huntsford—" she began but halted as she moved away again.

"Don't you think it's time you started calling me Nick?" His voice dropped to a low, devious whisper. "You've done so before." He reached for her hands, and they circled each other.

She glared at him.

"Obviously not," he muttered.

The couple moved into a turn, and Lord Huntsford gripped her tighter in order to guide her in the change of direction. Olivia ignored the fact that her skin underneath his hand felt scorched in spite of the many layers she wore.

"You smell like flowers," he announced suddenly.

"I don't think that's an appropriate vein of conversation, either, my lord," she chastised.

He leaned his head down until he was speaking almost directly into her hair. Olivia had to force her attention to her feet so she didn't lose her steps.

"You didn't enjoy my assessment of the weather, yet I'm not permitted to discuss anything personal. Why are you so standoffish?" Nick asked.

"I'm being proper," she defended.

"I wish you'd forget about being proper all the time."

She should rap him with her fan for suggesting something so scandalous. Instead, she admitted, "I wish I could."

Lord Huntsford furrowed his brow and stared into her eyes. "*I* wish I understood you."

"It'd be a waste of your time to try and figure me out," she warned.

"You wouldn't be willing to share any secrets, would you?"

She shook her head, wafting the smell of flowers around them.

"I enjoy a good mystery," he said conversationally.

"I'm afraid you'll be disappointed."

The dancers spun around them, each one seemingly lost in his or her own world. She glimpsed Finley's cousin Anna talking with a rather handsome gentleman on the other side of the floor. The sighting confirmed her fear that Finley would be lurking somewhere in the shadows. He was probably watching her and Lord Huntsford, seething with rage at her continued disobedience.

"I have to go now." The words, while hushed, came out in a rush.

"We're still dancing." His face betrayed his confusion.

"I'm sorry, I really must go. *Now*," she added, in case that part wasn't clear.

Nick's hands tightened on hers. His eyebrows pulled low, and his teeth were clenched. "You'll cause a scene if you leave now."

And she would. Olivia might not have spent her life twirling around the glittering ballrooms of London, but she was fully aware abandoning her partner in the midst of a set would put every tongue in attendance wagging.

But it might stay the one person's who worried her the most. There was a chance that she could still remove herself before Finley saw either of them. The hope was feeble, and the optimism most likely misplaced, but Olivia had to try.

"I'm sorry if I said something amiss." Nick's voice broke into her plans. "I promise to be on my best behavior." His disarming smile was genuine. But Olivia couldn't risk another moment in his arms.

"Good evening, Lord Huntsford," she said quietly, pulling her hand away from his.

Olivia didn't look back as she left the marquess stranded in the middle of the dance floor, surrounded by still-dancing pairs.

Lord Huntsford stalked away somewhere, and Olivia could hear the whispers following her as she found a lonely place to stand against the wall. She jumped as someone rushed up to her side, grabbing her arm. Turning quickly, Olivia was surprised to see Anna. The younger girl looked strikingly different. Her hair was artfully arranged, and she was dressed in an evening gown that complemented, without overwhelming, her pale complexion. It was evident that whoever had chosen the dress had superb taste.

"Olivia, isn't this wonderful?" Anna practically twirled beside her.

Obviously, Anna hadn't seen the debacle on the dance floor, nor been exposed to the murmured suggestions filtering through the crowd as to the reason why. Otherwise, she would have begun the conversation by asking if Olivia was in her right mind.

Olivia could have answered the question without hesitation.

She certainly wasn't.

Olivia smiled wryly, wondering if something was wrong with her for never having been so enthusiastic. "It is beautiful, isn't it?"

"I think I've had more fun the past hour than I have my whole time in London." Anna's eyes were positively twinkling.

"I'm glad you're having a good time." At least one of them was.

"Oh, yes. It's my first ball ever. I'm so glad my mother let me come, and Cousin Julian agreed to escort me." Anna pulled a face at the last comment then shrugged. "Mama wasn't coming so it had to be him, or else I'd still be sitting at home."

"I'm sure he's honored to escort you." Olivia didn't believe that, but perhaps it would make Anna feel better.

Anna looked down shyly, reminding Olivia so much of the girl she had seen just days ago. "He's afraid I'll embarrass him. He's already told me what will happen if I do."

Olivia wondered what would happen, but she didn't want to upset Anna. Apparently Finley spent most of his time threatening others.

She put her arm around Anna's shoulders. "Don't worry. I've been to these events before. I'll help you if you wish."

Anna smiled in response.

They stood in companionable silence for several minutes, watching as the dancers took the floor for a waltz. Luckily, since Olivia and Henri had arrived late, she still had spaces on her dance card, which meant she didn't have to worry about going anywhere for a while. She was content to stand there and do nothing.

"The waltz is next. It always looks so romantic." Anna sighed.

This made Olivia laugh. "It's not quite so romantic when you're worried about your partner crushing your slippers. Or if the gentleman doesn't like bathing. There are drawbacks to being so close to someone."

Anna wrinkled her nose. "Still, I should think I'd like to be held in a man's arms as he twirled me around the room."

Olivia laughed again, wondering if this was what it was like to be an older sister, getting to hear such unguarded, humorous statements.

"I should probably warn you—" Anna interrupted her thoughts "—my cousin is planning to seek you out this evening."

"Oh, really?" She tried to keep her voice light, but dread filled her.

"Yes. He told me if I saw you I was to come and tell him

immediately." Anna chewed on her lower lip. "He'll probably be upset when he realizes I didn't do as he told me."

Olivia wrapped her arm around the young girl. "We won't worry over that."

"But—"

Olivia laughed uncomfortably. "He won't be mad at you."

The reassurance was enough to calm Anna's nerves, and she relaxed her grip on Olivia's arm.

"Olivia," Anna whispered insistently. *"Olivia."*

Olivia turned to follow with her gaze where Anna was discreetly pointing. Her heart pounded an irregular beat when she noticed who her friend was motioning at. Lord Huntsford.

"Why is that man staring at you like that?"

Olivia tried to feign ignorance. "Like what?"

Anna dropped her voice so they wouldn't be overheard. "Like he's planning on marching over here and sweeping you away."

Olivia really wanted to ask Anna how she recognized such a look, but then stopped herself.

"I think he must be looking behind us," Olivia offered, to distract from her furious blush.

Anna took her statement in earnest and turned around searching for someone standing behind them. "There's no one back there, Olivia." A pause. "He is rather dashing and handsome," she sighed.

"No, he's not," Olivia said automatically.

"Are we looking at the same man? Because I can't really tell how anyone wouldn't think he was handsome."

Olivia did everything she could think of to turn the conversation. The last thing she wanted Anna accidentally letting slip to her cousin was that the marquess was glowering at her from across the ballroom.

"I've seen you with him before—at the theater," Anna said, finally realizing why Nick looked familiar.

"Oh," Olivia muttered. "I guess you're correct."

"Of course I am." Anna grinned. "I have an extremely lucid memory."

Marvelous.

"So, is he courting you?" Anna asked.

Olivia fanned herself, feeling incredibly warm. "No. He's simply a friend of my brother."

"That doesn't really explain the look." She gasped again. "Maybe he's secretly in love with you. How wonderful! He's so handsome, maybe he'll ask you to marry him. I can already see it. The wedding will be beautiful." Olivia wouldn't have been surprised if the young girl began twirling around the room.

"I don't think we're going to be getting married." She forced another laugh, trying to keep her voice light.

Anna's face fell. "It's because of my cousin, isn't it?"

It would be so simple, and would solve so much, to tell her yes, but Olivia couldn't bring herself to do it. "It's because he's nothing more than a friend."

Anna pondered that for a while, her lips pursed as though she were trying to solve all the problems of the world.

"Are you sure it's not my cousin?" Anna finally asked again. "I'd hate for you to waste your time with Julian, when you could be with someone like *him*," she said, pointing out Nick again.

"My relationship with your cousin has nothing to do with the marquess."

"If you say so," Anna said doubtfully.

Olivia remained silent, too unnerved by Nick's steady survey of her to concentrate on much else. She wished he would go away. He certainly was causing a spectacle. Several other attendants at the ball had already noticed his rather focused gaze. That, coupled with her leaving him in the midst of the quadrille would have the gossips overwhelmed with work.

There were no doubt many ladies already tittering behind

their fans, predicting the procurement of a special license. Henri's friends would claim that the marquess and the earl's sister would be the unequalled match of the Season. Two extremely powerful families, melding together. It was almost Shakespearean. Like Romeo and Juliet, perhaps.

It would do everyone well to remember they all died in the end of that one, though.

Anna's partner for the next dance, a charming young man, came to claim her, and Olivia was left standing awkwardly by herself.

Olivia felt the burst of breath against her bare neck before she realized someone was behind her.

Chapter Twenty

"**Y**ou shouldn't be standing all alone," Lord Finley whispered into her ear. She was grateful they were concealed in the shadows. "Unless you're hiding, of course," he continued.

"Sometimes I enjoy solitude," Olivia muttered.

"You don't seem very happy to see me. I would have thought a couple of days without my presence would have had you pining for me."

"You would have thought incorrectly, then."

He growled something unintelligible, but Olivia was fairly certain it was a rather vehement curse. "You don't want to make me angry, do you, Olivia?"

"No," she said automatically. She might *want* to, but doing so wouldn't be wise.

"Hmm." His breath made her want to recoil. "If that's true, prove it to me with a waltz."

Olivia started at his suggestion. The waltz may have gained acceptance in London ballrooms, but to dance it, unmarried and with an unattached man, was significant.

Or scandalous.

Perhaps in her case, it would be both. And there would certainly be no keeping that juicy tidbit a secret from Marcus.

She was well and truly trapped. Nothing but acquiescence

would appease Lord Finley, or else, he'd create the second scene of the evening.

"I would be honored to dance with you," she lied.

Finley took her hand and led Olivia onto the floor where the other couples were already dancing. This was their first dance together. In the books she read, this would have been a momentous occasion. A chance for the young couple to realize how perfectly they matched each other. Instead, all she could think of was that his hands on her caused no searing lightning along her veins—like Lord Huntsford's did.

At the thought of his name, her eyes searched the room for him. It took her a few moments to locate him in the crowd. She regretted her search the moment she found him. He was still glowering at her from across the crowded floor.

Olivia stumbled and grabbed Lord Finley tighter to keep from spilling onto the floor. And she winced as she clutched at Finley, certain she had smashed his toe.

"I never realized dancing was so difficult for you," he mocked. His eyes burned with his desire and lust, but something else lurked there as well. Something darker. Anger? Jealousy? It was difficult to say.

"I'm sorry. I merely lost my footing." She attempted to reinstate the distance between them, but Finley had used her lack of grace as an excuse to pull her closer. There was no propriety in the way they were dancing now.

"You needn't make excuses to me. If you want me to hold you closer, all you must do is ask." His grip tightened until she was practically wincing in pain.

"I'll bear that in mind for the future," she said between clenched teeth.

"See that you do." The statement held an air of finality, and Olivia forced her eyes and thoughts away from Lord Huntsford and his anger. She had more than enough to deal with right in front of her.

But Finley had already noticed where her attention lingered, or on *whom* it lingered. "Is there something between you and Huntsford I should know about?" Finley's voice was tight with anger. A muscle ticked furiously in his jaw, and his eyes cut back and forth between Olivia and the marquess.

"I've no idea why you would ask such a question."

"I've heard rumors. Apparently the attraction simmering between the two of you has not been lost on other members of the *ton*." The hand around her waist pulled, bringing her even closer.

"You know how people like to talk. If it weren't about me, it would undoubtedly be someone else." She managed a mirthless chuckle.

"I believe I told you I don't like being made to look like a fool."

"That was certainly not my intention."

"But it will be your result. I have made my opinion on this matter clear. There should be no gossip or cause for talk."

"I apologize if my actions have cast any unpleasantness on you. There is nothing between the marquess and myself." Her tone was obedient enough, but Olivia practically choked on her own words.

Her humble plea for forgiveness must have soothed Finley's remaining temper because he regained a bit of his contrived joviality. "You are forgiven. And I don't completely blame you. You simply need a firmer hand guiding your steps."

That made her want to cast up her accounts, but she nodded anyway.

"I'm afraid it's become stifling in here," Finley murmured as the waltz ended. "Shall we take a turn in the outside? I hear Ashburn's garden would shame the whole of England."

Olivia's eyes darted quickly across the ballroom, trying to find where the marquess had gone. Dancing was one thing, but leaving with Lord Finley wouldn't be omitted from a

conversation with Marcus. Mercifully, Nick was nowhere to be seen. Henrietta also seemed to be mired so deeply in her conversation Olivia doubted she would notice if the roof fell upon her. So, Olivia placed her hand around Finley's arm and allowed him to escort her out into the moonlight.

They had disappeared.

Nick had abandoned his watch for two minutes, and Finley managed to abscond with Olivia. Marcus would likely shoot him.

Nick had received Marcus's note that afternoon, explaining he had more business to attend to at his estate and that he would be gone close to a fortnight. Marcus had asked Nick to keep an eye on Olivia.

So Nick, after hearing from his aunt that the young lady was indeed planning on attending the ball, had come as well. And he'd found it impossible to stay away from her. To be cold to her. To be angry with her.

Until she left him in the middle of their dance.

And now. Well, now she was missing. With Finley.

Nick sought respite on the terrace. After having scanned the crowd, he had little hope Olivia and Finley were inside. Perhaps Olivia had simply gone to the retiring room, and Finley had taken his leave. But no, it was still early, and Finley wasn't one to leave while prey was still milling about. Nick peered down into the garden below, admitting—if it were not for all the uproar—he would be enjoying the view immensely. The moonlight cascaded through the trees and alighted magnificently on the flowers.

It was a perfect evening. And while Nick supposed he should be tearing apart the Ashburn home looking for his friend's sister, he needed a moment to breathe. He began moving slowly down the steps to the garden, delaying his rescue mission to regain his composure. He wouldn't let Olivia know his pride

was wounded by her abandonment. He would need to be a greater master of indifference and coldness.

Yes, he thought as he strolled a little farther into the hedges. He'd be circumspect in all his dealings with women from now on.

He'd be nothing like that couple practically inhaling each other behind a tree. He'd be...*what?*

The moonlight glinted off a strand of the girl's russet hair, and he *knew.*

Olivia considered herself a rational person. Which was why, when Lord Finley asked her to accompany him out in the garden, she thought of many reasons why they should stay inside, and then once they were out on the terrace, many reasons why they should stay there.

After descending the stairs to the garden below, however, she gave up trying to stay put. Silence reigned as they walked through the garden. As they passed a particularly gnarled tree, Finley stopped and pushed her against the trunk.

"I'm through waiting," he told her. His eyes burned with a frightening and intense heat. His hands gripped her waist and pinned her to the rough bark of the tree.

Her dress would be ruined after this.

She lifted her chin a few notches, meeting him in the eye. "Just a little more time."

"You've had time."

"Marcus still isn't ready for such an announcement. It'll crush him."

"All the better." Finley grinned.

He crushed her to him, his eager mouth smothering her own. Olivia squeezed her eyes shut, not wanting to look at his face right above her. She wormed her hands between their bodies and tried to push him away. He wouldn't budge. She jerked,

trying again to get away and felt the fabric of her dress catch on the bark and rip. The seam of her sleeve tore away.

"Sto—" She tried to yell as he ground his mouth against hers. Olivia beat her small fists against his chest, but Finley was obviously so intent that nothing would move him. "St—" She tried again.

Her hands scrambled for purchase, something heavy and blunt she could knock him out with, but there was nothing nearby. No vases. No volumes of poetry. The best she could do would be to try again to throw him off of her. But he outweighed her by a good many stone.

She kept her mouth clamped shut against his, which made him more determined. She clutched at his lapels, hoping to gain some momentum and thrust him away.

And both Olivia and Finley were so enwrapped in their own drama neither one heard a very pensive marquess nearby. And neither one saw the look of disbelief when the marquess realized who the two trysting lovers were.

But both heard his next words. "Get away from her!"

Finley's mouth lifted, and he swung his head around to face off against the newcomer. "Huntsford," he spat.

Nick was stalking Finley, moving slowly, but resolutely. Like a lion circling his prey. But to his credit, Finley didn't move an inch. He repositioned to shield Olivia's body with his own. It would have been a chivalrous gesture if not for the gravity of the moment.

Or the fact that this was his fault.

"I—I can explain," Olivia began, drawing a deep breath and preparing to launch into a very delicately worded chronology of the night's happenings.

"Step away from her, Finley," Nick demanded. Not surprisingly, it was as though Olivia had never spoken.

Fine. She'd try again. "There really is a very simple…"

"Silence!" Nick roared.

And with a decidedly unladylike squeak, she shut up.

"You have got thirty seconds to explain why I shouldn't kill you right here," Nick told his adversary, who was quickly losing whatever flare of bravado had initially seized him.

Finley found his voice, but the words sounded strained. "You'd kill a man over a simple kiss?"

"Yes."

Olivia wouldn't have been surprised if Finley fainted. Nick, seeing his advantage, pressed it. "Now, use your remaining fifteen seconds to get out of my sight. I don't expect to ever have this conversation with you again."

Huntsford then closed the distance between them with two strides. He grabbed Finley by the cravat and jerked, a little harder than necessity demanded. "And if I suspect you have even thought about mentioning this evening, you won't have to worry about conversation with anyone, ever again."

The baron gulped audibly, and with a quick look at Olivia, perhaps to silently apologize for fleeing, Finley took his leave.

Olivia swallowed hard, feeling very much like an unruly child who was about to be taken in hand. After several futile attempts to muster some courage, she gave up and stared at the ground.

"Come on. We're leaving, too," he said.

"I'm not going anywhere with you." She grasped tighter at the torn pieces of her dress, shame heating her face.

"So, while you feel comfortable enough to promenade in a garden at midnight with a known rake, you won't allow me to see you home safely?" Anger threaded through his voice.

Olivia wisely refused to answer.

Nick gripped her elbow, causing Olivia to wince at the suddenness of his gesture, though his touch remained gentle. Impersonal and cold, but gentle. "This isn't something I'm willing to discuss with you," he said.

He steered her toward the back of the garden, prepared to ferret out a simple escape route. She wanted to say something—anything—that might make him less angry. But the situation *was* rather tawdry-looking.

Unexpectedly, Olivia pitched forward, having caught her shoe on some hidden obstruction in the ground.

"Oh!" she cried out as Nick's arms wrapped around her, pulling her tight against him.

And for the second time during the evening, Olivia found herself pressed against a man out in the Ashburn gardens. He held her for a second, looking at her with blank eyes.

His entire expression was a mask.

He lowered his head slowly down to her, apparently preparing to whisper some vital information. His face was a breath from her own, and completely beyond her volition, she closed her eyes, half hoping for and half fearing a kiss.

And also for the second time that evening, Olivia didn't hear approaching footsteps on the walk.

She also missed the arrival of four ladies directly in front of them on the path.

"What?" And then. "Come along, ladies. I have accidentally led us down the wrong path. Tricky moonlight. My prize roses are *this* way."

Nick hastily withdrew from her and turned to face the four women, belatedly realizing the front of Olivia's dress was in shambles. When he remembered, the marquess angled his body to cover Olivia's side.

The hostess, Lady Ashburn, tried to maneuver the others away from the suspicious pair.

"This way, this way," she said loudly. "I have something I *must* show you over here."

The other three ladies, who were hidden in the shadows and unrecognizable, were valiantly fighting off their hostess's efforts.

"Could it be?" tittered one.

"No. Surely…"

"But it is!" Came the excited reply.

"The Marquess of Huntsford and the Westin girl," another of the women supplied helpfully.

The three ladies edged closer, perhaps hoping to gain a better look at the wayward pair. As the moonlight illuminated them, Olivia recognized all three as acquaintances of Henrietta and knew then she and Nick were both well and truly caught.

Olivia, who had always prided herself on never fainting—not even as a tactical strategy—suddenly felt the edges of her vision blur. She vaguely heard the tittering and gleeful whisperings of their discoverers, but she paid them no mind. Perhaps if she focused on one particular point, it would make her feel less dizzy. Olivia also didn't give a thought to what Huntsford was thinking. He stood staunchly beside her, that much she knew, but he was silent. Perhaps he was also trying to muddle out a likely excuse for their whereabouts and her appearance.

"Ladies, I hope you will excuse us for a moment," Nick broke into their chattering smoothly, and all the voices stopped at once. "My betrothed has torn her dress on a low-hanging limb and needs to repair it."

Olivia, still reeling from the events of the last few moments, failed to grasp the full import of his words. Apparently, so did the three senseless women in front of them. Lady Ashburn was the only one among them who seemed to have immediately taken hold of his meaning, and she smiled discreetly.

Nick guided Olivia by her elbow, intending to escort her out the back garden entrance.

One of the ladies finally sputtered. "Did you say *betrothed?*"

Nick nodded.

As the three went into raptures at being present for the announcement of the Season—unaware their very presence

had precipitated such a drastic measure—Nick asked for
Lady Ashburn to inform Henri they were leaving, then bustled
Olivia to the carriage.

Olivia was oblivious to the flurry of activity around her. She
was mute as Nick led her by the shoulders and helped her into
the conveyance.

All she could do was wonder if she'd single-handedly
destroyed both her and Marcus's lives.

Chapter Twenty-One

$\sim$

Nick forced his eyes away from Olivia, who looked utterly dejected, as though he had taken her last farthing and booted her onto the streets.

Was she that opposed to marrying him?

The thought was far from flattering.

Nick wondered why he didn't feel panicked. He understood the ramifications of what he'd done. He and Olivia *would* be married now. There would be no other way to salvage her reputation after what the ladies had witnessed in the garden. No one would care if the appearance wasn't the actuality.

Olivia needed a marriage. Without one, she'd be a pariah.

Well-bred ladies, even women of lesser social position, would be justified in turning their backs on her...a public and humiliating shunning. If she refused to marry him, Olivia would have difficulty finding another gentleman willing to marry her after such a disgraceful spectacle.

Nick couldn't allow that to happen to her. She didn't deserve to feel the brunt of the *ton*'s censure. While—admittedly—her own foolish actions instigated most of the evening's happenstances, she was young. And, it seemed to Nick, he was willing to forgive her almost anything.

Chancing a look at his soon-to-be bride, he noticed she was

white-lipped and sitting painfully erect. Her frame appeared so tight and brittle he thought, if he touched her, she might crumble entirely. While she looked in his direction, Nick was certain she didn't see him.

Should he say something?

Tell her everything was going to work out?

Assure her he didn't mind the marriage?

Nick didn't feel the slightest twinge of fear or anxiety about what he'd done. He actually felt…victorious. His feelings for Olivia were undeniable. They would be happy together.

If she gave him a chance.

But she seemed to be making a habit out of rebuffing him. She'd turned him down in favor of Finley. *Finley.* Nick needed to discover the trick to getting rid of the pesky baron permanently. Finley wouldn't leave Olivia alone just because she was betrothed. In truth, the lack of attainability might be even more attractive to the rake.

Thinking of the snake made him wonder what actually happened in the garden. Olivia had yet to say, and her staring ahead in stony silence didn't seem a promising step toward disclosure.

"Are you going to say anything?" he asked gently, wondering briefly if she might be in shock. Her lips trembled as though her teeth were on the verge of chattering together. It wasn't cold, but he began to feel around under the seat for a blanket.

Finding one, Nick placed it across her lap. "*Can* you say something?" His tone was harder, but not intentionally. Worry gave his words an edge.

Slowly, her eyes seemed to focus on his face, and he realized he'd misjudged her mood. Olivia wasn't shocked…she was furious.

"Do you realize what you've done?" she growled.

Nick managed to keep his tone mild. "I believe so."

"You've ruined my life!"

He fought the irrational surge of anger. Of course she was upset and lashing out. He was the closest target and able to weather the emotions without reacting. "I'm sorry you feel that way," he said quietly.

The quieter he became, the louder she grew.

"I'm not marrying you." Her tone was intractable, final, and Nick thought it best not to point out she was acting like a child.

"Yes, you are."

"You cannot force me to the altar. The church requires my consent as much as yours."

She had him there. If Nick couldn't get her to acquiesce, she would willingly ruin herself because of her stubbornness. Taking a few moments to pray silently, Nick waited, hoping the right words would come to him.

"This will be good for both of us," he said finally.

"You don't know me well enough to judge that," she said hotly. "This marriage will ruin my life."

"You've said as much already." He tried not to let her words sting. But it wasn't working.

Sighing in frustration, she sank deeper into the seat, rubbing her temples with her fingertips. "Don't worry. Marcus will be home in a few days. He'll help us sort this problem out."

Nick was one more protest away from losing his temper. "There'll be nothing left for him to 'sort out,' as you say. We *will* be married."

She snorted. "I don't know how many different ways you wish me to say no, but if you'll provide me with a number, I'll be happy to accommodate you."

"You'll be ruined if you don't marry me. I won't let that happen just because you're being stubborn."

"I'm ruined already."

Nick shook his head. "There will be talk, but the gossip

will die quickly enough once we are wed. You'll be properly married with the protection of my name."

She said nothing.

He leaned across the carriage, catching her hands between his. "I will take care of you, Olivia. You'll want for nothing."

Her eyes filled with skepticism. "You wouldn't care that I don't love you? That I can never love you?"

He dropped her hands, surprised over how much those words hurt. Nick should have known while Finley was in the picture he'd have problems getting Olivia to cooperate.

Her heart was, apparently, out of his reach.

How had he allowed himself to believe he and Olivia could be happy together when she would always be pining for Finley?

This time, as he addressed her, his own voice was cold and devoid of emotion. "You *will* marry me. And if you leave me no choice but to tell Marcus the truth about what happened tonight, I will."

Her protestations stopped immediately.

"I'll hate you for this," she said after several blissful moments of silence.

Nick was surprised at the venom in her voice. "I suppose I'll have to take the chance. I will not abandon you to the wolves," he said.

"I'd be in better hands," she spat.

While he knew she didn't mean it—at least he hoped she didn't—the last insult was better aimed than the others.

The carriage stopped in front of Olivia's home, and Nick, seized by a very ungentlemanly impulse, simply threw the door open and watched her struggle to dismount by herself.

"I'll call upon you tomorrow, and I expect to be granted entrance." He didn't have to add the *or else*. The unspoken threat hung, festering in the air between them.

Olivia barely acknowledged he had spoken, instead turning

her back on him to walk to the door. But for a moment she paused and looked back toward the still-open entryway into the carriage.

"I trust since you have my capitulation, you'll have no need to tell my brother about this evening?" While she tried to hide it, the vulnerability gleamed in her eyes.

Nick nodded curtly, thinking his voice might betray him. He wanted to call her back, to hold her until the pain in her eyes vanished.

But he didn't.

After watching her safely inside, he signaled the coachman to continue home. As the carriage rumbled past the row of houses, Nick wondered if Olivia would ever come to care for him.

Even just a little.

"You naughty, naughty girl," Henrietta chided as Olivia made her way to the breakfast table the next morning. She'd wanted nothing more than to hide in her room, pretending as though last evening had been a horrible nightmare. But the duchess had called upon her before the sun had really had a chance to rise, and Olivia had invited her friend to eat with her.

"What, Henri?" she asked, pretending as though she had not heard her the first time.

"I had to hear about you and my nephew from someone else. Imagine my embarrassment at having to be told two people close to me are planning to wed and I had not the faintest idea." The duchess paused briefly to take a breath.

Olivia seized the opportunity to interject. "The announcement was unintentional. After a rather unfortunate circumstance, Lord Huntsford decided to make his declaration public."

Henri's eyes sharpened at the mention of the unfortunate

circumstance, and Olivia knew as surely as she was sitting there, Henri had already been privy to the juicy details.

"Well, it is rather romantic," Henrietta said.

"Yes, well the marquess quite literally refused to take no for an answer."

Henrietta sighed dreamily. "Why, my child, I couldn't have done better for you if I had snagged the prince regent himself."

Olivia wondered how the duchess was planning to take credit for the events that transpired in the mockery of an engagement. Unless, of course, Henri was more cunning than anyone suspected.

In a flash, Henrietta whipped out a small writing pad and commenced scribbling notes. "Now, it's a shame your brother has not yet returned. I need him to contact whoever's in charge of these matters to see if we can't book Westminster Abbey for the wedding." She paused her movements. "I suppose I shall have to plow ahead under the assumption your brother will be able to handle the task to my satisfaction."

Olivia cautiously began, "Isn't it a bit soon to be planning the wedding?"

Henri looked as though Olivia had suggested that one day women would be running around in breeches and driving horse-less carriages.

"Well, let's plan for something small, then. Maybe here at my home," Olivia said quickly before Henrietta could begin weeping over the missed opportunity to throw a gala. Olivia hoped to avoid a public spectacle or uproar…at least until she could find a way to extricate herself from this mess.

As expected, Henri looked horrified. "I refuse—absolutely refuse—to allow my only nephew to be joined in matrimony to the woman I would love to claim as a daughter in the privacy of a *home!* We wouldn't want everyone thinking you are ashamed of the match." She waited a moment. "Or that circumstances

are such that God wouldn't be pleased at the event taking place in a church."

The duchess looked at her shrewdly.

"I don't think God has a preference where we wed, Henri," Olivia said. Was God upset with the mess she'd gotten herself into, however? She sent up a silent prayer asking for a way out of the latest fiasco.

"Well, *I* certainly do! And it'll not be here in this squalor." Henri gestured around the dining room, and Olivia strained to see how anyone could mistake the finely appointed furnishings as anything remotely resembling squalor.

Henrietta continued with her furious list making. "Now, I was thinking the first things the guests would see would be a sea of roses as soon as the doors to the church are thrown wide."

Olivia groaned. It was painfully obvious she was going to be forced to sit and listen as her well-meaning friend handled the meticulous details. She just prayed the older woman wasn't foolish enough to think Olivia would let her choose the dress. Although…Nick might well run from the altar if his intended waltzed down the aisle in something the shade of a pumpkin.

Olivia picked at her plate, half listening to the duchess's single-handed debate on the virtue of pink versus white roses. So much swarmed in her mind Olivia felt dizzy from the activity.

Salvation came in the form of Gibbons at the door. "You have a caller, Lady Olivia."

She nearly knocked over her chair in her haste to escape the duchess. Olivia didn't bother to ask who it was. She would have gladly endured tea with the Viscount Danfield just to have a few moments of not having to speak about the "tremendous news." But Olivia remembered her manners at the door and turned to look at Henri.

"Go on," the duchess said with a dismissive wave. "I'll be here waiting for you when you're done."

Olivia stifled a groan.

Moments later, she entered the sitting room to find Nick standing by the fireplace. His presence—while not necessarily welcome—was expected.

"Rather early for you to be about, isn't it, Lord Huntsford?" she asked, taking a seat on the chair farthest from him.

"Is it?" he asked, not yet moving from his position.

"Yes, I thought you would need to sleep in this morning. I can't say with surety, but I would imagine ruining lives is quite tiring." She didn't bother to hide the irritation in her voice. She might well be corralled into this marriage, but she wasn't going to be docile and compliant about it.

Nor was she going to stop and think about why she was so angry with the marquess. Truthfully, her own actions had instigated this entire affair, and she supposed most young women would be grateful for the marquess's interference and assistance.

But not her.

If she were looking for a fight, however, Lord Huntsford didn't appear as though he was going to oblige her. He crossed the room to stand in front of her. "I think perhaps I bungled things last evening," he said simply.

"That's an astute observation."

He ignored her. "I realize nothing about this has been the least bit conventional. But I hope you'll allow me a bit of tradition now."

She didn't have time to ask what he meant before he knelt down before her. "I realize most women want poetry, and flowers, and romance," he said, "but I think you would see through the fripperies. I know this marriage isn't something you planned for yourself, but I sincerely hope you will join me in making the best of our lives together."

Nick reached up and lifted her hand from her lap. "Lady Olivia Fairfax, I would be honored if you would consent to become my wife." He took something from his pocket and slipped it on her finger. Something cold and heavy—a complement to the feeling of dread gripping her.

Olivia looked down, preparing herself to be unimpressed by whatever she saw on her finger. But it didn't work.

The ring was stunning, a large sapphire set in the midst of a circle of diamonds. The gems caught the sun and cast little shining points of light on the closest wall.

She drew an involuntary breath. "It's beautiful," she said.

Tears sprung to her eyes, and she didn't bother to try to hold them back. The situation was so inconceivably—and unjustly— ridiculous. Were Olivia any other woman, this would have been the happiest moment of her life. Instead, she was embroiled in a farcical charade of a betrothal…a *second* charade of a betrothal.

Nick had only to glimpse her tears before bolting upright and wrapping her in his arms. He murmured words to her she couldn't make out—ones undoubtedly meant to comfort. And Olivia wanted nothing more than to lose herself in the embrace, to forget about Finley and his threats.

But that was impossible. She knew, better than anyone, the serious ramifications of marrying Nick, or even agreeing to an engagement. How then could she feel anything but sorrow?

Stemming the tide of tears and composing herself took several moments. It was better by far for her to be angry rather than sad, Olivia decided. If she were able to convince herself Nick cared nothing for her wishes, she could remain distant and aloof. But the Nick who thought enough to procure a ring, even for their sham of an engagement, was too complicated for her to handle.

Olivia needed to buy some time until she figured out how she was going to undo this mess.

"I think we should discuss the terms of our arrangement." Her voice was shaky, and she coughed to cover the fact.

Nick looked at her warily but nodded his assent. "All right."

"My first term," she began, "is for you to walk into the other room and find a way to pry your aunt away from my table. I've no wish to discuss wedding plans today."

He smiled. "Do I get to propose a counterterm?"

Olivia thought about this. "I suppose."

Nick's grin grew wider. "A kiss?"

"Certainly," she agreed.

"Really?"

"I assume you wish the kiss first?" she asked.

Nick nodded slowly, still looking ill at ease.

"And if I grant your request, you'll handle mine?"

He nodded again.

"Very well," she said on a sigh, rising from her seat and standing in front of him. "Whenever you are ready," she announced. She daintily held out the back of her hand.

Nick laughed but took her hand and pressed his lips to her bare skin. "You have bested me," he said with a smile. "Now, I shall go slay the dragon for your fair ladyship."

He left the room, and Olivia flopped into a chair. She held the back of her hand to her own lips.

And she pretended—just for a moment—she wasn't going to have to ruin everything.

Chapter Twenty-Two

Olivia tossed and turned for several hours that evening. She could tell the moment the rest of the house went silent and retired for the night. But she remained awake and lucid. Marcus would be home in less than a week. And she had no ready excuse to give him for the chaos he was sure to discover when he returned.

She was no closer to a solution that involved not marrying the marquess, nor was she anywhere near a plan that meant she'd not have to honor the agreement she'd struck with Finley. It had been a dangerous bargain with the baron. She'd known it from the beginning but hadn't realized how much she'd be losing in the end.

When she closed her eyes, hoping nerves and pure exhaustion would win in the epic battle between sleeping and not, Nick's was the face she saw. She envisioned the way his mouth quirked when he found something funny. And his were the hands she felt lingering against her cheek though they were physically far apart.

Would it be that way after she and Finley married? Would she look at her husband and instead see the man she was growing to wish she *could* marry?

A commotion from downstairs caught her attention just as her eyes were closing on something promisingly like sleep.

Olivia pushed her unbound hair back from her face as she sat up. "What?" she asked the empty room.

Throwing on a robe and belting it securely, she opened the door to her bedroom, looked both ways down the hall and stepped out when she found it empty. *Should I grab a candelabrum, a weapon against whomever might be intruding?* But she discarded the thought. Creeping unnoticed downstairs would be difficult enough without having to heft the weight of a heavy weapon.

"His lordship has given me explicit instructions not to let you enter," Gibbons's voice rose up the expansive stairwell to her.

Finley.

It had to be. Marcus wouldn't deny entrance to anyone else, and the baron was the only person with enough gall to come to her house at—she looked at the clock—one in the morning.

Finley's voice was lower in his response, but Olivia could still make out the words. They sent chills skittering across her back.

"Your lordship has no authority over me," he informed the butler. "I demand an audience with your mistress, now."

Olivia, struck for a moment by the very unlikely humor in the situation, wished she could see Gibbons's face after being dismissed so summarily.

"You, sir, are drunk," Gibbons declared. "And I no more intend on letting you see my mistress than I plan on letting you sleep off your drink on the front steps."

After Gibbons's observation, Olivia noticed Finley's words *did* sound slurred. It was difficult to tell where one syllable ended and another began. *Wonderful,* Finley in her house at all was more than she wanted to deal with. Finley after he'd been imbibing was another thing entirely.

"You should probably let your mistress decide if she wants to see me or not," she heard Finley saying. "I believe you'll find she's most eager to oblige me."

Olivia, poised at the top of the stairs, warred with indecision on whether she should descend. Or, like a coward, retreat to her chambers and allow Gibbons and the able-bodied footmen to deal with the problem of the drunken baron.

Before Gibbons could edge in a retort, Finley's voice came in clearer, as though he had turned his head toward the stairs—knowing she was at the top, listening in.

"I think you'll find she's most agreeable to come down. And if she hasn't done so in two minutes after you deliver my request to see her, then I think she'll realize she's misjudged my generous nature," he said, now sounding threateningly lucid.

"I'll not be delivering any kind of message for you." Gibbons's outrage rang through every word.

Olivia gave the ends of her sash a yank, fortifying herself against what was likely going to be an unpleasant confrontation. The twenty-six stairs down to the entryway suddenly seemed thrice the number, and Olivia thought of about as many reasons why she should turn around and lock herself back in her room. But she forced one foot in front of the other until she'd made it down the flight.

Gibbons had his back to her, and without wanting to startle him, she laid her hand on his shoulder. The butler whirled to face her. "It's all right. I'll see him."

"I don't think it's wise, my lady." His words were clipped.

Olivia tried to look imperious, which was rather difficult considering she was attired in nothing but her nightgown and robe. She also tried to ignore Finley's eyes on her, scorching through the layers of clothing she wore.

"Am I not in charge of this house when my brother is away?" she asked Gibbons.

His nod was curt.

She turned her attention to Finley. "I'll see you in the morning room." Then she turned her back on him as though he ceased to exist to her.

Once Finley had stalked off, Olivia looked back at Gibbons. "I can handle him," she assured the butler, but she wished her voice sounded more confident.

"Your brother won't be happy to hear of this," Gibbons said. But the ominous words didn't have the desired effect. Marcus was either going to come back home to discover she was engaged to his best friend, or he'd eventually find out she was marrying Finley. She could hardly fear her brother's inevitable displeasure now.

"Go to bed, Gibbons," she said kindly. "He won't hurt me," she told the still-skeptical-looking servant.

At least she hoped he wouldn't.

Olivia didn't wait for Gibbons to move away before she went to join Finley in the morning room. But she did have enough presence of mind to call out, "No eavesdropping," over her shoulder as she walked away.

She had no delusions Gibbons would obey her command.

"What do you think you're doing here?" she asked Finley without preamble, as she closed the door behind her.

"That's a nice look for you," the baron said instead, taking in her appearance with a long, lingering look. "You'll wear that once we're married." It wasn't a request but a command.

"Let's talk about why you're here right now, and not what you think of my attire." She crossed her arms over herself in an attempt to add an extra barrier between herself and her future husband's probing eyes.

Finley dropped any pretense of good humor. "You know why I'm here."

Of course she did. But she wasn't going to be the one to begin the conversation.

Apparently, Finley didn't mind leading the discussion on her

indiscretion and accidental betrothal to another man. "Did you not think I would hear about you and Huntsford?"

Olivia refused to cower from the anger in his tone. Finley was the one responsible for the disastrous scene in the garden. She wouldn't take the blame for something he had begun. "No, I knew you would find out."

Her frankness must have flustered the baron because he blinked at her several times. "How could you allow such a story to circulate?"

The baron was perilously close to seeing her temper ignite. "What exactly did you think would happen after you led me out there and then tried to maul me against a tree?" she growled.

"You should never have left with Huntsford," he accused.

"*You ran!* Need I remind you it took nothing more than an angry look from Lord Huntsford for you to flee.…"

He stalked up to her, grabbing her shoulder with a bruising grip. "I. Did. Not. Run."

Olivia had passed the point where her tongue was guarded by her better sense. "Yes, you did," she goaded. "You were frightened as soon as Nick looked at you."

She could tell she'd spoken too much by the look in his eyes.

Finley called her a word she'd only ever heard a few of the servants whisper to one another. He grabbed her face in one hand, squeezing until her lips puckered, and she felt as though he would loosen some of her teeth. "Did you call him Nick?"

It must have been a burst of insanity, but she found it funny he would fixate on that. "I did, *Lord Finley.*" His grip on her face mangled the words, but he understood well enough.

With no warning, he released his hold and slammed the back of his hand against her cheek. Her head snapped to the side, and she gasped for breath. The air in the room seemed to grow thin and sparse. Her hand went automatically to the throbbing skin. She tasted the warm bitterness of her own blood.

Finley stood a foot from her, his shoulders heaving and his face an ugly, mottled red.

Olivia could think of a hundred things to say to him. A hundred different ways to convey her disdain and anger, but she bit each hateful word back. Instead, she raised her chin and smiled.

"You may make me your bride," she said slowly, clearly. "But you will never have me." She didn't understand her own words, but apparently, Finley did because he reared back his hand again.

The sound of a pistol being cocked stopped the newest threat.

"If you so much as try," a voice said, "it will be the last thing you ever do."

Olivia could have fainted in relief at Nick's unexpected presence. Finley froze, his arm suspended in mid-swing. She felt, rather than saw, Nick moving closer to her, stepping between her and Finley.

The pistol in his grip didn't waver, nor did his voice. "Leave. *Now.*"

Olivia's accusations of cowardice must have been playing through Finley's mind because he refused to budge. "You're the one who needs to be leaving."

"Olivia is my betrothed. She is also under my protection while her brother is away. You have no right or claim to be here. She is *mine*." Nick's gun moved the smallest bit toward the baron's chest.

"Plan on calling a magistrate to send me away?" Finley asked, clearly torn somewhere on the line between bravado and insanity.

"No." Nick's voice was a calm, rational counterpart to Olivia's mounting hysteria. "I'll kill you."

The marquess's voice was cold, devoid of any emotion, of any logic telling him he couldn't very well follow through on

his threat. She began to fear for him, wondering how much of the man she saw right now was a remnant from his war experiences. She could only see him in profile, and then solely by the dim light of the candles flickering in the room.

Nick's jaw was clenched so tightly it looked as though his teeth might shatter. Olivia's feet moved toward him before her mind could caution her against the wisdom of her actions. Her only concern was to keep Nick from blowing Finley's fool head off his shoulders.

Her hand touched the arm of his coat. "Nick," she said quietly, but he didn't turn to look at her. "Let's put the gun down. Finley's leaving now."

"No, I'm not," Finley called out.

Olivia silenced the baron with a wave of her hand.

Nick still had not moved, his features and stance as rigid as any marble statue. So Olivia, much like Nick had done for her, moved to put herself between the two men. She doubted Nick would shoot *her.* And hopefully, Finley would be quiet once he realized how dangerous this situation could be for him.

But what she had not thought about was Nick would actually get the opportunity to see her face. Her face that was bruised and cut from Finley's earlier strike.

Nick noticed immediately. The gun didn't drop or waver, but his eyes fell to her cheek. "He's already struck you?" The voice was strangled, mingled with anger and violence.

Her rescuer didn't wait for her to answer. The condemning evidence made her confirmation unnecessary. Nick was around her before Olivia knew what was happening.

Nick pressed his gun under Finley's chin, tilting the baron's head back with the weapon until Finley looked most uncomfortable. Olivia began praying diligently that Nick would find the restraint not to shoot the baron. Not that he probably didn't deserve some sort of punishment, but Nick didn't need a death on his conscience.

God must have agreed with her.

Rather than pulling the hair trigger, Nick jammed Finley's head backward a bit more. "I could shoot you," he threatened in a deceptively soft voice. "And I probably should."

But the gun was gone as quickly as it had been there. "Get out, before I change my mind."

Finley must have decided during the interchange that he had no more desire to risk his life because he stalked past the marquess. As he attempted to shoulder past Olivia, he muttered, "I'll return later to finish our discussion."

The warning was the last thing she could be concerned about. Though the front door had slammed closed, Nick stood in the center of the room, rigid and staring as though he could see through the wall and out to where Finley had departed. As she watched him, Olivia took in his attire. He wore a greatcoat over a rumpled lawn shirt. And while his breeches and boots didn't seem out of order, the entire ensemble had the look of something hastily thrown together.

"How did you know to come?" she asked. The words broke the silence, but didn't break through his haze. Olivia wondered if he was going to answer.

"Gibbons sent for me when he saw Finley's coach pull up outside." He turned to face her finally. "You should have waited for me to get here."

"I didn't know you were coming," she defended, trying to dispel some of his anger.

"Then *you* should have sent for me."

He never would have gotten her message because he would have already been on his way. Olivia decided not to mention that.

"Come here," he said, but his voice was a question, not a demand. He moved to sit on the settee, leaving her enough room to sit beside him.

She could think of many, exhaustive reasons to refuse.

But she didn't.

"Does it hurt much?" Nick asked as he touched the side of her face. Vainly, she wondered how badly it would bruise, and then, practically, wondered how she was going to explain its presence to other people. Her brother especially.

She supposed, however, Nick would be more than willing to pass the story on to her brother.

"Not too much," she answered, then hesitated. "Please don't tell Marcus."

Nick nodded, giving her his vow. He stroked her face with the back of his fingers, and the light touch elicited a small flinch of pain from her. "I could kill him," Nick said.

Olivia knew he wasn't talking to her. Nor was she going to answer. She had every suspicion Nick would be chastising himself later, and she'd not add any guilt or responsibility onto him.

She was suddenly so tired she couldn't think past the next syllable she wanted to say. But she mustered the strength to turn and look at Nick.

"May I ask a favor?" She dimly thought her words sounded slurred.

He nodded, although he still seemed lost in his private contemplation.

"May I rest against you? Just for a moment?"

Nick didn't answer. Instead, he wrapped his arms around her, pulling her back until she was cradled against his chest. Olivia wasn't sure what happened to the pistol…wasn't sure she wanted to know, either. Sometimes ignorance was wisest.

Chapter Twenty-Three

Nick knew as soon as Olivia's breathing leveled to a deep, even pattern that Olivia's fatigue had won its battle against her desire to remain awake. With exorbitant care, he rose from the settee. His future bride didn't object when he lifted her in his arms and cradled her against his chest. Instead, she snuggled against him, as though burrowing for warmth.

Nick was tempted to sit again. To hold this woman until the sun rose and he was forced by propriety to leave. But soon enough, he wouldn't have to part from her, wouldn't have to whip his horse into a lather riding across town to save her. No, she would stay with him always, and he would protect her.

Gibbons was waiting outside the door when Nick used his free hand to open it.

"Thank you, my lord," the servant whispered. Relief etched itself across every line of his expression. "I feared what harm would come to her while we waited for you."

"You were right to send for me," Nick assured him. "And she, unfortunately, has met with harm enough."

Gibbons looked at his mistress's face, and the color drained from his own. "Baron Finley did that?" he asked.

Nick nodded, although confirmation hardly seemed neces-

sary. "Will you show me to her chamber? Your lady needs sleep now."

The butler nodded and led the way upstairs. Nick walked past him, into the bedroom, and laid Olivia on the bed. He pulled the blankets over her, trying to ignore the stab of emptiness he felt once she was out of his arms. Gibbons didn't follow him in, nor did the old man leave his post at the open doorway. Nick smiled at the servant's protectiveness.

He contented himself with brushing a kiss across her cheek, and Olivia sighed in response. Whatever latent anger was still bubbling inside Nick lost some of its intensity at the innocent noise. He forced himself to walk away from the bed, to walk out the door, even though he felt he was leaving part of him behind.

"Should I send word to his lordship?" Gibbons asked.

"When is he expected home?"

"No more than a few days hence."

Nick thought. He'd given Olivia his word. Further, Olivia was soon to be his wife, his responsibility, and he'd handled the threat.

Besides, he and Marcus had enough to discuss once the earl returned.

Nick wondered if they would still be friends once the talking was done.

"Leave it be," Nick finally said. "The damage has been done, and Marcus might well not take our word that his sister isn't gravely injured. It wouldn't do for him to leave from the country in the middle of the night and show up on Finley's doorstep demanding satisfaction."

Gibbons nodded in agreement.

Nick could have made myriad excuses as to why he needed to stay by Olivia's side. Fear Finley might return. Concern she would be worried and frightened even if he didn't.

A pure and simple desire not to let the woman out of his sight.

But he bade Gibbons a good night—for what was left of it—and went to retrieve his mount and head home.

The space and distance would be good for him. They would give him an opportunity to cool his anger and bloodlust. He'd not felt this way—this consuming urge to violence—since his time early days in France. Back then, he'd been idealistic about his missions and convinced of his divine right to vengeance. But with age had come temperance. And it had been so long since he'd felt that surging and mounting desire to pull the trigger, the intensity had been nearly overwhelming. For a moment, Nick had not known himself what he was going to do…what he was capable of doing.

That had frightened him.

But he'd let Finley live.

Whether Marcus would have extended the same mercy was a different story. But Nick knew as much as he wanted to, and as justified as he might have been, he couldn't return to the man he used to be. He wouldn't have his future wife look on him with horror and fear.

Thinking about Olivia caused a pang in his chest. When he thought about what would have happened had he been delayed by mere minutes…

It wouldn't do him any good to dwell, he decided.

One thing was certain, however, he and his intended were going to have a lengthy discussion.

Very, very lengthy.

And very, very soon.

Nick wasn't sure why Finley felt he had the right to show up at Olivia's home in the middle of the night, but Nick was more than willing to set the situation straight for him. And while he couldn't understand what ties existed between Olivia and the baron, he was fully prepared to sever them.

* * *

Marcus arrived exactly five days later.

Olivia wasn't waiting at the door to welcome him but he heard a loud commotion coming from the drawing room. She must be in there.

"My lord," Gibbons greeted.

Marcus grinned. "You know, Gibbons, I almost missed you while I was gone."

"I can assure you, my lord, you were alone in your suffering." But the butler's grin belied his words.

"Is my sister in?" Marcus asked, fairly sure the answer was a yes.

"Last I checked, my lord." Something about the old man seemed out of character.

"With her suitors?" Marcus chuckled, heading in the direction of the sitting room.

"Not in several days, my lord."

The young earl puzzled at the statement but didn't bother to ask for a further explanation.

Marcus was rounding a corner when he almost tripped over a lady.

"Beg your pardon, my lady," he said with a dramatic little bow.

"Oh! Lord Westin. How wonderful to bump into you." The short, pudgy woman was near sixty, but she blushed as she raked her eyes over the young man.

"The pleasure is mine." He made a move to leave, but she put a hand out to touch his sleeve.

"You must be positively thrilled!" she trilled.

"Um, yes. Yes, I am." Granted, he was glad to be home, but Marcus thought her enthusiasm a bit overdone.

"I've been saying all along it would happen. And it was very gratifying to be proven correct." She smiled at him, waiting for a response.

What lunacy had transpired during his absence? "Yes, I can see how it would be."

The older woman leaned closer to him, dropping her voice to a whisper, although there was no one else about. "And I wouldn't worry about the bit of gossip circulating about the two of them in the garden. Granted it was—from all accounts—a bit risqué. But betrothed couples can, of course, be given a bit more latitude and forgiveness."

A distinctly sour taste filled Marcus's mouth. "Of course," he ground through clenched teeth.

The woman patted his arm. "I'm sure you are pleased your sister is finally marrying so well. Even if everything has been in a bit of a rush, it's better than sitting on the shelf."

Marcus saw red. "If you'll excuse me, I must meet with my sister—about wedding arrangements."

This made the woman titter all over again, but Marcus barely paid her any heed as he vaulted the stairs up to his sister's rooms. Fury stole over him, and he needed to talk to Olivia before he lost all control.

Olivia was reclining absent-mindedly on the settee in the sitting room adjoining her bedchamber. A book rested across her lap, but she'd not glanced at its pages in several hours. She'd closeted herself in her chambers most of the time. The bruise on her cheek was fading quite nicely, and along with the rice powder she applied throughout the day, it was almost impossible to tell it was still there.

A quick knock came at the door, but before she could call out, it flew open.

"What have you done?" Marcus shouted as he entered.

After the barest of glances at his face, she realized he *knew.*

Without sparing a moment for a greeting, she asked, "How did you find out?"

Her brother nearly took the door off its hinges as he slammed it shut. "Does it matter? Did you honestly think you could keep your foray a secret from me? That I wouldn't hear as soon as I stepped inside the house?"

"Gibbons?" she gasped, bubbling with righteous indignation at the thought of the old man breaking her confidence.

"No. It wasn't Gibbons," he said tightly. "But I see I am to add him to the list of traitors in my own home."

Olivia said nothing. She fingered the fringe on her shawl, unconsciously unraveling the threads in her anxiety.

"How could you?" The hurt was evident in his face. Olivia felt the stab of guilt—as sharp as any knife.

Marcus continued, "There will be no marriage. You might as well pack your belongings because we'll be returning to Westin Park."

Relief washed over her. If Marcus wasn't going to force her to stay in London and marry Nick, then she could always find a way back from the country later, and devise an excuse to explain her departure to Lord Finley.

"What will you do?" she asked.

"Simple," he said, striding toward the door. "Kill your fiancé."

Olivia jumped to follow him. She doubted that Marcus would kill his best friend—even over her—but she didn't want her brother rushing off in a fury and ruining his friendship with the marquess.

"Marcus!" she called as she trailed behind him in the hallway. "Stop! Nick and I meant no—"

He stopped his path toward the stairs but didn't turn to face her. "Nick?" he asked. "Did you say *Nick?*"

His voice had dropped to a whisper, and Olivia was afraid to answer.

"Did I just hear you say Nick and you…?" he asked again.

"Yes," she croaked, wondering if the revelation of the other

person involved in her public shame would make it better or worse.

"So you weren't caught in a compromising situation with Finley?" His back was still turned to her.

"No." *Because of Nick's intervention.*

"Instead, you were found with my best friend?"

"Yes," she admitted. "But it isn't what it seems—"

"Enough!" he roared. "Stay in your room. And don't bother packing until I return from Huntsford's."

Olivia took a few steps forward, wanting to lessen the blow somehow. "Marcus, remember he's your friend."

"He was" was all the young earl said before descending the steps and leaving the house.

As Nick sat in his study, he attempted to make sense of his estate accounts, but every time he looked at the numbers, the figures melded together, jumbled or otherwise made themselves impossible to read. His heart wasn't in his work. It was across Mayfair at Olivia's house. In the days waiting for Marcus to return, he'd become a permanent fixture there. Her brother was due home today so Nick had forced himself to stay away.

Nothing in recent memory had been quite so difficult.

"I should shoot you," Marcus bellowed as the door flung open. Nick's butler Mathis was hot on the earl's heels, breathing hard after the mad dash up the stairs.

"I'm sorry, my lord. I tried to stop him," the butler panted as the younger man strode up to the desk.

"It's all right, Mathis. He's expected."

The butler bowed stiffly and exited the room.

"Stand up," Marcus growled.

"Why?" the marquess asked coolly.

"Because I can't very well hit you if you're sitting down."

Nick sighed. "I have no wish to fight with you."

"Then you shouldn't have mauled my sister." Marcus edged closer.

"Is that what she told you?"

"No. She tried to protect you in spite of your sins."

That, Nick supposed, was slightly gratifying. Since she had extracted his promise that he wouldn't tell Marcus what had occurred, she could have easily cast Nick to the lions and blamed everything on him, secure in the knowledge that having given his word, he would not contradict her. "All I can do is ask for your forgiveness."

Marcus sat down heavily in a chair. "Well, you don't have it. I trusted you with her. Thought she would be safe with you." A mirthless laugh. "Apparently, I was throwing her to a hungrier wolf than Finley."

Nick hated not being able to tell his friend the truth. Marcus would then abandon his lust for vengeance against him. But he would do nothing to break Olivia's trust.

"I've offered for her," Nick said instead, "and she has accepted. Everything is put to rights."

"In society's eyes perhaps," Marcus allowed. "But not with us."

"Given the circumstances, it was the best I could do."

"So what am I to do?" Marcus asked. Some of his anger seemed to dissipate with his forceful exhale. "Allow my sister to marry you, and condemn her to a loveless union? Or do I forbid the marriage, and let the gossips eat her alive?"

"I hardly think marriage to me would be so disastrous."

Marcus studied his old friend closely. "It would be for her. Olivia deserves to be with someone who loves her."

Nick reached over and grabbed the decanter of water sitting on the edge of his desk and poured himself a drink. "I like and admire your sister a great deal.

"I will treat her well," Nick added after Marcus remained silent.

There were several more beats of uncomfortable silence, and Nick sipped aimlessly at his water, trying to still his emotions. Would Marcus forbid the match?

Marcus stared at him before sighing in resigned defeat. "I guess there's nothing to be had for it. The news is already circulating, and it would look worse for Olivia if I forbade the marriage."

The iron fist gripping Nick's heart eased.

"I've already procured the special license," Nick said. "I think this business should be finished quickly." Another sip. "Your sister and I discussed having the ceremony two weeks after your arrival." Well, *Nick* had discussed...Olivia had listened in stony silence.

Marcus stiffened again. He seemed irked at being left out of the proceedings. "I suppose there's really no choice in the matter."

Marcus stood up to leave. "I'll expect you to call on me tomorrow in order to finalize arrangements."

Nick nodded.

Marcus walked toward the door but before pulling it open, turned to face his old friend. "I hope you know this is the end of our friendship."

"I was afraid it would be," Nick said.

Chapter Twenty-Four

Marcus and Olivia rode home from church service in relative silence the following Sunday.

The minister's words from the sermon about truthfulness rung in her ears, tormenting her for withholding the truth from Marcus about what had happened in the Ashburn garden. It was unbearable to see Marcus so needlessly angry with his friend.

"I enjoyed service this morning," she began.

"I'm glad."

"I guess I'd never thought of honesty quite that way." The minister had explained, by using Colossians 3:9–10, that as a new believer she had to strive to live up to different standards.

> Lie not to one another, seeing that ye have put off the old man with his deeds; and have put on the new man, which is renewed in knowledge after the image of him that created him.

By not telling Marcus the truth about what had really transpired in the garden, she was acting like the old Olivia would. Marcus nodded as she was thinking. "I find God continuously

reveals new things to me. I can take the same scripture, read it three times and come away with three different messages God wants to speak to me."

"In the interest of being honest with you, I think I need to confess something." Olivia stared at the passing scenery so she wouldn't have to look at him.

He watched her expectantly. Olivia was loath to continue; Marcus was just beginning to look at her without growing angry. But she knew as soon as she told him about Finley's actions in the garden, his temper would ignite again. And while it would mean Nick would be free from the anger, Olivia would be bringing it fully on her own head.

There was nothing to be done for it, however. "I allowed you to think certain things about what happened when you were out of town the other evening."

Marcus's confusion was plainly written across his face. "Yes?"

"Lord Huntsford *was* in the garden with me the night of the Ashburn ball, but only after he found me there."

"I have a feeling I'm not going to want to hear the rest of what you have to say," Marcus murmured.

"Probably not. I know what I did was foolish, and I hope you'll accept my apology."

"I still am not sure what you're apologizing for."

She breathed deeply. "Lord Finley was the one who brought me to the garden. Nick found the two of us and, once Finley left, Lord Huntsford was going to escort me home. That's when the ladies came upon us."

Marcus's jaw clenched, but Olivia forced herself to continue.

"Obviously, the situation didn't look at all proper. So Lord Huntsford decided to tell the women we were engaged in an effort to salvage my reputation."

Finished with her story, Olivia folded her hands in her lap and waited for the impending explosion.

It wasn't quite what she'd expected.

"Who are you?" Marcus asked sadly.

"What do you mean?"

"I've never known you to take foolish risks, and whether you would agree, being anywhere with Finley—especially a secluded garden in the middle of a ball—is extremely foolish."

"I know. I wasn't trying to be daring, or foolish, but Finley asked…"

Marcus's jaw clenched. "So you would rather do what Finley asks than what I ask?"

Olivia's exasperation began to show. "You don't know anything. You'll have to trust that I never wanted to cause trouble for anyone. Not for myself, and especially not for you and Nick."

Marcus shook his head and slumped deep into his seat. "You realize what you've done, do you not?"

Olivia nodded.

"Not only did you allow yourself to be compromised…by someone I've repeatedly told you I don't want you around, but you also forced my closest friend to sacrifice his future to play the knight chevalier."

Olivia fidgeted. "I didn't ask him to announce a betrothal! *He* chose that course of action, not me."

Marcus looked angry enough to throw something. "What else was he supposed to do, Olivia? Stand aside and allow your reputation and honor to be cast heedlessly into the ether?"

"Finley would have stood up with me."

"Finley. *Finley!* I grow sick of the man's name." Marcus was yelling at her now, but Olivia wasn't going to point out that fact. "What proof do you need?"

"Proof of what?"

"Of his disreputable character. Would you like me to scour the countryside and find a legion of young ladies like yourself who will attest to the heartache and pain he has caused them?"

"It's not that way between us," she defended, more for her own sake than Finley's. Frankly, she agreed wholeheartedly with Marcus's assessment of the baron's character, but in order for him to stop with his endless attempts to dissuade her, she needed to try and convince him Finley was capable of making her happy.

The task before her appeared impossible.

"Is that so? Then, pray tell, what is it like?" Marcus asked.

"He wants to marry me."

Marcus scoffed. "We've already discussed this," he said. "You don't need to be married to someone like him."

"Well, you obviously felt you can't trust me to make my own decisions, since you refused him on my behalf before you even permitted him to ask me."

"I believe you've illustrated rather effortlessly why I distrusted your judgment," Marcus snapped.

The barb hurt.

Marcus's visible disappointment hurt worse. She'd undertaken this whole scheme to protect him. She hated that she was upsetting him all the same.

"I didn't mean what I said," Marcus said quietly after several moments of silence between them. "I don't want to fight with you. I love you," he added with a ghost of a smile.

"I know you do," she said softly.

"Can we, for right now, put this business behind us? I'll make my peace with Nick, and you'll continue planning the wedding."

Marcus's face was so hopeful, Olivia didn't have the heart

to crush him. She nodded rather than speaking the truth he'd eventually have to hear—that Finley would be her groom, not Nick.

"I do believe you'll be happy with him." Marcus reached across the carriage and grabbed her hands. "If I thought you wouldn't, the threat of scandal—no matter how large or destructive—wouldn't be enough to convince me to allow the union. But, as it is, I don't have to worry over that. The two of you will be content together."

Too bad, Olivia thought, *we'll never get the chance.*

Nick didn't glance up from his paper when a shadow fell across his table at White's.

"May I sit?" Marcus asked from above him.

At the voice, Nick lowered the paper enough to look at his once friend. He'd not spoken to Marcus beyond finalizing the wedding arrangements. Part of him wondered if his old friend was returning for round two or if he had another purpose in mind behind his arrival at their club.

"Of course," Nick said, indicating the chair across from him. "I was about to order luncheon."

Marcus nodded, looking as uncomfortable as Nick had ever seen him. But he pulled the chair out and seated himself without another word.

"How is everyone?" Nick asked to break the silence. It wasn't as though he hadn't seen both Marcus and Olivia the day or two previously.

"They are doing well. Your aunt is keeping Olivia quite busy with preparations."

Nick chuckled. But at the same time, he felt the familiar knot of unease in his stomach. He doubted the tension would pass until he and Olivia were truly and unalterably wed. Until then, he feared his feisty betrothed would find some way to extricate herself from their agreement.

That was the last thing he wanted.

"Aunt Henri is beside herself with something worthwhile to do. I can only be grateful she realizes I am completely immune to her wedding detail excitement," Nick said.

"Olivia told me what really happened." Marcus's announcement was abrupt and startling—at least for Nick.

He couldn't find the words to ask his next question.

"I won't be confronting Finley, if that's what you fear," Marcus said. "But I must also apologize to you for believing the worst."

When he recovered from his surprise that Olivia had confessed, Nick waved off the words of apology with his hand. "What else were you to believe? Every shred of evidence incriminated me. I'm simply glad you know the truth. Keeping it from you was a burden."

"I won't force you to marry Olivia," Marcus said quietly.

Nick's breath caught. They both knew the impact of what Marcus was saying. If Nick was allowed to cry off the engagement—not that he was considering doing as much—Olivia would never be able to show her face in polite society again.

Marcus continued, "I can remove her to Westin Park. She doesn't care much for town anyway. And while there is nothing I'd like more than to call you brother in a true sense, I can't—won't—ask you to atone for another man's sin."

"You don't plan on accepting Finley's suit for her then?" Nick asked, sure he already knew the answer, but needing to hear the words.

"I would sooner Olivia and I both bear the full brunt of the *ton*'s censure. Their disapproval will pass. Marriage to Finley would ruin the rest of her life." Marcus looked at Nick, waiting for him to no doubt sigh in relief and run out of White's rejoicing over his freedom.

Nick had absolutely no plans to seize the ready escape.

Marriage to Olivia was an idea that had grown increasingly

appealing. And just thinking about *not* spending the rest of his life with her made his chest ache. He wanted to be the one to hold her when she was upset, protect her when she was in danger and rejoice with her when she was happy.

Which was, of course, why the next words came out of his mouth. "I want to marry your sister."

Marcus looked surprisingly hopeful, as though he'd not allowed himself to believe Nick's feelings for Olivia could be real. But something in his friend must have pressed him to be sure. "I won't think badly of you. It is my fault you and Olivia were in a position to be found that way, and I owe you a grave debt. I'll not pay it by taking away your freedom."

"Marcus, perhaps you didn't hear me. I wish to proceed with this marriage to your sister. I will treat her well, and I certainly am not bitter about the event in front of me. Can you not agree it must be God's hand leading this?"

Marcus nodded. "I could think of no one I would rather entrust my sister to, and I'm sorry there was a misunderstanding between us."

"Now that all is well between us, I can actually look forward to whatever ceremonial pomp my aunt and future wife have waiting for us." Nick liked far too much the way the word wife rolled off the tongue.

If he were falling for his own fiancée, well, who could possibly fault him for that?

Chapter Twenty-Five

Olivia pulled on her glove with a firm yank, then she smoothed the skirts of her dress, adjusted the ribbon on her bonnet and checked her reticule.

Gibbons watched the unnecessary fanfare with a mild interest. He couldn't possibly know her nerves prevented her from marching out of the house and back out into society. From the moment she and Nick had been found in the garden, she'd been careful not to put herself places where she might find herself the object of attention.

But she needed a few items from Bond Street, and while she could have sent Sarah with a groom, Olivia had decided it was time to lift her self-imposed exile.

As Gibbons finally opened the door at his mistress's nod, Olivia straightened her chin and marched out the door.

And right into Anna Finley.

"Lady Olivia," the young girl stammered, her hand raised as though still ready to knock on the door.

"Anna?" Olivia asked, gripping the girl by the elbows to steady them both.

"I was coming to see you," Anna said. "Obviously," she added with a self-deprecating smile.

"Come in," Olivia invited, pushing the door back open and leading the girl inside.

"It's so lovely in here," Anna breathed.

"Thank you. Come have a seat." Olivia led them past several doors until they were in the morning room.

Anna sat but looked uncomfortable.

"How are you?" Olivia asked gently. For the first time in their acquaintance, Anna seemed awkward around her. Perhaps the news of what happened at the Ashburn's with Nick had made her question the kind of person Olivia was.

"I'm fine." But the twisting of the reticule in Anna's hands belied her words.

"It's good to see you. It's been since…"

"The Ashburn ball," Anna finished for her.

Neither one spoke, and Olivia was prepared to offer to ring for tea when Anna broke the silence.

"Olivia, I'm so happy for you," the young girl blurted.

The admission caught Olivia unaware. "You are?"

"Yes." She nodded fervently. "I heard about what happened, and that you're getting married. I think it's wonderful! It's to *that man,* isn't it?"

Olivia's mouth was open in shock, and Anna didn't wait to hear her answer.

"I know Mama said I'm not to congratulate you because it's scandalous what happened, but you're my friend…aren't you?" she paused her rant long enough to look at Olivia.

Olivia nodded. She was still mute.

"And I know the gossips are saying all sorts of horrid things, but I told Mama it was all perfectly innocent." Anna's tone indicated she'd brook no argument.

What had Olivia done to deserve such a steadfast champion? And what fluke of heritage had gifted Anna into the same family as Finley?

Since they were on the same settee, Olivia didn't have to

stand to embrace her friend. "Thank you," she said. "I'm so glad you came by to see me."

Anna pulled back. "Oh, right. Julian was at the house when Mama and I were talking about me coming to see you." She pulled a face. "He wanted me to bring you something."

Olivia carefully kept her face neutral. "What would that be?"

Anna pulled the strings on her purse and fished around inside. Finally, she pulled a folded piece of parchment out.

"I don't know what he wants," Anna said with an apologetic shrug.

Olivia knew she should wait to open the letter until she was alone—had the distinct feeling her face would show every emotion she felt once she read the words. But she didn't want to sit there through the rest of the visit, morbidly imagining what was contained in the missive.

"Do you mind if I just glance at it?" she asked Anna.

Anna shook her head. "Not at all."

Olivia's hands trembled as she unfolded the letter.

It was short, and to the point.

Denounce the engagement. Leave London. Finley would meet her in the country, and they would be married without delay. By a minister or a blacksmith in Gretna Green.

And of course, she knew what would happen if she didn't.

He'd underlined the last part several times, leaving a heavy ink spot at the end of the emphasized line.

"Olivia?" Anna asked, "Are you all right?"

Olivia managed a nod, but she wasn't certain how reassuring that was.

Anna patted her on the back, like a mother soothing an upset child. But Olivia still had enough presence of mind to realize Anna seemed to be upset as well.

Olivia realized the reason why a few moments later.

"I should never have agreed to bring it with me," Anna said with a huff. "What vile things did my cousin have to say?"

"It's nothing," Olivia dismissed, hastily refolding the letter and tucking it under her skirts. "Nothing at all."

Anna looked skeptical.

"Did you enjoy the ball?" Olivia asked suddenly because she knew Anna would be distracted from the letter.

"So much," Anna gushed.

The next half of an hour was lost to Olivia. She knew she made appropriate comments and responses, but her participation in the conversation ended there.

How could she possibly feign enthusiasm when she was thinking about how she was going to hurt the man she wished she could spend the rest of her life with in favor of the man she never wanted to see again?

Olivia agonized over what to do. She didn't want to stay around the house because it depressed her, and there weren't many places around town she wished to go to. Her Bond Street expedition was abandoned for fear of running into Finley.

Which was why she surprised herself by asking Sarah to accompany her to the Duchess of Leith's house. The coachman pulled up outside the townhome, and Olivia waited several moments before opening the door and descending the carriage steps.

She had no rational reason for wanting to see the other woman, and she knew as soon as she officially rejected Nick, the duchess would probably not want much to do with her. Perhaps she wanted to be the one to break the news to her, so she could gauge for herself how the woman was going to react. Or perhaps—and this scenario was more likely—she wanted a bit of understanding and commiseration. She might not be able to share the full story—or any of the important parts—with her,

but Henrietta seemed the type of woman to offer both sympathy and understanding.

Olivia could use a healthy dose of both.

But then Olivia's paranoid nature began to take over. What if the duchess had a temper? What if she became enraged Olivia wouldn't be marrying her nephew?

Olivia had never before been thrown out of someone's home. She supposed, however, certain things in life were inevitable. And as the future wife of Lord Finley, she knew there would be places she wouldn't be welcome. In her time in London, she'd discovered the baron didn't command the respect or admiration he'd always claimed to.

She also supposed it was a good thing she didn't much care for societal affairs.

The formal butler, one who made Gibbons look like a traveling circus act, admitted her immediately into an elegantly appointed room. And surprisingly, there wasn't a single splash of chartreuse among the color scheme.

The duchess greeted Olivia warmly when she came in to meet her.

"It's so lovely to see you dear," the duchess said as she gave Olivia a welcoming hug.

"I hope you don't mind I came by unannounced." Olivia twisted her reticule in her hands, worried about what the older woman would do once she heard what Olivia had to say.

"You are welcome here anytime." Henrietta motioned for Olivia to sit and then called for a tea service.

"What's troubling you?" she asked Olivia, once she took her own seat. "You look pale."

The rice powder, Olivia thought to herself. She was still wearing it to cover the small traces of the bruise left on her cheek. "I don't know how to begin." Olivia occupied herself with smoothing her skirts, hoping to avoid having to look at the kind countenance of Nick's aunt.

Henrietta leaned forward in her seat. "Are you feeling well?" The duchess was too much of a lady to mention the circles under Olivia's eyes and her look of desperation.

Olivia didn't need to hear someone tell her how she appeared. She'd seen her own face in the mirror often enough to have the image burned into her mind.

"I'm afraid I have upsetting news."

The tea arrived, and Henrietta efficiently prepared their cups while Olivia waited in silence. After she had passed a teacup to Olivia, the older woman nodded her head to encourage Olivia to continue.

"I won't be marrying your nephew." The words tumbled out in a rush, and Olivia wasn't sure they were understandable.

"Whyever not?" Genuine distress colored the duchess's features.

"It's complicated. Nick is blameless, though. I don't want you to think he's the reason I'm calling off the engagement."

Henrietta sipped her tea. While Olivia couldn't prove it, she was relatively sure the duchess was stalling for time.

"What did Nicholas have to say?" Henri asked finally.

Olivia bit her bottom lip with her teeth, worrying at it until she couldn't put off answering the question any longer. "I haven't told him yet."

Olivia thought Henrietta was going to choke on her beverage. "You haven't told him you're not marrying him?" she sputtered.

The ungraceful reaction somehow made Olivia feel even guiltier. "No, I haven't. Well, not in so many words. He can be rather insistent about things. So he refused to take my initial no for an answer."

The sound of the older woman setting her teacup back in the saucer made a delicate *clink*. "I know you might feel as though you don't know me well enough to answer, and I

certainly understand. But can I ask why you feel you can't marry Nick?"

"My reasons have nothing to do with your nephew in particular. And I feel badly about having to deny him. He has become a friend to me."

The duchess seemed to be trying to come up with a simple explanation for Olivia's problem. "Are you afraid of getting married, my dear? I know you must miss your mother terribly now. You should be getting ready and sharing the experience with her. She should also be the one to tell you what to expect now that you're going to be a wife."

Olivia's eyes misted at the mention of her mother. Henrietta couldn't have anticipated the reaction her words would have. The thought made Olivia sad, of course, but it also made her angry. Were it not for her mother, she never would have had to make this difficult decision.

Olivia had to continually pray God would help her conquer the anger she felt. While perhaps she was justified, the emotion wasn't edifying.

"I'm sorry, I should have known not to say anything about her." Henri moved closer as though she was going to offer solace.

Olivia didn't bother pulling out a handkerchief but wiped the few lone tears away with the tips of her gloved fingers. "No, think nothing of it. Her absence pains me still—" in more ways than anyone would ever know "—but she isn't the reason why I cannot marry your nephew."

"Child, I wish you would come out and say it. I can't help you if I don't know what the problem is."

"I can't speak about it. At least not now," Olivia answered honestly.

Henrietta pursed her lips. "This isn't about the bit of ugliness circulating about Nick, is it? Because while I can't divulge

a confidence, I can tell you not to believe a negative word about him."

"I don't. I know him well enough not to pay any mind to the idle gossiping of the *ton*."

"Nicholas is a good man," Henrietta affirmed. Her solid nod made it clear she would brook no arguments on the subject, not that Olivia had any to offer, of course.

"I know he is. He is a good friend to me." Or at least, he had been.

"Does your brother not approve of the match? I thought the two were friends as well."

It would be so nice to be able to tell someone the truth. She doubted Henrietta would judge her, or her mother harshly, and obviously, the woman could be trusted to keep a secret. But Olivia didn't want Henri to feel any sense of responsibility or feel Olivia was asking for any kind of help.

So she stayed silent.

"I can't really discuss why I'm not marrying Lord Huntsford." Olivia leaned forward, took the elderly lady's wrinkled hands in her own. "I'll tell you something I can't even tell Nick." She dropped her voice to a near whisper, saying, "If I had a choice, it would certainly be him."

Henrietta opened her mouth, perhaps to ask why Olivia felt she couldn't decide for herself.

Olivia rushed on. "Please don't make this any harder for me. You have to know I would love nothing more than to be able to call you my own aunt. I know you'll probably want nothing to do with me after this, and I'm not sure I'll be allowed to see anyone. But please know I think you are a wonderful woman."

The duchess shook her head. "Olivia, dear, I'm afraid you're not making much sense. From the way you're talking, one would think you're planning on being kidnapped, or worse."

Oh, worse—much worse.

"You'll have to forgive me. Marcus tells me it's in my nature to be dramatic," Olivia said, hoping to ease Henri's mind.

Henrietta grasped at the explanation desperately. "That must be it. Your nerves are simply overwhelming you. I suggest you go home and rest. Everything will look clearer in the morning."

Olivia didn't contradict her. Henrietta would discover soon enough that Olivia meant what she had said. Olivia would have to rest in the knowledge she'd at least tried to prepare the duchess for what was going to happen.

Chapter Twenty-Six

Olivia sat in the empty morning room. Ever since the announcement in the *Times,* her ardent, dedicated suitors had ceased calling on her. So, she thought with a wry smile, there had been some benefit to the charade.

She knew Nick would be coming to see her as he'd warned her the day before to expect a visit. He'd sounded cordial enough—so obviously Henri had not yet talked to him. Perhaps the duchess thought Olivia had changed her mind. That in the time since they'd spoken, Olivia had realized the foolishness of her thinking.

So, while Nick was coming over to finalize their wedding plans, she intended to break the engagement for good.

Nick entered the room with a smile. Olivia had to force herself not to study him too closely. He was, as always, impeccably dressed. The man could have stepped directly off a fashion plate.

"Good morning, Olivia."

"Good morning to you as well. I trust you had a pleasant evening."

He nodded, waited until she took a seat and then sat in the chair closest to her.

An awkward silence descended. Neither one seemed to want

to bridge the conversational gap. Olivia knew she should go ahead and break the news to him, but she wanted to stall. She was half afraid of his reaction, half reluctant to end the fantasy once and for all.

Nick noticed her discomfort. "Is there something on your mind?" he asked.

She wished she could shake her head and assure him everything was all right. But lying—to either him or herself—would cause problems later.

"I can't accept this." Olivia slipped the ring off her finger with more hesitation than she would have expected from herself. Over the past several days, the cold weight had grown comfortable. She felt bereft without it.

Nick's brows furrowed in confusion. "You already have."

"I should never have agreed to wear it," she amended. The beautiful sapphire was clenched tightly in her fist. But she forced herself to open her hand over the table. The ring hit the polished wood with a *thunk* that resounded and echoed in the now-silent room.

"Do you not like it? I can go to a jeweler's and have something else made—something to suit your taste."

Olivia wanted to snatch the ring off the table and put it back on her finger. Doing so would have erased the vulnerability in his eyes. "It's a lovely ring," she assured him.

But the bauble remained where it was.

He looked at his discarded gift to her when he asked, "Why exactly are you returning the ring?" His voice was quiet, and Olivia couldn't tell if he was angry or upset. Or both.

The deep breath didn't have the steadying effect she hoped for. "I can't accept your ring because I can't marry you."

Nick stood and gripped the back of his neck with his hand. "Are we back to this?" he asked. "We've discussed the matter. You have no choice but to marry me."

Olivia wanted to argue, but was certain that, as before, he'd remain firm in refusing to listen to her arguments. She knew he wouldn't let her go easily.

"I've tried to tell you we will not be getting married. The only person who is having difficulty accepting that is you," she said.

Nick crossed his arms and leaned against the wall. "Is that right?" he asked skeptically. "Then what, exactly, do you plan on doing? What will you do when no one will speak to you because your reputation is in tatters?"

"It won't matter to me by then."

"What do you mean, 'by then'?"

She prayed God would be merciful and give her the strength to do what she had to do. And she turned her head away from him, not wanting to see his expression when she told him the one thing that would end their relationship.

"I'll be married by then."

While she wasn't looking at him, she could hear his sigh of relief. "All right. Put the ring back on, then, and we'll forget we ever had this conversation."

"I won't be married to you," she clarified.

"You won't be married to *me?*"

"No."

"Who then? Who do you plan on making your husband?"

Olivia looked at him, trying to appear stern; otherwise, she was afraid her eyes would well with tears. "Do you even need to ask me that?"

"You must be joking."

Olivia shook her head. The sadness threatened to overwhelm her, and her resolve wavered. Did she really have to cave to Finley's blackmail? Would it be so bad for Marcus to know the truth about their mother? He was a grown man, had a strong faith and perhaps he wouldn't be as surprised by the news or

her duplicity as she feared. She could confess and not have to worry about Finley divulging the secret to him. She could marry Nick and have the life she'd not allowed herself to believe was possible.

Finley wouldn't stop at telling Marcus, however. He would make good on his threat to expose the shame to the rest of England. And now with Marcus's workhouse reforms gaining support, the objective would be jeopardized if something like their mother's suicide was to become public knowledge.

So she had to be firm in her resolve. Nick would find another bride eventually. A fine lady who wasn't forced to carry around years' worth of her own regrets and others' mistakes.

Olivia didn't need anyone to tell her she wasn't good enough for the marquess.

That much was startlingly clear.

Nick had spent a few moments in shocked silence. "You *aren't* planning on marrying Finley." It was phrased as a statement rather than a question.

"Yes, I am."

Nick pushed off the wall and walked to stand in front of her. "Imagine the further damage it would do to your reputation. The two of us were seen together in a compromising position, and yet you plan to marry an entirely different man."

"I've told you, I don't care about what everyone else thinks. As long as Julian is happy, then I am as well."

Not entirely a falsehood. If she could keep her future husband pacified, her life would be much easier.

"Do you really mean that?" Nick speared her with his eyes. They seemed to bore through the layers of pretense. He was searching too deep, and she was afraid of what he might see if he kept looking.

"I do."

Those were the words she wished she could ultimately say to

him. Olivia turned to walk out of the room, afraid if she stayed she'd give herself away. Blinking back tears, she thought she was close enough to doing that on her own.

But Nick grabbed her hand as she tried to walk past him. He didn't pull her back, just held it tenderly as though they were walking through the park together. She stopped.

"Do you not feel anything for me?" he asked.

His question would have to remain unanswered. She couldn't lie to him. But if she told him the truth, he'd never leave her in peace. His pride and nobility wouldn't allow it.

"If you *do* feel something for me, how can you even consider marrying Finley?" His voice was raw, and the words grated on her.

"He's the man I need to spend the rest of my life with." She tugged on her hand, but he wouldn't relinquish his grasp. "Please let me go," she whispered.

"This can't be the end of it. If you don't want to be with me, I can accept that, I suppose. But I can't accept you marrying *him*."

The round-and-round was making her so weary all she wanted to do was march up the stairs to her bedchamber and sleep the rest of the day. "You don't have a choice in the matter."

"Do *you*?"

Startled, she looked at him. "What do you mean?"

"I wonder if you've been blinded by whatever lies Finley has told you. I can't imagine you, or any Godly young woman, would want to tie herself to a man of his character for the rest of her life." He brushed his hand against her cheek, where but days ago, a black bruise had marred her countenance. "He struck you. He cares nothing for you. Is that how you're supposed to spend the rest of your life?"

Who but God could know what she was supposed to do?

And while Olivia feared God would be disappointed when she married the baron, Reverend Thomas had assured her He was a forgiving God. And surely He would see she had no choice but to do what she was planning to do. Her mother had committed a crime, and Olivia had to serve the sentence.

"It is my decision to wed Lord Finley. Please don't ask me any more questions."

"Why? Does it bother you that I don't believe you're in love with him?" Nick pressed.

She didn't answer but to whisper, "Please let me go."

He relinquished his grip on her hand immediately, but Olivia couldn't find the willpower to move away from him.

"I want us to be friends," she said quietly. The very idea was laughable. She wanted to accept the life he offered her, a life by his side, but she couldn't. And being his friend would mean she would eventually have to witness him losing his heart to a woman, getting married and raising a family, which would injure her beyond words. Perhaps being friends, she thought to herself, wouldn't be such a good idea.

Nick apparently agreed. "I don't think I can just be your friend. Not when I've been expecting to be so much more."

"I'm sorry, then. I'm sorry I hurt you. It was the last thing I ever wanted to do. I lo—" She stopped herself in time.

Had she been about to admit she loved him? Had those three little words been so close to slipping out and ruining everything?

Olivia realized it was true.

She *did* love him.

Loved him more than she ever thought possible or ever dreamed. Which made her future all the more grim. She would sacrifice a life with the only man she'd ever loved in order to be with someone she loathed.

Olivia almost hated her mother in that moment.

Anger—hot, roiling and destructive—bubbled to the surface. Perhaps she'd never fully come to grips with what her mother had done to the family. She'd been so concerned with how the secret would have affected her brother she'd completely forgotten to consider her own heart could become a victim.

One act of selfishness had enough strength and magnitude to devastate her.

And this righteous fury gave her the cold callousness she needed to finally turn her back on Nick…to walk to the door fully expecting it would be the last time they'd ever have so intimate a conversation.

"You can change your mind," Nick insisted.

"I will be marrying Julian, Lord Huntsford, and I will not discuss it further." The words were clipped and stiff, a complement to the stiffness and rigidity of her back.

Nick was muttering to himself, and Olivia could tell he was angry. "Your brother won't allow the match," he threatened.

"I don't need his permission to go to Gretna Green." The two would probably have to wed in Scotland. Since she'd not been able to convince Marcus to allow her to be with Finley, he was sure to object to any union between the two of them. If he knew about it in time, of course.

"So you've decided?"

Olivia nodded.

Nick walked past her. "I suppose I'll take my leave, then."

He paused for a moment as he passed the table with the ring. In a motion so quick Olivia would have missed it had she not been staring at him, his hand snatched the engagement ring and pocketed it.

"I'm sorry," she whispered, her eyes misting over completely.

He looked at her, narrowing his eyes in study of her features. Then he nodded, turned and left the room.

* * *

Nick flicked the reins, spurring his horse onward. Another flick and the steed picked up speed until both animal and master were flying through the farthest reaches of Hyde Park. He couldn't think beyond his anger. He was angry at her, angry at himself and furious with the meddling Finley who seemed to turn up at every corner. Here he was preparing to dedicate the rest of his life to a woman, something he'd never contemplated, and she'd practically thrown the ring back in his face and told him she'd rather be wedded to an unscrupulous rake.

Nick knew he was being irrational, knew he was going to have to seek forgiveness for his sudden burst of temper, but reining in the emotion seemed impossible. Olivia should be preparing to marry him, he fumed inwardly. But it seemed Finley had bested him.

Was that why it rankled so much?

Was he merely feeling as though he'd been in competition and was bitter over losing?

Were that the case, it didn't speak too highly for him, but Nick thought there must have been something more at work.

Olivia was a friend.

Or she had been.

Even now, she was the sister of his closest friend, and regardless of his own pride, he wouldn't want any young woman of his acquaintance trapping herself in a relationship with Finley.

And, of course, he didn't want Olivia to have to wed someone who so obviously didn't love her.

A man who loved a woman wouldn't have coerced her into going to a secluded garden.

A man who loved her would have known even the barest hint of scandal would have completely ruined the young lady's reputation and damaged her chances at a good life.

A man who loved her would have treated her with the utmost care and respect.

A man who loved her a fraction as much as he did…

Nick pulled so hard on the reins the horse whinnied in protest and slammed to a halt. But Nick was too lost in his own mind to dismount. The horse and rider sat still in the midst of a grassy field.

Did he love her?

Nick had never been in love before, so he wasn't sure what it was supposed to feel like. The poets, the ones who wrote sonnets and epics in honor of the wonders of the emotion, all seemed to think loving another gave the person wings with which to soar over the trials of life.

But Nick had never felt so low.

Nick had had enough sitting outside like a lovesick fool. He needed time to think about this latest revelation, time to figure out if he were simply being reactionary. Of course, he was wounded that Olivia didn't want to marry him, especially considering he'd grown used to—and rather fond of—the idea. But this feeling of angst was something deeper than bruised pride.

"What are you doing?" Marcus asked as he leaned against the door frame and looked into her bedroom.

Olivia's portmanteau was on the bed, and she was walking back and forth from her closet to the bed, carrying armloads of clothes and shoving them in the carrying case.

"Packing," she answered.

"Are you planning on going somewhere?" he asked with an amused half smile.

"Home."

Marcus sighed and pushed away from the door. "Are we back to this again? The wedding is less than a fortnight away. We

will return home right before the ceremony." The plan was for Reverend Thomas to officiate at the small ceremony at Westin Park.

"There will be no wedding." *At least not to Nick,* she added silently.

Marcus came to the bed, grabbed some dresses and headed back into the closet. "Yes, there will be." His tone was firm.

She ignored him and continued her haphazard packing.

He put his hand on her shoulder to stay her from returning for more garments. "It's a sound match," he told her. "Nick wants this wedding. He is a good man. You'll be taken care of."

"Have I been so troublesome that you are so eager to be rid of me?" she snapped. Her nerves were frayed, and her tongue sharper than she intended.

Marcus's face fell. "Of course not. I love you, but you will marry eventually anyway. And I couldn't think of anyone better suited to you."

"I've told you, I will not marry him."

"Why the sudden change of heart?"

Olivia looked away from her brother, not wanting to see his disappointment. "Please. Would you have me marry a man I don't love?" She was careful in wording her question.

Marcus didn't have anything to say. "You know what this means, don't you? You'll be ostracized."

"All the more reason to return home. I hate it here. And you've been gone more than you've been in town. Is this not best for us both?" She held Marcus's hand, wanting the power of touch to sway his mind.

"I can't understand this," he said helplessly.

"Just trust me. My life will be ruined if I marry the marquess."

Marcus obviously found it difficult to argue with such dramatics. He sighed in defeat. "I will see you home, but

I will probably have to return in order to finish matters at Parliament."

She hugged her brother, squeezing with all her might.

"I think you're making a mistake," he told her. His frown, etched into his face.

"I know," she said as the door shut behind him.

Chapter Twenty-Seven

On her hands and knees in their father's old study, Olivia scoured the floor, looking for her lost earring. Where had the thing gone? She smoothed her hands across the carpet, trying to catch the feel of it before the trinket was stepped upon. Perhaps it had fallen farther under the desk. She scooted along, trying to feel ahead with her hands.

With a few more scoots, she was completely under the desk. And still no earring.

Were she in any mood to find humor in herself, she would have laughed at the picture she presented. Thankfully, Marcus was out and not due back at the house for some time. Not that he would be in the mood to look for her. They'd been back at Westin Park for three days, and he'd only had a handful of words to speak to her.

And even though she'd sent the baron a missive letting him know she'd returned to Westin Park, Finley had yet to send word.

The waiting was making her anxious.

She began backing up, resigned to having to search all over the stupid study for the earring. Without looking, she raised up so she could stand and walk normally. Unfortunately, she had not cleared the desk.

"Ow," she yelled, rubbing the back of her head where it had come in sharp contact with the wood.

There was no blood, she noted, pulling her hand down to check her fingertips. She'd certainly be contending with a headache later, however.

There had been a clicking noise though, she thought, after she hit the wood. Her hands groped underneath the desk, looking for the place where she'd come in contact with the desk.

There was an open compartment.

She chuckled to herself. Marcus had become more secretive than she'd given him credit for. Curiosity over what was in the compartment was a sure temptation to her, but she resisted the urge to look. She would simply close the door back, and he would never know she'd been this close to his secrets.

She had to smother a laugh. What kind of dire secrets could Marcus really have?

She found out when the folded piece of paper fell out of the compartment and onto the floor.

Something about the page looked familiar.

Of their own accord, her hands reached out and picked up the paper, meticulously unfolding it in order to see what was contained within.

She didn't have to read the words in order to know what it was. The familiar slashing handwriting called to her the moment her eyes rested on it.

It was her mother's letter.

The letter Finley had claimed to have.

The letter she'd ruined her future for.

She couldn't process it. It was too much information to take in. How had Marcus come by the letter? Why did he never say anything to her? How had it been safe for so long when she had thought it was lost to the possession of a man who would use it against her?

She took the letter, and on shaky legs, crossed to the sofa. Sitting down heavily, she clasped the paper in suddenly ice-cold fingers.

Marcus found her there when he arrived home. "What are you doing?" he said on a laugh, before he saw the expression on her face.

When he finally noticed the grim set of her mouth, the laughter died in his throat. "What do you have?" His voice was hoarse. He didn't need to ask. He knew what was clutched in her hands—what he had tried so hard to hide from her.

"This," she said, holding up the page, not bothering to look at him.

"Where did you get that?"

"I could ask you the same thing." Her voice was tight.

Was she angry with him? He almost shook his head at his own foolishness. Of course she was. She'd have every right to be after what she'd discovered.

"Mother left it for me." There was no need to shelter her any longer, it seemed. She had read the worst of it.

She rose and turned to look at him then, and her eyes were haunted. He hated himself for what he'd done to her. "In the rosewood box in the library?"

How did she know? "Yes," he answered cautiously.

"Mother didn't leave it there."

It was his turn to be confused. "She didn't?"

Olivia shook her head.

"Who did then?"

"I did."

"You did what?" he asked.

"I put it there. I found it with her, and I hid it in the box." Her words started coming faster until Marcus had to strain to keep up with the flow of conversation. "I didn't think anyone used the box anymore. I thought it would be a safe place."

She laughed, a broken, heartbreaking sound. "I thought no one would ever find it there."

Marcus didn't understand. How did she know about the letter? What was she talking about?

Her eyes were brimming with tears. "Don't you understand?" she asked on a sob.

He shook his head, hating to admit he was still confused.

"How long have you known?" she asked.

"I found out the day before the funeral."

Her eyes flashed fire. "This whole time? This whole time I've lied and pretended, and you knew?"

He stammered, but no words came out.

"I've thrown everything away to protect you." The words were harsh but not accusatory. "I've worried and sacrificed." Marcus had the distinct impression she was no longer talking to him. It was as though she were having a private dialogue with herself, and he just happened to be in the room.

"You knew," she said, her voice torn somewhere between irony and horror. "This whole time, and you *knew*."

He wondered if perhaps she had run out of phrases to say.

Marcus, ever the diligent, concerned brother, took her arm and led her to the settee.

She waited until she felt the piece of furniture behind her legs before sitting down heavily.

"You need to calm down, Olivia."

"You knew," she said again. It seemed to be the one thing she could push past her lips. Her disbelief was so great she feared she'd never be able to form a coherent thought again.

Marcus looked tormented. "I'm sorry I never said anything. How was I to imagine you would know as well? Mother had covered her deed so well, I thought you would never have to know."

"Mother covered her deed? Explain."

"Mother must have broken the window before she did…it.

She wanted us to think she'd been murdered. It was easier than the stigma of her suicide. I thought it would be easier for you, too." He kneeled down in front of her, his eyes beseeching, asking for forgiveness.

But she had nothing to forgive him for. It was herself she was most upset with. For years, she had carried a lonely burden that her brother had apparently shouldered in silence as well. Had she but had the faith in him to confess the truth, all of her pain could have been avoided.

When she thought about it, the situation was so absurd she feared she might start laughing and never stop.

"Olivia," Marcus asked again, "are you feeling unwell? You're beginning to frighten me."

"Mother didn't care enough to hide her intentions. *I* made it look like someone had broken in and killed her," she said almost soundlessly. "Yet everything I did to protect you was worthless—you already knew."

"You…?" he began, but she held up a hand to stop him.

"When Finley told me he had the letter, I looked." She turned to him with beseeching eyes. "You have to believe me. I would never have agreed to his scheme if I had known the truth."

"Slow down," her brother's voice was urgent. "What are you talking about?"

She turned her own eyes to him, eyes holding years of secrets and shame. "When Finley asked me to marry him, I said no. But then he told me he had the letter. He said he would make it public—would ruin our reputations—if I refused to be his wife. So I said yes. Even though I knew the match would upset you, I said yes—so I could protect you. And instead, I just made things worse."

Her brother seemed to be struggling to absorb what she'd just told him.

But she couldn't give him the time to come to it gently. Now

that she had revealed the truth, the words tumbled out of her mouth without any stopping.

"It is I who must apologize to you. I've lied for so long, any time I thought about telling the truth, the situation seemed too far gone to know where to begin."

Marcus raised himself off the floor, reaching out and enveloping her in a hug as she stood. He squeezed her tighter than he ever had, and while the hold bordered on the verge of being painful, she didn't say a word.

"We were both foolishly trying to protect the other," he said. "There is nothing to forgive."

A new, sudden, sickening thought occurred to her. She'd destroyed her chance at marriage with the one person in the world she loved all for the sake of an unnecessary lie. The truth of it staggered her.

"I need to sit," she gasped.

"Olivia?" But Marcus's voice suddenly sounded like it was coming through a tunnel. The edges of her vision were blurring black as well.

"Olivia?" The pitch was higher, but the sound was farther away.

Then she heard nothing.

For the first time in her life, she'd fainted.

Marcus carried Olivia to her old bedchamber, called a servant to watch over her and barricaded himself in his study. The revelations of the morning were still swimming in his mind, making him feel as though he was no longer in touch with reality.

How had he *not* known what Finley was planning?

When the baron had approached him at Westin Park asking for Olivia's hand, Marcus should have seen through Finley's anger at being denied. Marcus had, of course, suspected Finley's finances were not what he wanted everyone to believe

they were, but he'd never imagined Finley possessing the gall to blackmail his sister.

To blackmail her with something he didn't even possess.

How foolish had Marcus been not to anticipate the threat, or to see through Olivia's sudden fascination with someone so unscrupulous?

Marcus's first reaction was to head straight for London…and pummel Finley. Yet while that might have been instantly gratifying, Olivia's well-being had to be his primary concern.

And Marcus knew just who could help his sister.

Hours later, Marcus, dusty from a breakneck horse ride, marched up the steps to the Marquess of Huntsford's country estate. He said a prayer of thanksgiving that Nick had sent a message to let him know he would also be retiring to the country. London was too far away to make it in time. But as it was, Marcus had only to travel a short distance to find and retrieve his friend.

After three raps, the butler warily pulled open the door.

"My lord," the man greeted.

"I'm here to see Huntsford," Marcus said curtly.

The butler looked torn by indecision. "I'm not certain he is available…" But he let the sentence die as Marcus narrowed his eyes.

"See if you can't make him available." Marcus had to be careful to rein in his temper. Unleashing his fury at Finley on his innocent friend would make matters worse and upset Olivia when she found out.

Well, she was going to be upset enough after she found out he had come to play the mediator. There was no need to give her extra impetus to be angry with him.

Mathis disappeared, leaving the front door open but without having invited Marcus in. But Marcus took the lack of a closed door as an invitation to enter anyway. He stood rather awkwardly in the front hall, wondering what excuse Nick was

going to give as to why he couldn't see him. Not that an excuse would matter much to Marcus; he planned on having his say whether Huntsford was inclined to listen or not.

"His lordship will see you in his study," Mathis said as he descended the stairs.

Marcus was in such haste he didn't stop to thank the butler. He took the stairs two at a time, suddenly eager to help the soon-to-be-wedded pair mend their lives together.

Nick wondered what Marcus's visit meant. Was he here to berate him for what had happened with Olivia? Or to offer unsolicited counsel? In truth, Nick didn't feel like entertaining guests, but he could hardly turn his oldest friend away. That was why, against his better judgment, he'd told Mathis to send him up. And if it was a lecture he was coming to deliver, Nick would rather get it over with.

There was no knock at the door, no pretense of asking permission to enter. Marcus looked like a man sent on a holy crusade, solemn and determined to overcome any obstacle in the path of his mission.

"You look awful," Marcus said without preamble.

Nick could feel the stirrings of a laugh in his chest, but he restrained the urge. "I'm sure you will forgive me if I don't thank you for the observation."

"I'm not here to flatter you, anyway," Marcus returned brusquely.

"Why *are* you here then?"

"I've got something of yours I think you might want back."

"What would that be?" Nick asked, interested in spite of himself.

"Your fiancée."

Nick tried to ignore the sudden furious pounding of his heart.

Of course, Olivia was with her brother. He didn't think she'd run to Finley. Right?

"Last I checked," Nick began, "we were no longer betrothed."

"Don't you want to mend things?"

"I don't think it much matters if I would like her to come back. She has to make her own choices."

Marcus appeared to ponder before delivering his own verdict. "Stop acting like an idiot."

"Excuse me?"

"Look, Olivia has some things to tell you. I won't take that right and obligation away from her. The fact is she needs to be the one to say them, and you need to hear them from her. But both of you need to stop acting like idiots in order to clear things between you."

"Should I assume you have given her a similar lecture?"

"Not precisely. Not yet," Marcus smiled sheepishly. "I've no wish to lose any more of my artifacts, especially not over my own head."

Nick thought this through. He loved Olivia. That seemed to be the only thing he could say with any certainty. But just because you loved someone didn't mean she automatically returned the sentiment. The poets heralded the pain of unrequited love, and Nick could understand now what the fuss was all about.

The question was, did he want to fight for her? He felt God had groomed him to be Olivia's other half, and he knew God had ordained a marriage to be a lasting commitment. He also knew that as a husband he was to love his wife and be willing to sacrifice anything for her. But all of his desires and wishes would pale in comparison to whether she wanted to give him a chance to prove his loyalty and devotion to her.

But he had to try.

"She's your sister," Nick began slowly, wondering how his

request for information would turn out. "What do you suggest I do to make things right?"

Marcus's smile was swift and mischievous. "How are you at wooing?"

In that moment, the camaraderie between the two men seemed to be at once perfect and unbroken. "I've never had to woo a former fiancée before, but I suppose it shouldn't be too far outside the realm of my capabilities."

"Excellent," Marcus decreed. "I'll wait here while you gather your things to leave."

Chapter Twenty-Eight

"Olivia," Marcus called softly, sticking his head inside her private sitting room.

She looked up from her position on the couch, where she had been, while not quite sleeping, at least resting. After her uncharacteristic fainting spell, the servants seemed unwilling to let her do anything but walk to a place to sit down. Which she had done for the whole day. And she still had yet to be released and given freedom.

"Where have you been?" she asked in genuine curiosity.

"I've been out getting you a present."

"A present?" she echoed.

"Would you like to see it?" he asked, and she wondered over the obvious laughter in his voice.

"I think so," she said slowly. Surely this wouldn't be like the presents he had given her when they were children, which included dead rodents, bugs and, once, a particularly fearsome-looking garden snake.

"All right. I'll send it in, and I will leave you alone," Marcus continued. Truly, this was growing more unusual by the second. "Oh! I'll be downstairs should you need me."

And with the cryptic offer, he disappeared from the doorway. Olivia started to rise, rife with curiosity and eager to see what Marcus had acquired that was making him act so strange.

Nick entered the room.

"I'm afraid I'm not much of a present," he said with a self-deprecating smile.

Olivia was speechless. She stepped backward until she could feel the couch against her legs, and then sat rather indecorously.

"Is your silence a joyous one?" he asked hesitantly.

If there were words needing to be said at that moment, Olivia could scarcely think of what they might be. All she knew was her heart seemed to be thrumming with more passion, more strength than it had for the past several days.

Nick was muttering under his breath, and Olivia had the absurd impression he was scolding himself, over what she didn't know.

"Let me start over," he said, coming closer to her. And when he kneeled before her, Olivia had to remind herself to breathe.

"I've missed you." His words were soft, gentle and nothing like the tirade she had expected when they finally saw one another. He should be enraged! She'd broken the engagement. But there were no recriminations in his manner, no anger toward her.

"Have you?" she asked with wonder, hating the way her voice sounded so quiet, so hopeful.

He nodded. "More than you'll ever know."

"I thought you might like to be rid of me," she said. The words were a test, and she held her breath, waiting anxiously for what he would say.

"Never."

She exhaled. And hope—something fragile and tenuous— budded within her.

Could it really be? Could it be that Nick, the man whom she had scorned, had treated so badly, wanted her back in his life?

"I—" she began.

"Did—" he started at the same time. A pause followed where neither one wanted to interrupt the other, so they just sat there. "You go ahead. There is plenty of time for me to say what I would like to tell you."

"I haven't been honest with you," she said shakily. Could she really do it? Could she trust someone else with the information she was about to share?

Nick nodded encouragingly.

His open, honest expression gave her the resolve she needed. If she ever wanted any kind of future with this man, ever wanted to mend the bridges she had single-handedly destroyed, she had to say it.

"In fact, I've been lying from the moment I met you."

Still there was no condemnation in his eyes. No shock. No horror.

Perhaps he would forgive her yet.

Olivia looked down then, not able to face him when she made the startling pronouncement. Perhaps it was cowardice, but if she didn't have to look at his face, the words would be easier to say.

"I haven't meant to hurt you," she began again. "I haven't meant to hurt anyone. And while my lies are by no means justified, you have to understand I lied to protect those I love. *Everyone* I love," she emphasized. The cowardice had been defeated by a strain of bravery.

"It doesn't make it right. And I can't undo what I have done, but I want you to know my goal was to…" She took a ragged breath. Articulating her motivation was more difficult than she'd imagined. How could one put into words all of the pain

she had endured alone in order to safeguard others from the ugly truth of reality?

Nick took her hands, and while still kneeling at her feet, he brought the two, cold hands to his lips, kissing them softly. "Perhaps it would help if you tell me what you did," he suggested with so much softness and understanding, she thought she might weep. "I know your reasons were pure."

"I don't love Finley." The words were so quiet she wasn't sure she had spoken them aloud. Were it not for his gentle murmur of encouragement, she would have sworn she'd merely thought the truth. "I never loved him."

She chanced a glance at Nick's face. His eyes were bright and smiling.

"Marriage to him was the last thing I ever wanted." She thought over those words. "Nearly the last thing I ever wanted. I agreed to his arrangement because I feared what he would do if I did otherwise."

Confusion warred with dread in Nick's face.

"Finley knew my mother wasn't killed by an intruder." This was the confession that had the potential to unravel everything she had worked so hard to disguise. *Lord, give me the strength to speak the truth.* "She killed herself."

She paused then, giving him a moment to absorb the full impact of her words. He'd announced his engagement to someone whose mother had committed the most grievous of sins.

And his reaction was as startling as she had imagined it might be…but for another reason. He rose from his crouched position and sat beside her. In one swift move, she was cradled in his strong arms.

"My darling," he murmured into her hair. "I'm sorry."

Unshed tears threatened to blind her, and the sobs she'd kept in for so long clawed and grasped to break free. "I made it look like a robbery," she confessed. Listening to the steady pounding of his heart imbued her with a strength she had not

thought herself capable of. "I thought no one knew. I didn't want anyone to know. I didn't want anyone to ever have the vision of her I still…" She shuddered. She broke off, horrified by the memory.

"There was so much blood. So much blood. I couldn't get it out of my dress later. I had to throw the gown away. But no one questioned. Not even Marcus. I thought my job had been thorough and convincing."

He smoothed her hair, rubbing the errant strands back from her face. "You are very brave," he whispered.

"No, I'm not," she argued. Never, never did she want anyone, especially Nick, to think her actions were born out of some courage she didn't possess. The truth was much uglier. She had pretended and lied because she was so afraid of anyone finding out the truth.

"I would disagree. You shouldered this burden all alone. For years, you've sacrificed yourself so no one would have to know."

She turned her face into his shoulder, not wanting him to see the tears that had slipped through.

He pressed her tighter to him. "You've had to carry this all by yourself for so long," he soothed. "You must be so tired."

The simple observation, something that was so obvious and true, caused the floodgates to open. Years' worth of tears and grief poured out from her very soul and soaked his shirt.

She wasn't sure how long she sat cradled in the arms of the one person she was afraid would have rejected her. And while she didn't want to be premature, it didn't seem as though he was going to hold the revelation against her.

After some time, she raised her head to look at him. "I never wanted to be with Finley." Her voice held all the fervency that had been building inside her. "Never. But I couldn't allow myself to imagine a life with you was possible. He swore he

had proof of my mother's crime. He said if I didn't marry him he would expose her shame."

Nick's arms tightened again, and Olivia could tell from the ragged intake of his breath that he was angry. Very angry.

Nick said nothing for a long time. And the fear Olivia had allowed to rule her life began to creep back. Perhaps she had imagined his understanding. They had been betrothed after all; perhaps he felt it was his duty to comfort her.

"Do you hate me?" she asked in a quiet voice.

"Do I hate you?" he repeated. He sounded stunned. "Out of everything you've told me today, that is the one thought I can't abide you having." He grasped her by the shoulders, pulling her firmly around to face him. "I could never hate you. I could never—not when I love you so much."

"You love me?" The incredulousness and wonder in her tone were hard to miss, and she didn't bother trying to disguise her awe. She felt like someone who had been given a too precious gift and was afraid it might disappear at any moment.

"Have I not said it before?" His smile was wide. "I know I've thought it a thousand times."

Olivia could scarcely believe what he said. The words were so sweet, so precious and yet so unexpected.

Nick looked at her expectantly, and Olivia thought fear colored his features. "Do I dare ask what you feel for me?" he questioned.

She moved her mouth, but no words came out. "I'm afraid to say what I feel," she confessed. "I'm afraid because once the words are spoken I'll never be able to call them back."

Nick's grin was swift and gave her the final spurt of courage.

"I never wanted to love you," she said with a half smile. "In fact, I wanted anything *but* to fall in love with you." She laughed, the freedom and joy of the moment suddenly impacting her more than she thought it would. "But I was an idiot,"

she said, echoing Marcus's early sentiments. "And I do love you. So much so I can't find the words to tell you."

"Does that mean you'll marry me?" Nick asked with a smile.

Olivia, true to what she said, couldn't find the words to say yes, so she merely nodded.

Well…nodded and then pulled his head down to hers, their lips meeting and melding in a long, overdue kiss.

Finley didn't have any furniture in his sitting room. Marcus tapped his foot impatiently as he waited for the baron to appear. The butler had tried to turn him away, but Marcus had insisted on waiting until Finley returned from whatever errand he had been running.

Not surprisingly, once Marcus made it clear he wasn't going to be leaving until he was granted an audience, the butler remembered that his master had not yet left the house.

But Finley was taking his time coming down to see him.

Marcus would have taken a seat, but there wasn't one thing in the room to sit on.

This didn't surprise the young earl, either.

He had known for many years Finley was living largely beyond the means his father had left for him. Years spent gambling, purchasing drink and paying outrageous amounts for smuggled goods from France had drained the modest family coffers. Finley's father had shared with Marcus's father—several times before either of the men's death—his concerns over the future of his son.

Obviously, those fears had been well founded.

"Well, this is an unexpected pleasure," Finley sneered as he entered the room.

Insults and scathing set-downs immediately sprang to mind, but Marcus had to remind himself that regardless of the person Finley was, Marcus still had a testimony to maintain.

Finley shifted his weight nervously. "Are you here for something in particular?"

Marcus would need to repent later for the amount of enjoyment he was getting from Finley's discomfort. "I thought you wanted to marry my sister. Did you believe you'd never have to see me?"

"In a perfect world…" Finley muttered, but let his voice trail off.

Marcus reached into his coat and withdrew a thick stack of papers. "Do you have time?" he asked with more cordialness than he felt, and he held up the papers to indicate he planned on reading.

"I don't have much of a choice, do I?"

"No. But thanks for your indulgence. Just give me a moment to collect myself." Marcus thumbed through the notes. "I've made quite a few trips lately on your behalf," he said as he scanned the papers.

"You have?" Finley asked—suspicion clear in his tone.

"Yes. It's taken me all across England it seems. Ah, here we are. The first paper here is from London Tailory. I don't know if you're aware, but you owe them quite a bit of money." He named a figure, which would have made someone with half a mind blanch.

Finley managed to look abashed and angry at the same time. "And?" he asked in a tight voice.

"Well, it seems the Town Haberdashery is also waiting for you to pay your tab with them." Marcus shook his head sadly. "Unfortunately, this sum is nearly three times the other."

Marcus leafed through another page. "Well, under normal circumstances, I wouldn't set foot inside the establishment that holds your largest note, but in the interest of finding out what kind of man wanted my sister's hand in marriage, I made an exception. I was most disappointed in what I found." Disappointed, but not wholly surprised, he added silently.

"What exactly are you trying to do?" Finley made a quick move to try and grab the stack from Marcus's hands. The earl, however, was able to snatch them away in time.

"I am simply trying to give you my reasons."

"Reasons for what?"

"For refusing to allow you to so much as see my sister again."

Finley's grin was so self-confident Marcus wished he were a violent man. While it was certainly not proper for him to think, and certainly not to admit to even himself, he would have—in the moment—loved nothing more than to permanently erase the man's smirk.

"That will be difficult to accomplish once we are wed," Finley gloated.

Marcus wrinkled the papers when his fingers clenched instinctively. "It is unfortunate for you that my sister will be wedding another."

Finley paused. "I believe you are misinformed."

"I see you don't read the paper."

The muscles in Finley's jaw ticked furiously. "That was a misprint."

"It certainly wasn't," said a third man.

Both Marcus and Finley turned to the new addition to the room. Nick stood just inside the door, arms crossed over his chest and leaning against the door frame. He watched the baron with a largely disinterested gaze.

"What are you doing here?" Finley asked, taking the words away before Marcus could ask himself.

"I thought perhaps you wouldn't be willing to take no for an answer," Nick said to Finley.

"Who are you to speak for anyone?" Finley stepped closer to Nick, and Marcus took several steps backward, willing to watch until he felt it was time to reveal what he knew.

"I'll be Olivia's husband in a few days."

Marcus thought Finley looked as though he badly wanted to throw something across the room—perhaps at Nick, or even him. "You lie. Olivia will marry me. She knows what will happen if she doesn't." He brushed past them as though he were going to leave.

Nick stalked after Finley, and Marcus thought he saw a glimpse of the predator who had hunted traitors and enemies during the war. Had Marcus not known Nick, he might have been afraid for his own well-being.

"And what, pray tell, will you do if she doesn't walk down the aisle with you? Threaten her with more of your blackmail? Strike her again?" Nick moved within a breath away from Finley, who now at least had the sense enough to seem regretful over his choice of words.

Strike her? "What's that about, Nick?" Marcus asked. "Has he hit my sister?" His voice was deceptively mild.

"Oh, yes," Nick said without tearing his gaze from the baron. "I should have shot him then, I suppose. I might have, had I known the other ways he was tormenting the woman I love."

Finley looked suddenly unsure. Very unsure.

Marcus leaned against the wall. He was curious to see how Nick would react to whatever Finley had to say. And he thought it best to repress his own white-hot anger.

"I don't think this is any of your concern," Finley told Nick. The words were probably meant to sound brave, but the quivering voice gave the fear away.

Nick gripped Finley by the front of his waistcoat. "What you don't seem to understand is anything involving my future wife is my concern."

Finley's face lost all its color, and for an amused moment, Marcus thought the man might faint.

He half hoped he would.

Finley seemed to rally his remaining courage. "Olivia is an adult. She understands her actions and decisions have consequences."

"As do yours," Marcus interjected into the conversation. It was time to put an end to this foolishness. Finley wouldn't be admitting his error, and Marcus was likely to lose what remained of his temper.

"We know you've been blackmailing Olivia," Nick said again for emphasis.

"We also know what you've been threatening to expose," Marcus said.

This seemed to surprise the baron. "You do?" he croaked.

Marcus nodded. "I also know your claim of having proof is a lie."

"The letter exists," Finley argued. "I've seen it with my own eyes."

Marcus shrugged. "Do you have it to prove what you're saying?"

Finley wasn't one to admit defeat. "It doesn't matter if I don't have the letter. The bare mention of your mother's suicide will turn everyone against you."

Marcus waved the papers in front of Finley's face. "Perhaps you've forgotten your own dubious reputation. I'm sure your creditors will be interested to hear you've completely depleted your bank accounts and are in danger of losing everything. In another month, this beautiful home will have to be sold."

Finley trembled with rage. "How would you know any of that?"

"You should have taken me seriously when I said I would do anything to stop you from pursuing my sister. I didn't quite realize the depths you would plumb to get your way, but I was smart enough to do a bit of research on you."

Everyone in the room knew the consequences of what Marcus was suggesting. Once the creditors realized everything

Finley could have gotten his hands on was already gone, and the baron was in danger of losing the roof over his head, they would begin to call in their debts in order to be the first ones who would receive the money.

They would descend on him like vultures scenting blood. And Marcus knew, after thoroughly checking the people Finley owed, many would be unwilling to wait for the magistrate before taking matters into their own hands.

"The marriage would have given me all the money I needed to save the estate." Finley shot a disgusted look at Nick, and then turned to Marcus with beseeching eyes. "You wouldn't want to see Father's home sold to the highest bidder, would you? I know how much you respected the man."

"Yes, I did respect him. That's why I've already spoken to my solicitor about making the purchase as soon as the estate comes on the market. I've been assured I'll have the first option to buy because the land abuts my own."

Finley smashed his fist into the wall, obviously aware he had well and truly lost. "So what am I supposed to do?"

"First, I must ask you to stop putting holes in my wall. As for the rest, I suppose that would be up to you. You can either keep your silence, or you can talk. I'm afraid you won't get to enjoy seeing your public ruination, however, because you'll be sitting in debtors' prison."

Nick contributed his own suggestion. "You should probably leave the country...tonight. The thought of you distresses Olivia, and I cannot abide that. And I believe I've made clear several times what I'm willing to do to protect the woman I love."

"Where will I go?" Finley whined.

"I don't care," Nick answered. "But I'll find out if you're not on a ship tonight, and I'm certain you won't like what Marcus and I will have to do if you refuse to see reason."

The two friends left then, and as they walked past the bewildered butler, they heard the sounds of Finley throwing something against the wall.

"Think he'll take your suggestion?" Marcus asked as they descended the stairs together.

"I think he's probably packing now," Nick said with a grim smile.

Chapter Twenty-Nine

It was the day.

The day Olivia had almost missed out on and then thought would never arrive.

She'd woken with the roosters. And then she'd paced the length of her bedroom countless times, wondering how long it would take for ten o'clock to arrive.

Too long, she thought later.

Eventually, the time passed, and Olivia's nervousness gave way to excitement, and then impatience.

She was ready.

She'd been ready for quite a while.

Olivia rode to the church with Marcus, who seemed rather quiet to her.

"Something on your mind?" she asked as the carriage pulled up in front of the small but beautiful country church.

"Home won't be the same without you," he said with a sad smile.

"At least Gibbons will be there," she said with a smirk.

"Comforting," her brother muttered. "Very comforting."

The two walked into the back of the church together, and Marcus excused himself to go speak with Nick.

Olivia could think of nothing but the man who was soon

to be her husband. Once she saw him, all other thoughts and concerns fled. She truly was going to be the Marchioness of Huntsford, forever tied to the one person she had never expected to love, but now couldn't imagine living without.

Olivia studied herself in the full-length mirror. And for probably the first time in her life, she was fussing with her appearance. She wanted everything to look perfect for Nick. The dress didn't disappoint. It was a light green, trimmed with silver and delicate pearls. The modiste in London had nearly expired with nerves when Olivia had requested the dress be made in a matter of days, but the finished product was stunning.

And her hair. Well, it would never stay where it was supposed to. So in the interest of not having to fight to keep it in a tight chignon, she'd let the wavy tresses trail down her back in a tumble of curls.

"You look so beautiful." Henrietta dabbed at her eyes as she handed Olivia her simple bouquet.

The flowers, something Henrietta had insisted on providing for Olivia, were wrapped in a silver ribbon. The white roses exuded a pleasing fragrance, so she sniffed them discreetly before turning back to her friend and soon-to-be aunt. Olivia was actually surprised at the modest arrangement. She'd half feared the bouquet would be too large for her to carry by herself. And she was also pleased to note there wasn't one tawdry color in the mix.

"Thank you." Olivia embraced her, uncaring if the tight hug would wrinkle either of their dresses. "And thank you for standing with me. It means the world to me."

"I can't tell you how much your asking meant to *me*." Henrietta glanced at the tall clock. "I think it's time."

Marcus approached from Olivia's other side. "You make me feel like an old man," he joked as he wrapped her hand into the crook of his arm.

Olivia swatted at him.

"You really do look lovely. Our parents would be sad they missed this."

"Don't make me cry," she warned him, fighting back the tears.

"Are you happy?" he asked with a smile. He already knew the resounding answer to that.

"Happier than I've ever been."

"Good." He guided her to the closed door of the church, which was just barely blocking the sound of the beginning of the wedding music.

"Ready?"

She could only nod. Her heart was in her throat. She wanted to remember every moment of this so that she could one day tell her children exactly how she felt when she was preparing to marry their father. The music was lovely, and as the doors to the church were thrown wide, Olivia blinked several times in surprise.

Flowers covered every spare inch of the sanctuary. It looked as though someone had planted a garden overnight in the building.

Olivia looked at Marcus, her forehead wrinkled and eyebrows pulled low.

Henrietta saw the look. "That was me. I know you said you didn't want any decorations, but I assumed that was because you were afraid there wasn't enough time."

Olivia dragged Marcus over to the woman and kissed her cheek. "It's perfect."

"Your wedding should be," Henrietta said with conviction.

The musician had begun to repeat the wedding march, banging a little more purposefully on the keys.

"I think someone needs to start walking," Marcus said with a chuckle, "before Mrs. Jones breaks the pianoforte."

They stepped forward and Olivia could feel the moment that

all eyes turned to the back of the church. She fought the brief rise of nerves. Henrietta went first in the processional, and Olivia tried to ignore the curious stares and instead worked to peer over the crowd and the duchess to see Nick.

He was waiting at the end of the aisle for her, and looking more handsome than he ever had

Their eyes locked, and he smiled his beautiful smile at her.

Olivia didn't wait for the cue, didn't know if she was supposed to be walking already, and took off down the aisle.

"Are you sure you want to do this? You seem reluctant," Marcus commented with a touch of humor in his voice as they made the procession toward the awaiting marquess. Olivia knew she was nearly dragging her brother down the aisle of the church. And while decency and demureness warred within her, her desire to join Nick at the front was too strong to allow her any sense of decorum. The sooner she made it to the front of the sanctuary, the sooner they could begin their lives as husband and wife together.

Those sitting around, the small gathering of friends and family who had come to witness the ceremony, also seemed to notice her haste. Quiet chuckles could be heard throughout the sanctuary. That was, when they could be heard in between the loud gasping sobs of Gibbons, who was sitting on the first row.

As Olivia and Marcus passed him, Olivia reached out her hand and laid it on the butler's shoulders. He grew more emotional at the simple touch. He pulled out a piece of snowy-white linen and loudly blew his nose into the fabric.

When Olivia finally stood in front of Nick, she thought that perhaps he looked even more eager than she did. And as she took his hand, the rest of the congregation around them seemed to fade into the distant shadows.

Reverend Thomas smiled benevolently at both of them, and Olivia—without thinking—dropped hold of her future husband's hands and nearly leapt forward to embrace the older man.

"Well, now." he seemed surprised by her show of affection.

After a tiny squeeze, she turned back to Nick who looked more amused than shocked.

"We can begin now, Reverend," Olivia said quietly, without realizing her voice was carrying to the farthest corners of the church.

"Thank you, child," he said with a grin. "We have all come together to witness the union of two of God's children who have found love in Him, and each other."

The couple smiled at each other.

Olivia barely heard the rest of the time-honored wedding vows. She repeated after Reverend Thomas when prompted and listened with bated breath as Nick made his own declarations. She couldn't believe she'd made it to this place, with this man.

When Nick placed the band on her finger, Olivia was aware of Marcus coughing quietly into his hand. She didn't need to look at him to know he was crying.

She would tease him for that afterward.

Later, the wedding-goers would proclaim the couple the match of the Season, perhaps even the decade. And while the simple ceremony had been held in a modest parish church—something highly unusual considering the rank of those involved—all who were privileged to attend said they'd never before seen a service quite so elegant.

Or floral.

Nor, they said, had two people been so obviously in love. They were willing to forgive the bride's haste, the brother's tears and the butler's hysterics.

All in all, everyone agreed, it was a perfect day.

* * *

Nick's estate was every bit as elegant as she'd expected it would be. The house was massive, with a beautiful reflecting pool in the front. The gardens—something Nick had pointed out as their carriage rounded the semicircle in front of the house—stretched for what seemed like miles. Yes, Olivia thought with satisfaction, she was going to like it here.

There must have been fifty or more uniformed and liveried servants waiting outside for the master and new mistress to arrive. Olivia tried to memorize the faces as she was introduced to the men and women, but knew that it would take time before she could recite their names without error. The staff had been welcoming and excited to have a new mistress of the house.

Stepping inside, Olivia was gratified to see that whoever had decorated—she suspected it was Nick himself—had impeccable taste. She wanted to see the rest of the house, curious to become acquainted with her new home. Olivia wasn't given a tour, however. The most she saw of the house was what was on her way to their chambers.

All of her personal items had been delivered, and she noticed her copy of *Twelfth Night* sitting on the little stand by a comfortable looking chair. She walked into the dressing room, saw her brushes and other personal items and sighed with pleasure. Olivia marveled over how different, and better, the small things looked in the new setting. Would she never cease to be amazed at how completely and wonderfully her life had changed?

She hoped not.

Olivia thought she would be nervous, or even a bit sad, to be leaving behind her old life. All she found was an incredible joy and anticipation over the future bliss stretching out before her.

She looked at the miniature of her mother that Nick had insisted be placed on the dresser, and for the first time in a long while, she had a return smile for the painted lady.

She wouldn't condone what her mother had done. Her suicide was a perfect example of the destructive power of love. Her mother had been wrong, you couldn't love a person too deeply. But you could love them more than God, and when that happened, the relationship became unhealthy and damaging.

She hoped her mother had found peace in the last moments, but she'd never know. She did know, however, she couldn't allow her mother to continue to govern her life—even unintentionally— from beyond the grave.

"I forgive you, Mama," she whispered to the picture.

"What was that?" Nick asked, coming behind her and wrapping her in his arms.

She breathed in deeply, enjoying his nearness. "Hmm?" she asked dreamily, thinking they could stay like *this* forever and she'd not have any complaints.

"I thought I heard something," he said.

"Oh, that. I was talking to Mother."

He pulled back a bit and looked at her. His brows were pulled together, and a tiny smirk played at the corners of his mouth. "She wasn't answering back, was she?"

"Not this time."

"Not this…?" The playfulness in his face quickly gave way to puzzlement.

Olivia laughed, the loud sound echoing off the walls. "That was a joke."

From the security of his arms, she felt free to admit, "I accepted my mother's apology. She made one, in her letter."

She felt, rather than saw him nod his head.

"I don't have to live in the shadow of her shame," Olivia continued. Taking a deep breath, she looked up at her husband. "Just as you don't have to live in your father's."

His face was somber, but he nodded his head. "I know that now. I promise no more running."

She smiled. "No more running, for either of us," she agreed.

Neither spoke for several minutes. "I could stay like this forever," Nick said as he rested his cheek atop her hair.

"Me, too, my lord."

"I believe that's Nick to you, Lady Huntsford."

"Finally," she breathed, thinking how long and hard the road to get to this place had been.

"Yes, indeed." He kissed her, his mouth gentle on her own, and Olivia changed her mind. They could stay like *this* forever and not have any complaints from her.

"God is good," Nick murmured as he pulled away from her.

"Yes, He is." Her agreement was so swift and certain that he had to laugh—joyously. They had come such a long way in their short time together. Nick said a quick, silent prayer of thanksgiving. God had granted him what his heart had not been optimistic enough to desire.

Nick leaned down slightly so he could kiss his wife. "Have I told you in the last ten minutes that I love you?"

She smiled, an expression mirroring his own happiness. "Yes. But I don't mind hearing it one more time."

So he told her again…and again…and again…

* * * * *

Dear Reader:

I've had Nick and Olivia in my head for the past ten years. These two have been squabbling and falling in love in my imagination for what seems like forever, which sounds crazy but seemed completely normal at the time.

It's been nice to set these two lovebirds free.

I adore Regency England for its customs of courtly romance, lush scenery and beautiful dress—I am a woman after all. But I also love writing about Regency England because I find these fictional people are not so different from modern-day folk. Olivia's grief over her mother's suicide, Nick's unfairly gained reputation, Marcus's duty to his family—and others—and God's supremacy and care for His children are all universal emotions and truths. They can touch any of us, at any time… regardless of what period we live in or what clothes we wear.

I pray this story has blessed you in some way. And I hope you are as happy to read Nick and Olivia's tale as I was to write it.

Blessings,

Mandy Goff

QUESTIONS FOR DISCUSSION

1. After her mother commits suicide, Olivia finds herself questioning the goodness of God. What events in your life have made you question your faith?

2. At sixteen, Olivia conceals her mother's suicide in order to protect her brother, Marcus. Discuss whether there is ever a situation where deception would be justified.

3. When Olivia is honest about her anger toward God, Reverend Thomas responds with a kind and nonjudgmental attitude. How does this loving approach begin to help Olivia repair her relationship with God?

4. When Nick returns to England, he finds he is the subject of much gossip and speculation. Why does he choose not to defend himself to the gossips? What biblical explanation is there for his choice?

5. How hard would it be if you, like Nick, knew people believed lies about you? How would you react?

6. Both Nick and Olivia have been shaped by shameful family secrets. What is the difference in how they choose to cope with the legacy?

7. God assures us that we are not tainted by the sins of our parents. Have you, because of a difficult family background, ever harbored fears that you are doomed to repeat your parents'—or others'—mistakes?

8. In an effort to protect her good name, Nick plans to marry Olivia after the suspicious meeting in the garden

with Finley. Why does he believe protecting her honor is more important than the pain he might experience by marrying a woman who is possibly in love with someone else?

9. In Regency England, arranged marriages—especially among nobility—were common and a way of generating monetary or social benefit to the involved parties. What would the challenges be in a marriage that wasn't founded on love?

10. Nick is a master of restraint. He must initially fight his attraction to Olivia because he knows she isn't a Christian. He also must rein in his desire to pummel Finley—on a continual basis! How important is self-control in a Christian's life?

11. The Bible likens a person without self-control to a "city broken down without walls," (Proverbs 25:28). Why is it crucial for believers to always watch their behavior and actions?

12. Although he is attracted to her, Nick is initially opposed to any serious relationship with Olivia because she does not share his faith. Why is the Bible so firm on not marrying unbelievers? What kind of problems could two people of different faiths have in a marriage?

13. After Olivia becomes a Christian, Nick feels confident that God is leading him to marry her, but she rebuffs him because of her agreement with Finley. This makes Nick doubt what he feels God is saying to him. Have there been times you've been convinced God wanted you to do something, even though things aren't exactly going as planned?

14. Because of his relationship with God, Nick commits to marrying Olivia and doesn't waver in spite of Olivia's rebellion and Finley's interference. How far would you go to honor a commitment? Where would you draw the line and say, "enough is enough"?

15. The concept of reaping what you sow is prevalent in the scriptures. Is Marcus and Nick's handling of Finley at the end of the book a just punishment for the blackmailing baron? Why or why not?

HISTORICAL

TITLES AVAILABLE NEXT MONTH

Available March 8, 2011